THE TAMAR

Creative Texts Publishers products are available at special discounts for bulk purchase for sale promotions, premiums, fund-raising, and educational needs. For details, write Creative Texts Publishers, PO Box 50, Barto, PA 19504, or visit www.creativetexts.com

The Tamarind Tree
by Mike Paterson-Jones
Published by Creative Texts Publishers
PO Box 50
Barto, PA 19504
www.creativetexts.com

The following is a work of fiction. Any resemblance to actual names, persons, businesses, and incidents is strictly coincidental. Locations are used only in the general sense and do not represent the real place in actuality.

ISBN: 978-1-64738-102-8

Chapter 1

Giles Smith was born on a large estate in Devon, England in 1868. He was the only son of Matthew Smith, head gamekeeper on the estate of Sir Paul Grantham-Smythe, one of the minor nobilities found scattered over the English countryside. There were only two gamekeepers to act as guardians of the wildlife over an area of some fifteen hundred acres of wooded hills and open valleys. His mother, Mary, had been a chamber maid in Farrant Manor, a reasonably imposing Georgian mansion on the outskirts of Chumleigh Waterford, northwest of Exeter.

Mary died when Giles, or Gilly as he was called, was only four, to be raised solely by a father whose life revolved around breeding pheasants and controlling vermin like foxes. Left much to his own devices, a young Gilly discovered, as soon as he learnt to read, the world of books. By chance, Sir Paul learnt of Gilly's fondness for books and gave the young boy the freedom of the Farrant House library, but only on Saturday mornings. Gilly soon learnt that the world was a far larger place than his quiet corner of Devon and full of exciting people and places.

Gilly passed from grade to grade at the village school. He always passed with flying colours without overexerting himself. His education could have ground to a halt if it wasn't for an extreme stroke of luck. Sir Paul Grantham-Smythe decided to run for parliament. One evening over a game of billiards at Farrant Manor, it was suggested to him that his chances of election would be greatly improved if he were to make a generous and visible gesture to the locals of the constituency. Sir Paul wrestled with what he might do until it came to him that he should offer a scholarship to a deserving boy to continue his education beyond elementary school.

The scholarship was announced with a lot of publicity and was well received in the district. Sir Paul found Gilly in the library one Saturday.

"How would you like to continue your education after primary school, boy? "he said.

"Very much, sir", answered Gilly.

1

Sir Paul said no more and walked out of the library and so it was that, without any competitive selection, Gilly found himself as a boarder at Exeter Grammar School the following year. Gilly excelled in the academic side of his new life and at sport. However, he did not fit in socially. Attempts to bully him were generally short-lived as he was big for his age. On several occasions, visits to the sickroom by prospective bullies with bloody noses, were reported to his housemaster, who was disinclined to act against a boy who had the apparent patronage of Sir Paul Grantham-Smythe.

Gilly continued to be an avid reader and in his senior school years liked nothing better than to curl up in the corner of the house common room with either a book or a current newspaper. He became enchanted with Africa. He read all he could about it, especially what he could about The Cape Colony. He was fascinated with a part of Africa which had a recorded history going back several hundred years and was also the apparent gateway to the wilder Africa to the north. One person about whom he read avidly, was Cecil John Rhodes. He admired the man who had gone to Africa as a sickly seventeen-year-old and had become a successful businessman and millionaire at eighteen years old.

Gilly decided he would, as soon as possible, get to Cape Town and let luck guide his path from there. He worked hard and left school with a good education, very few friends, but with the edges of his rural west country accent rubbed off and the ability to further modify his accent at will. When necessary, he could make himself sound much like his fellow school pupils. This ability was to stand him in good stead in the future. After finishing at Exeter Grammar Gilly went home to his father. His father was proud of his son, slightly in awe of him, and totally at a loss as to what to do with him. Gilly solved this problem for him.

In his determination to raise enough funds to get him to Southern Africa, Gilly talked himself into the job of an assistant to a cider maker in the village. The job paid enough for him to save a goodly portion of his wages and his knowledge in cider making was to be of great value in the not-too-distant future. The company that made the cider found out that Gilly was good at mathematics and gave him an extra job, helping with accounts on a Saturday for extra pay. Sir Paul also gave him paid employment every Sunday morning, cataloguing the modest manor house library.

1888 found Gilly on board the Union Line S.S. Athenian on its way to South Africa. Two years of hard work had earned him savings of nearly £25. A third-class ticket from Southampton to Cape Town cost him a small portion of his savings. He leaned over the rail looking at the fast-receding English shoreline. He had been sad to say goodbye to his father, but knew that his father would only miss him until the next event involving poachers or pheasants occurred. Gilly was excited as he watched white top waves tumble over under a gloomy sky

The voyage was uneventful. Gilly kept very much to himself. He did however have to share his cabin with three other men, the price to pay for travelling third class. Deck space for the Athenian's riff raff was limited, but Gilly found a place between two lifeboats where he could be alone and could read one of the books on the Cape Colony, he had managed to buy at a secondhand bookshop in Exeter. The food was not great but at least filling.

On the seventeenth day, the imposing sight of Table Mountain came into view. Gilly could hardly contain his excitement. He could see the "tablecloth", the layer of cloud that rolled over the top of the mountain and then melted away in the midday sun. Below the mountain was the city with its docks, commercial centre and then nearer the mountain and running a small way up it, the residential areas.

The third-class passengers had plenty of time to admire the city of Cape Town as they were the last to disembark from the ship. Gilly went ashore carrying his leather suitcase with straps given to him by Sir Paul. Though it was not new, it contrasted with the cardboard suitcases and canvas bags that bore the possessions of his fellow passengers. As he trod on African earth for the first time Gilly felt he was taking the first real step to fulfilling his dream.

He made his way on foot into the city and was surprised to find that Cape Town was bigger than he had expected, and he was further surprised to see so many large buildings from where he stood in Adderley Street. He wandered along the street taking in the atmosphere and surveying the crowds of people who passed by him. He saw people of obvious European heritage, Blacks and even the brown skinned people who had learnt from his reading, to be descendants of slaves brought from Malaya to the Cape by the Dutch. When he eventually reached Hout Street he turned right and then kept his eyes peeled for number 76. One of the crew on the ship had told him of a boarding house run by a rather fearsome woman of mixed European, Cape Malay heritage who ran a small but clean and cheap boarding house in Hout Street.

Gilly rang the bell that hung outside the solid teak door of a whitewashed building. He waited for about a minute and then the door opened, and he was faced by a woman of average height and considerable girth. She glared at him and said something in a language which he failed to understand.

"I am sorry, I don't understand. I am looking for Mrs. van Rooyen. I need a place to stay," blurted Gilly.

Mrs. van Rooyen looked him up and down and then said in understandable English, "bloody Rooinek! I have one room you can have, but only if you can pay me now. The room is one shilling a day. For one shilling and sixpence you can eat with the family at night, and I make you some bread and cheese for the day. You want it?"

"Gilly just stared at the large woman who stood a foot shorter than him and mumbled," thank you, thank you. Shall I give you ten shillings and sixpence now?"

With this he handed Mrs. van Rooyen five coins. Mrs. van Rooyen first stood and gazed at the sky while she checked his arithmetic and then counted the money before putting it into a pocket in her apron.

"Goot, come!"

Gilly followed her into the house. As the passed through a parlour and then along a passage towards the rear of the house he was pleased to see that all was neat and clean. He was shown into a small but adequate room with a bed, small wardrobe and table. On the table was a glass jar in which were some flowers he was later to learn were proteas, local to this part of the Cape. Mrs. van Rooyen left him in his new accommodation but not before she had informed him that supper was at six.

Gilly pulled aside the curtains on the window and gazed out the back of the house. Not too far away was Table Mountain standing majestically in the cloudless sunshine. He could see no 'tablecloth' now. He lay on the bed to test how comfortable it was. It was fine. He retraced his steps to the front parlour where Mrs. van Rooyen was sitting presiding over tea with her husband and two teenage children who she introduced to him. They all just smiled, obviously unable to speak English. Mrs. van Rooyen offered him tea, but Gilly declined. She felt in her pocket and gave him a key, obviously for him to gain entry to the house.

"You go out, you lock."

Gilly thanked her and took the key. He went out into Hout Street and stood there examining his surroundings.

Since he had plenty of time before he had to face the van Rooyens and other guests for dinner at six, he made his way into the centre of Cape Town. He found himself heading in the direction of Three Anchor Bay and Sea Point according to signs along the unpaved road. A horse drawn bus approached and Gilly took the opportunity to continue his exploration as far as Sea Point at a cost of one penny. He wandered along the sea front at Sea Point and watched a scattering of families on the beach, men and children mostly. swimming close to shore. The women, the mothers and wives, appeared to be unwilling to enter the sea in their voluminous beachwear, witness to Victorian modesty even in far off Cape Town

Having indulged himself with an ice cream and having seen all he could of this part of the Cape of Good Hope coast, he paid another penny to get himself back to Cape Town. He had to run half the length of Hout Street to make the six o'clock deadline at Mrs.van Rooyen's. Gilly enjoyed his dinner, a Cape Malay spicey dish with rice. He was not introduced to the other guests but did get a couple of encouraging smiles from a well-dressed middle-aged lady who only appeared to speak Dutch.

After dinner Gilly went to his room. To start with he just lay on the bed and reflected on the day, his first in Africa. He was pleased with himself. He was a bit overawed at the life goals he had set himself. He admitted that he felt a little insecure and did miss his father. Beyond the window of his room the sun was setting, and the details of the mountain were becoming less easy to discern. Before he fell into a deep sleep, he decided that the following day he would find a bicycle to purchase and then see what he could do to earn some money. He dreamt of a ship being chased by a fiery sun below a black and menacing mountain.

Mrs. van Rooyen greeted him in a slightly more friendly way and handed him a brown paper bag of sandwiches. Gilly worked his way back into the city centre by a route different to that he had used the day before. He found a bicycle shop that sold new and secondhand bicycles. After lengthy negotiation with a tall young Dutch speaking man who seemed to speak no English but did understand money, he bought a bicycle in good condition for seven shillings and sixpence. Noting the smile on the bicycle seller's face as left on his bicycle, he wondered whether he had made a good buy or not.

Riding along Darling Street he noticed a bookshop. He stopped, leant his bike against the wall outside the stop and looked in the widow. There were books, lots of books new and old, poorly displayed, but what caught his eye was a modest sign written in beautiful copperplate announcing that Mr. Ezekiel Goldblatt was looking to employ an assistant with good references and extensive knowledge of books. Gilly stepped confidently into the bookshop. Behind the small counter was a gnarled, grey-haired gnome.

"Please can I speak to Mr. Goldblatt, sir?" said Gilly as confidently as he could.

"You are speaking to him, boy", said the little old man "State your business!"

"I have come to ask about the job", said Gilly.

"Name boy?" said Goldblatt.

It was at this point that Gilly did something for which he could never find an explanation,

"Giles Elliott-Smith, sir" said Gilly shocked by his own garnishing of his name. The 'Elliott he had added was his mother's maiden name.

"Who wrote the Iliad" said Goldblatt.

"Homer" came the reply.

"And Anna Karenina?"

"Leon Tolstoy" said Giles, for that he was to be from now on.

"Have you ever worked with books, young sir "asked Goldblatt.

Giles had his answer ready. "Yes, sir, I worked on cataloguing the collection of Sir Paul Grantham-Smythe at Farrant Manor near Exeter in England."

Goldblatt looked Giles up and down. He was impressed with the young man in front of him and, forgetting to ask about references said," I'll give you a week's trial starting tomorrow at thirty shillings a week."

"Thank you, sir, I will be here tomorrow at eight fifteen." said Giles He had noted that the shop opened at eight thirty.

Giles walked down the shop steps and mounted his bicycle. He needed to do something and do it quickly. He had to change his name by deed poll. After enquiring the way to the government buildings from at least seven people, he eventually found himself in the Department of Registration of Births, Marriages and Deaths. Here he approached a young lady who not only spoke English but rather liked the look of the handsome young man in front of her.

Gilly explained his desire to change his name by deed poll. Twenty minutes and two shillings later Giles had applied to have his name changed, confirmation of which would be posted to him at 76 Hout Street. Giles walked out of the government building in a pleasant haze, bought a bunch of proteas from a flower seller and took them to the helpful young lady in the office. She said nothing but blushed a bright pink.

Giles cycled down to the docks and sat on a bollard near to where the Athenian was still docked. He ate his sandwiches which Mrs.van Rooyen had given him. They were delicious. He was later to learn that they contained smoked snoek, a fish commonly caught in Cape waters. He spent a happy afternoon wandering all over Cape Town on his bicycle. He reveled in new sights, sounds and smells. He got back to Mrs. van Rooyens well in time for dinner. Dinner was a fish curry which was good. When two of the other guests attempted to talk to him in broken English, he felt that that was an appropriate end to a highly successful day.

Chapter 2

Less than an hour before Giles had left the S.S. Athenian, another figure had walked gingerly down the ship's gangway. She carried no luggage with her. Servants would collect the two large trunks and two suitcases from the docks and transport them to the large Dutch gabled house situated in shady Newlands. She was a first-class passenger, a young woman, slightly built with long dark hair that reached her waist. Her name was Emily de Speville, seventeen-year-old daughter of Marcel de Speville, Attorney General in the Cape Colony Government.

As she stepped onto African soil, Emily felt relief that her three-year exile in England was over. The three years she had spent at the Maynard School in the St. Leonard's area of Exeter could now be committed to a far corner of her memory. Her father's sister, Aunt Mary, had been kind to her over all the school holidays and had even taken her on a grand tour of Europe. The staff at the Maynard had tried, she knew, to be understanding and be kind to the strong-willed girl from the Colonies, but she had never accepted the restrictive life in an upper-class girl's school in Victorian England. She had never stopped longing to be able to saddle up Bucephalus, and then let him have free rein to chase across the lower slopes of Table Mountain or across the sand of Camps Bay.

Emily spotted her father's doctors buggy from a distance. Her father stood next to it. Emily willingly forgot three years of instruction on how to be a lady and rushed to hug her father. He responded eagerly.

"My God," he said looking at his daughter who was now almost as tall as he was. "You have grown."

"And Father, you have shrunk!", said Emily.

"Fraid so, my Dear. Came in the buggy so we could talk before your mother takes over the conversation. Witbooi will be here just now to collect your luggage."

Emily did act as the lady she was meant to be and, taking her father's helping hand, climbed elegantly into the buggy. Marcel de Speville's buggy had been imported from the USA and pulled by his seventeen-hand bay gelding, Alexander, was reputed to be the fastest mode of transport in the Cape Colony.

As father and daughter travelled south along the base of Table Mountain they talked. Emily did most of the talking, wanting to know how her mother and brother, Reggie, were. She also wanted to know about the family's servants and their families. She was happy to hear that most of the household, in place while she was growing up, were still in service there except Daniel the butler, who had moved on and now presided over a grand house in London. Emily was very pleased to hear that Motsepe, the ageing gardener, was still alive and well, though moving more slowly than before. He was the one who had lit a fire in her, a fire that was fueled by the need for knowledge of the local fauna of the Cape.

As they drove the shaded streets of Newlands it started to rain, not unusual for the wettest part of the Cape. Marcel de Speville slowed the buggy so that the rain did not drive in under the buggy roof. The wrought iron gates to La Mercy were open and the buggy sped up the long oak lined driveway. The manicured gardens seemed not to have changed much in three years. De Speville brought the buggy to a halt below the house steps. On the first step stood an elegant middle-aged woman with dark but slightly greying hair, Emily's mother. Next to her was a handsome young man, also dark haired. It was Reggie, who was now sixteen and taller than either of his parents. On the next step were three faces from the past, dear Motsepe, Angela the maid and Mrs.Goosen, the cook.

The family were seated in the drawing room. Molly de Speville took over the conversation. She pumped Emily with a constant stream of questions not even waiting for full answers before launching the next question. In effect she was demanding a complete history of Emily's last three years in half an hour. Eventually Molly de Speville ran out of steam but before she did, she suggested that Emily must be tired and might benefit from a rest in her bedroom. `

Emily laughed, "All I have done today is to walk off a ship, sit in a buggy and try to get a word in with you, Mother. How could I possibly be tired?"

Mrs. de Speville, blushed and excused herself as she needed to talk to Mrs. Goosen about that evening's menu.

Emily's father also excused himself and went to his office. Emily looked at Reggie.

"What the hell do they feed you on at SACS and, talking of SACS, I want to know why you go there just down the road and I'm sent halfway across the world to complete my education.?"

9

"Easy Sis, SACS is the best and oldest school in Cape Town. No equivalent for girls!" said Reggie.

Emily threw a cushion at her brother and left the drawing room. She walked slowly round to the back of the house and strolled between two rows of azaleas towards the stables. Bucephalus was in his stable looking out of the open upper half of the stable door toward her. He whinnied and shook his head up and down as Emily approached. Emily put her arm around his neck and hugged him. Emily could not help herself. She went to the tack room and took his bridle and fitted it over his head. Bucephalus looked excited. He started to run and Emily, voluminous skirt and all, vaulted skillfully onto his back. Bucephalus took off round the lawn at the back of the house. He raced round and round and Emily cheered him on. The two staff members in the rear garden just stood and watched. Suddenly a window on the second floor of the back of the house opened and Marcel de Speville screamed," Stop, stop, girl. Have you gone mad? Come inside at once."!!

Emily dismounted, removed the bridle and put her horse back in his stable. She expected to be dressed down by her father, but it never happened, and the matter was never mentioned again.

Over the next few weeks, La Mercy became a silent battle ground. Molly de Speville devoted herself to trying to present her now eligible daughter to all the worthwhile elements of Cape Town society. She spent hours explaining to Emily that she was a member of a well-respected family who, though French Mauritian, 'Grand Blanc' of course, were, as of the last hundred years, members of the British high society in The Cape. As such, it was her duty to make a good marriage. Emily argued black and blue that she had no intention of getting married yet and if she did then it would be to a man of her choice.

Molly was determined and managed to get Emily to accept invitations to a couple of balls over the summer but that was as far as Molly got. What she didn't know, and Emily didn't tell her, was that at one ball, one chinless wonder of a youth had come up to her as she cooled herself on the stoep. He had tried to kiss her. Emily delivered a well-directed punch to his nose and the callow youth took himself off for repairs.

*****

10

Giles presented himself at the bookshop for his first day of employment. He was early and had time to sit on the steps up to the bookshop and watch other people hurrying to work. Ezekiel Goldblatt arrived at exactly half past eight. He looked pleased and almost surprised to see Giles. Once in the shop, Zeke showed Giles round the modest three-roomed business. There was the shop itself, with two display windows and a stockroom which looked to Giles like a wordy version of hell. Finally, there was a small office with a door into the service lane at the back of the property.

Mr. Goldblatt seemed unsure as to what he and his new assistant should do. It was Giles who suggested that he sweep the shop and dust the stock. Goldblatt seemed happy to retire to the office and make two cups of coffee. An hour later the shop was considerably cleaner, and its owner looked pleased. At this point a customer entered the shop, a well-dressed man who greeted Ezekiel and asked for any old copies of Hansard that they might have available. Goldblatt looked confused so Giles stepped forward and asked for what dates the Hansard was required. The customer said 'any'. He said he would return the next day to see what they had found.

Zeke was the first to speak after the man left the shop.

"Do you know that that was our Attorney General. What is a Hansard?"

Giles had catalogued Sir Paul's copies of Hansard and explained that Hansard was a record of British Parliamentary business.

"Might be some in the stockroom in some boxes I have never ever opened." Said Goldblatt.

Giles searched the unopened boxes in the stockroom and found three volumes of Hansard dating back twenty-five years. He left the books with Mr. Goldblatt and then applied himself to making the display of books in the two windows more presentable. Failing any direction from his employer, he decided that one window would be for new books and the other for secondhand. He spent a happy hour arranging books in some sort of order. While he had been doing the windows Mr. Goldblatt had served three customers.

Giles sat in the office to eat his sandwiches which were cheese and local pickle. They were good. When he returned to the shop Goldblatt returned from where he had been looking at the widows.

"Good, good, Giles. My Ruthie used to do the widows for me.!"

11

Giles later learnt that Ruth was Goldblatt's late and childless wife.

The Hansard customer, de Speville, returned the next day. He was pleased with the three volumes, but would have preferred some later volumes. Giles politely entered the conversation and suggested that he could arrange to have later volumes shipped from London, but it would take time, de Speville looked delighted and Goldblatt looked worried. After de Speville had left the shop, Goldblatt turned on Giles and demanded an explanation for his action with regard to supplying extra Hansard. Giles calmly explained that while working in the Farrant House library he had learnt of a house clearance business in Exeter who always had copies of Hansard on hand. He explained that a telegram could be sent to this business under his name as he knew the owner, and he was sure any suitable volumes they had would be sent on a 'pay later' arrangement.

At the end of Giles's first week, Mr. Goldblatt confirmed, with pleasure, that Giles had a permanent job. He said,

"You know young man you make me tired. You are always on the move, but you are good for this business!"

Giles's accommodation arrangement was working well. Mrs. van Rooyen still called him 'a bloody Rooinek' but in a gentler tone of voice. He now was getting to know the other boarders in spite of the language barrier. When Mrs. Van as he now called her discovered that he was good at figures she offered him the job of posting account items in her ledger for an hour twice a week in return for free dinners, an arrangement that suited both Giles and Mrs. Van. He did however wonder why only two boarders were recorded as paying guests. He assumed that the other two must have a family connection. He dug no further into the matter and Mrs. Van never offered an explanation.

*****

Life for Emily settled into a routine that was both pleasurable and problematic. She still had to spend hours on the defensive as she fended off her mother's tireless attempts to find her a prominent place in Cape Town society and a subsequent suitable husband. Emily estimated that her mother must have examined the families of every important and well-known family within a dozen miles of the city. However, whenever she managed to place herself out of earshot of her mother, she escaped to the garden and sought out Motsepe.

Motsepe was an old Xhosa who had been in the employ of the de Speville family for nigh on fifty years. He had watched Emily as a toddler tumble about the expansive lawns of the garden in the shadow of Table Mountain and had watched her father do the same. The bent wizened old man's home lay five hundred miles to the east. He never went home and seemed to have no family. His life was La Mercy and its manicured flower beds, orchards and verdant lawns. Motsepe was an expert on the local fauna of the Cape. He delighted in teaching young Emily all about 'fynbos', the indigenous plants of the Cape. Fyn was the Dutch for fine or narrow which described the leaves of many plants that had become adapted to the hot dry windy days of a Cape summer.

Emily liked to wander through her father's gardens at Motsepe's side as he wielded a pair of secateurs to remove dead leaves and branches from shrubs, hedge rows and trees. Every time he stopped, he fed her information on the plant on which he was working. It was not long before she had acquired her own pair of secateurs and helped Motsepe with gradually increasing skill. This action of hers received a certain amount of unspoken disapproval from some of the staff around and from her father and mother who watched her from windows of the house. Her father said nothing to her and cautioned his wife to do likewise.

Emily took her time to select an evening when her father seemed to have had a good day at work before she asked his permission to create a natural flower garden to be devoted to the indigenous plants of the Cape. Her father was not surprised at the request and suggested that a part of the La Mercy grounds behind the stables would be suitable. He went further and offered her the full-time services of the ageing Motsepe. He had been wondering for some time as to how to ease the duties of the old man without retiring him. Molly was not happy as it would no doubt remove Emily even further from her sphere of influence and diminish the chances of her marrying well. However, she held her council. Emily rushed to her father and planted a kiss on his cheek next to his prolific mutton chop whiskers.

Life was good to Emily. The natural garden progressed, and she accommodated her mother by agreeing to attend a limited number of social events to including a few balls. The number of potential suitors found by her mother declined rapidly as word got out amongst the Cape Town eligible bachelors to the effect that 'the de Speville girl was too hoity toity and reputedly an 'ice queen'.

Chapter 3

Life was also good for Giles. His contact in Exeter had located fifteen copies of Hansard, including several recent ones and had shipped them to the book shop. De Speville was informed of their arrival and presented himself at that establishment a day later. As it happened Zeke had taken a morning off to go and tidy up his Ruthie's grave and put some new flowers on it. Giles approached de Speville when he entered the shop and explained the owner's absence.

"Never mind who attends to me, where are the copies of Hansard?" said de Speville.

"Right here, Sir." Said Giles lifting a heavy box off the floor and onto the counter.

"And what do I owe Mr. Goldblatt?"

"Fourteen, including transport. "Replied Giles. He had added five pounds to the cost of the books and shipping. He thought that this amount was a fair charge for locating and obtaining the books.

"A lot, but hopefully worth it." Said de Speville. Please carry the box to my carriage," he continued.

Giles took the books to the carriage and returned to the shop. De Speville was still there looking at books on the shelves.

"Tell me, my boy, what you might suggest as a present for my seventeen-year-old daughter. Her birthday is coming up soon."

Giles thought for a moment and then went to a shelf where he withdrew two books, both appearing to be new.

Giles placed the two books in front of de Speville and said, "This book is a new white vellum-bound copy of Romeo and Juliet."

De Speville gave Giles an odd look before putting the book down. He picked up the other book. Giles explained that it was a first edition copy of Harry Hamilton Johnstons 'Travels in Africa' with profuse illustrations of plants. Giles had chosen this book because it appealed to himself. He was surprised then when de Speville said, "my daughter loves plants and I see this book is well illustrated. I will take it." He continued, "What is your name young man?"

Giles was conscious of the switch from "my boy" to "young man" and replied, "Giles Elliott-Smith, Sir."

"Where are you from and where were you educated? "Asked de Speville.

"Chumleigh Waterford in Devon and I went to Exeter Grammar School." Giles was aware that his accent had altered marginally to fit in with the subject of his middle-class education.

De Speville nodded approvingly and thought to himself, "Pity Emily cannot meet somebody like this presentable young man. If he had some pedigree, I would introduce them myself."

Taking the Harry Johnstone book with him de Speville left the shop. Giles was pleased with himself. He had made Zeke a handsome profit on the Hansard books and had found a good home for a book he had already read from cover to cover, being on his favourite subject, Africa.

Giles was happy with his life. He worked diligently from Monday to Saturday for Goldblatt and then Mrs. Van in his spare time. At weekends he made an effort to get out and explore the Cape Peninsular. He not only saw many new places but met many new people. He got to know an Ebrahim Agmat well, as the young man lived next door at 74 Hout Street with his parents. He was about the same age as Giles and spoke Malay, Dutch and English well. He appeared to have no visible means of support but always had at least some money to spend.

Giles and Ebrahim spent a lot of time exploring the streets of Cape Town and its environs together. Both young men were aware of disapproval they got from those bystanders who did not approve of racial intercourse. Neither of them cared. They enjoyed each other's company. Giles asked Ebrahim how he made money without a job. Ebrahim explained that he did a bit of 'this and that". He explained how kept a keen eye open for anything that was for sale and could be bought and re-sold for a profit. This included, on occasion, information.

Happy as he was, with his bank balance climbing steadily, Giles felt that he wanted his life and its prospects to speed up. So it was that, when Ebrahim told him of a piece of land at Tokai in the shadow of Table Mountain that was an untended apple orchard and for sale, Giles's mind started racing. 'Where there are apples there is cider' he thought. Ebrahim informed him that the orchard was one morgen, about two and a half acres in extent, and for sale for one hundred pounds. Giles didn't have a hundred pounds; only seventy-eight. He suggested to Ebrahim that the two of them should go into partnership and if it was feasible, make cider.

Ebrahim was happy to join Giles in the cider enterprise after Giles had told him of his previous working experience with a cider maker. On the following Sunday the two men cycled to Tokai and, after extensive enquiries discovered the whereabouts of the orchard. Ebrahim was visibly disappointed with what he saw. The orchard was overgrown with weeds and the apples on the trees were small and did not look appetizing. Giles examined a number of the apple trees before explaining to Ebrahim that the apples would still grow a bit before they were ready for harvest and most importantly, the apples could be small and not appetizing and still make good cider. Giles estimated that there were about two hundred trees on the plot.

Seated on the high tide mark on Muizenberg beach, Giles and Ebrahim made their plans. The matter of an apple press was easily solved. A cousin of Ebrahim had an old but usable winepress that could be easily adapted to crush apples. The wine press was stored in a small warehouse on the outskirts of Cape Town. Ebrahim was confident that he could get his cousin to part with the press for a couple of pounds. In addition, there were several old wine vats suitable as brewing vessels for the cider. As far as bottles and corks for the cider, Ebrahim assured Giles that they were freely available in a city surrounded by many wine producing farms.

When the discussion turned to what had to be done to make their business legal, Ebrahim insisted that he would have to be a silent partner. He explained to Giles that his typically Malay name on any official document would not be popular with the white dominated officialdom of the Cape Colony. Giles reluctantly accepted the wisdom of what Ebrahim had to say. On a lighter side, the two men decided that their cider should be named E and G Scrumpy. Giles explained that scrumpy was a term used in the West Country in England for a rough cider made from unselected apples. An excited and happy pair of men cycled their way back to Hout Street.

The next few weeks were busy ones for the future owners of E and G Scrumpy. Goldblatt was happy to give Giles two days leave to 'sort out some personal matters'. They made an offer of eighty pounds on the apple orchard, which was rejected, but a sale was agreed at ninety pounds. Two relatives of Ebrahim were engaged to clear the weeds and grass growing in the orchard. Ebrahim had to admit that the apple trees and their slowly ripening crop looked a lot better when not surrounded by unmanaged undergrowth. Giles went to the municipal offices to apply for a brewing licence. A stroke of luck placed the nice young woman from the registry office in the licence department on promotion. She blushed visibly when she saw Giles again and went out of her way to facilitate the issuing of a brewer's licence. She almost swooned when he expressed his thanks with a very large bouquet of flowers and a beautiful pair of gloves from an up-market shop in Darling Street

Once the brewer's licence was secured, Ebrahim directed Giles to a small printing business owned by another of his many contacts. A couple of hours at a drawing board and a design for the label of the scrumpy bottles was decided upon and a few days later Ebrahim and Giles were gazing, unashamedly proud, at the labels for their new product. They had decided to secure a lease on part of the warehouse where the winepress was, and make that part of the building their brewery. With an adequate supply of bottles and corks stored in their warehouse all they had to do was wait for the apples to ripen fully.

*****

Emily was sitting on a rock in her new natural garden and crying silently. Her father had not understood what she had set out to do. He had stated that the garden was a mess and that it was lacking in formal design and colour. She had tried to make him understand that it was her intention to create an area of indigenous plants, fynbos that was, in as natural setting as possible. He got furious and threatened to re-assign Motsephe to another part of the garden. Motsephe found her sitting on the rock and asked her what the matter was. Tears now flowing, Emily explained. Motsephe crouched in front of her in accordance with his tribe's rule that one should not address a superior from a higher position.

"Missy, "he said, "very few people from the northern lands can understand the beauty of Africa and its children, the plants and animals. They only see beauty in their plants and animals and want them around them in Africa. Roses and oak trees are beautiful but should not push away the proteas and ericas of the fynbos." Emily marveled at the understanding the wizened old man had of his homeland and its flora.

Motsephe continued "The old lion often attacks without understanding why he is attacking. Your father will understand in time.

Don't try and tell the old lion why he is wrong. Let him come to that conclusion himself."

Emily smiled at Motsephe, gathered up her skirt and walked slowly to the house as the southeaster wind dried her tears. Her father was not present. Her mother informed her that he had gone to town to look for a present for her birthday the following day. Molly told her daughter to not say anything about her garden for the moment. She would try to make her husband understand.

The next day dawned brightly and the dry north easter had dropped. Emily entered the dining room. Her parents and Reggie were already there and faced her with broad smiles on their faces. Her parents each kissed her and wished her a happy birthday. Reggie gave her a token kiss. On the sideboard were three beautifully wrapped parcels. Reggie rushed to steady a parcel which Emily could swear was moving. As she picked it up, the parcel burst open and there was a beautiful black Labrador puppy. Emily cried out in delight and hugged the little animal which responded by licking her face.

"Oh, Reggie its perfect and as I see he is a boy, I shall name him after you,"

Handing the puppy to her brother to hold, she picked up the biggest package on the sideboard. On it was a card which said' happy eighteenth birthday, your Mother. Tearing open the package she extracted a most beautiful turquoise dress with mutton chop sleeves and multi-layered lace collar.

"It's perfect, Mother." cried Emily.

You can wear it tonight when we go out to dinner." Said Molly.

Emily then picked up the third parcel which she suspected from its shape was a book. On opening the package, she found a book, Harry Hamilton Johnston's "Travels in Africa. She leafed through the book and discovered the copious illustrations. She loved them, especially when she saw that at least two of the plants illustrated were growing in her wild garden. She rushed at her father and hugged him tightly. She said nothing but, from the way he hugged her back, she knew her garden was safe. Motsephe was right.

That evening a carriage arrived at La Mercy to collect four passengers to transport them to the Perseverance Inn near the Parliament building in Cape Town. This establishment was established in 1836 as a rough drinking place, but was now regarded as one of the best places for the wealthier people of the city to dine.

Heads turned as Emily entered the dining room in her new dress. More than one young man looked, admired, recognized her, and knew from experience to leave it at that. The meal was good, and the wine flowed. Emily was, for the first time, allowed a full glass of wine, a privilege she decided was not enjoyable enough to warrant taking advantage of too often. Emily had been concerned about what to do with her little puppy, Reggie, while they were out for dinner, but she had happily left it with Motsephe to look after.

That night Emily lay back on her bed. It was hot but there was a slight breeze that she could feel on her uncovered body. She could just hear the leaves of the oak tree outside her bedroom window rustle. It had been a good day. She felt deliciously wrapped in the cocoon of love her family obviously had for her. Her work on her garden could continue with the help of Motsephe and lying in a wicker basket on the floor at the end of her bed was a warm black bundle of joy, her Reggie.

Chapter 4

Giles felt that the apples were almost due for picking and turning into cider. He was feeling guilty. He admitted to himself that, though he continued to work hard at the bookshop, during most of the time he spent in the shop, his mind was elsewhere. Zeke was a wise old man and recognized a silent restlessness in Giles. On a morning when the shop was empty of customers Zeke sat Giles down in the office.

"Tell me, Giles, what is on your mind these days?" he said.

Giles looked sheepish but was relieved to be able to tell the old man what was happening or was about to happen, with the cider project and he told Zeke all about his and Ebrahim's plans. When he had finished, Zeke smiled at him and said, "I soon knew that your mind was too active, and you were too ambitious to want to spend your life in a little bookshop. You have been good to me and for me. The shop is making nearly double what it was and, with you around I have less need to think about and miss my Ruthie. When you want to move on, let me know and I think I will retire back to the East End of London."

Giles didn't know what to say. He sat for a while with his head in his hands. "

"Mr. Goldblatt, I like my job here, but I want to do more. Do you think I could carry on at the shop working three days a week and Saturday mornings so as to give me two weekdays to build my new business? I will accept a cut in my wages and will work very hard on the days I am in the shop."

"That seems a good compromise. Let's drink a cup of tea to our new arrangement. Take a shilling out of the till and go and get us a couple of those fancy cakes from that new shop down the road." said Zeke.

The new arrangement worked well for Giles. The apples were ripe. He hired three of Ebrahim's relatives to pick apples. They picked the apples into wicker baskets which, when they were full, were emptied into a wagon drawn by a large Percheron horse that he had rented on an as needed basis. When the wagon was full, Ebrahim drove it slowly all the way to Cape Town to the warehouse. Batches of apples were then shoveled into a large metal basin where they were crushed using a road making tamper. The resulting apple mash then went through the wine press and the resulting cloudy liquid was directed into one of the thoroughly cleaned wine vats to spend days slowly fermenting.

When Giles judged that most of the sugars from the apples had been converted into alcohol, the liquid was filtered and bottled. Ebrahim and Giles contained their impatience for a week before opening a bottle and trying their scrumpy. Giles sipped his glass of the light gold liquid and smiled broadly before finishing the contents of the glass.

"Eb, we have done it!"

Ebrahim hesitated before tasting the cider. "Giles I am going to hell. I am a Muslim and shouldn't touch alcohol, but what the hell!" He downed his glass with relish.

It took the two men more than three hours to glue labels on the bottles which were then placed in crates rescued by Ebrahim from a rubbish dump. Ebrahim and Giles used a hand cart to deliver their first batch of cider to customers lined up by Ebrahim from amongst contacts, mostly Muslims who were happy to risk the wrath of their local imams. The cider was strong but good tasting and an instant success. By the end of the picking and brewing season Giles and Ebrahim were able to split a sum of seven hundred and eighty pounds.

Giles's life entered a relatively quiet period. He and Ebrahim had a stock of over two thousand bottles of cider stored in the warehouse, enough to satisfy clients for quite some time. There was little to do at the apple orchard except to periodically utilize casual labour to keep the weeds down. It was a Wednesday afternoon and Giles was pushing the handcart. He had just delivered three cases of cider to a hotel in Darling Street. It was hot and since he was only yards away from the bookshop, he decided to stop in and have a cup of tea with Zeke even though it was his day away from the bookshop. His decision to stop at the bookshop that afternoon was to be a decision that would affect the rest of his life.

Zeke and Giles sat in the office and talked. There were no customers until Zeke, who was facing the door to the shop suddenly jumped up and went to meet a man who had just come through the door. Giles turned in his chair and saw a slight man of medium height enter the shop. He had an insubstantial moustache and a retreating hairline. Giles knew immediately from pictures in the Illustrated London News, that he was facing none other than Cecil John Rhodes.

Zeke greeted Rhodes with," Good afternoon Mr. Rhodes. What can I do for you?"

"Afternoon Zeke, you old reprobate. You can introduce me to that young man I see in your office. I believe him to be Mr. Giles Elliott - Smith."

Giles stepped forward and proffered a hand. Rhodes took it hand and shook it vigorously before saying to Zeke.," I have need of the services of this young man. He comes recommended to me by Mr. de Speville the AG."

"Mr. Rhodes, both Giles and I are entirely at your service. "Said Zeke.

Rhodes made a move to enter Zeke's office. Giles and the old man followed him. He sat down. The other two men remained standing.

"What I am going to say must not go beyond these four walls at least for the moment, understood?" Giles and Zeke nodded.

"I want you, Elliott-Smith, to do some research for me. I need to know more about the African hinterland, in particular the area north of the Bechuanaland Protectorate. I want you to get books, maps, anything to do with the kingdom of Monomatapa, the Rozwi people and Chief Lobengula of the Ndebele. I will pay handsomely."

"It will be my pleasure, Sir, Mr. Rhodes." said a startled Giles.

Rhodes continued," You will drop off a sealed report for me once a week at Parliament."

"Yes, Sir." Giles replied. Rhodes shook hands with both Zeke and Giles and stepped out of the shop into the hot afternoon. Both Giles and Zeke sat down in a state of shock. It was Zeke who spoke first," you have just met a man, a great man who will, I am sure, prove useful to you one day, Giles."

Giles could do no more than nod in agreement. After discussing the matter with Zeke, Giles agreed that as his life was moving through a quiet period, he would devote all his time to helping Mr. Cecil John Rhodes. Lying on his bed that night and, starring out of his window at Table Mountain, felt an intense sense of excitement. He had met the man he had read all about and admired. More than that, he was hopefully going to be able to assist him. He slept well that night.

The next morning found Giles in Zeke's office making notes on all he could remember from the hours he had spent reading about Africa and in particular the southern part of the continent. He wrote down names like, David Livingstone, Reverend Robert Moffat, John Moffat and Lobengula. He then went with Zeke's approval to the public library in The Gardens area of Cape Town. The library was a fine new building with an extensive collection of books. As he approached the counter there was a young woman bent over a book. Giles almost hoped that his young woman of the registry and licencing offices had somehow been transplanted to the library, but it was not to be.

The library assistant looked up. She wore glasses and was not quite as pretty as Elsie, the name he had gleaned of his helper in the past. The library assistant was very accommodating, and she and Giles spent the next four hours going from library shelf to library shelf under the direction of the young lady, By the early afternoon Giles had accumulated a substantial pile of sheets of paper on which were his rapidly inscribed notes. When they had exhausted the potential leads in the library Giles decided that he would not buy flowers for the library assistant but rather something to eat as she had worked over her lunch hour. He went to a nearby hotel and persuaded the manager to have some sandwiches made for a modest financial inducement. Mary, the young woman in the library, was delighted with the sandwiches which she shared with Giles in a small office in the depths of the library.

From the library Giles went to the Telegraph office and sent off two telegrams. One was sent to Sir Paul Grantham-Smythe asking him for help as a constituent, in getting access to somebody in the Africa department of the Foreign Office. He used his new name on the telegram. A second telegram went to the headquarters of the London Missionary Society in London asking for the current whereabouts of Robert Moffat or John his son.

*****

Emily could hardly contain herself having to wait until after breakfast to go and take her new puppy into the garden. Having gulped down a meagre meal, she took Reggie into the garden and put him down on the lawn. The little dog examined his new surroundings for a while before heading for a flowerbed where he deadheaded several large zinnia flowers before being returned to the lawn. From then he was happy to follow Emily as fast as his little legs could go. Emily led him eventually to her garden where Motsephe was already at work weeding out non-indigenous plants.

Reggie was to follow the after-breakfast routine day after day and he grew fast until he could tear around the place faster than Emily could. Emily extended walks with Reggie to include the area above La Mercy and below Table Mountain. She and often, Motsephe as well, searched the virgin bush looking for more plants for Emily's garden. They gathered watsonia bulbs, took cuttings of ericas and proteas and dug up rare plants such as the disa found only in one place well up the mountainside, all destined to expand the collection of plants in the natural garden

It was on one plant collecting trip high up the mountain slope that Emily, Reggie and Motsepe came across a black spitting cobra. They had just rounded a sandstone boulder and the snake, disturbed in warming itself in the morning sun, launched itself at Emily. Reggie was fast off the mark and ran at the snake. The snake reared up and then in a split-second aimed a stream of venom at Reggie's eyes. Reggie howled in pain and ran to Emily. The snake took the opportunity to make its escape. Emily tried to comfort the dog without success. She wiped venom off the dog's face with the hem of her skirt. She then noticed that Motsepe had disappeared not to reappear for several minutes. Eventually he came running towards Emily and Reggie with a handful of some succulent plant he had found somewhere.

He took Reggie's head in one hand and with the other squeezed juice from the succulent leaves into Reggie's eyes. He kept doing this over and over again for quarter of an hour. Slowly Reggie seemed to get relief from the venom. Emily wiped the juice off the dog's face and looked at his eyes. They seemed normal and Reggie was now struggling to be allowed to run around. Emily looked at the old Xhosa and said," You are a genius, Motsepe. How did you know that plant's juice could deal with cobra venom?"

The old man smiled. "My father was a Nganga, an herbalist or witchdoctor as you people like to call them. He taught me all about 'muti' as we call medicines we get from plants and other natural things."

Emily thanked Motsepe profusely. He appeared to be embarrassed by the attention he was getting. Back at the house Emily told her parents about what had happened. Her mother got very agitated and didn't want her daughter to leave the house again. Her father calmed her mother and told Emily that in future, if she was in the bush she should move noisily as almost all snakes, if given enough warning, will move away. He

warned her that the one that didn't was the puff adder which stayed still
and relied on its camouflage. The defence against these snakes is to keep
your eyes always on where you were stepping. Her father examined
Reggie, the dog and pronounced him fully recovered from his brush
with the snake.

Emily went to her room and taking an unused journal from a drawer
opened the cover and boldly wrote:" Medicinal Plants of the Cape
Colony by Emily de Speville" and then underlined it. She had started
what was to become a lifelong interest. Every day that she collected
plants with Motsepe from there on, she recorded what he had to say
about the plant. She then sketched the plant and later painted it in
watercolour and finally, where she could, identified it by not only its
botanical name but also its Xhosa one.

*****

Giles was surprised to get a reply within twenty-four hours to his
telegram to the LMS. It was to the effect that John Moffat, son of Robert
Moffat, missionary and father-in-law to David Livingstone, the explorer,
had ceased missionary work and had entered the Colonial Service in
Bechuanaland. Giles was delighted with this news as in his notes from
the previous day's work at the library, he had the telegraphic address of
the Governor of Bechuanaland. He rushed off again to the telegraph
office and sent a message to the governor asking him to get John Moffat
to contact him via the office of Cecil Rhodes at the Cape Parliament
Building.

He then cycled as fast as he good to Rhodes's office and arranged
for his secretary to send a messenger to Giles at the bookshop with any
reply to his telegram. The secretary, a businesslike young man, had
obviously been briefed about Giles and was happy to help. Two days
passed before Giles got a telegram from Francistown in Bechuanaland.
John Moffat said that he was happy to assist Mr. Rhodes in any way he
could. He mentioned that he was well acquainted with Chief Lobengula
of the Ndebele tribe and would be happy to act as an emissary if required.
Giles decided that Moffat's offer to help Rhodes was important enough
for him to cycle to the Cape Parliament Building where he went to see
Rhodes's secretary. He was informed that Rhodes was in the parliament

chamber, but should be available in half an hour or so. Giles agreed to sit on a bench outside Rhodes's office until Rhodes was available.

Giles was daydreaming and was not immediately aware that someone was talking to him. He looked up to see Marcel de Speville looking down on him.

"Mr. Elliott-Smith what on earth are you doing here?" he demanded.

"Waiting to see Mr. Rhodes, Sir", Giles replied.

"And about what," de Speville asked.

"No disrespect, Sir, but that I cannot divulge." replied Giles.

De Speville looked surprised and walked away. He wondered about the very presentable young man to whom he had just talked. He also wondered what he had to do with Cecil Rhodes who was known as a plotter with lots of irons in the fire. He determined there and then that he would look into the young man's background to find hopefully some sort of pedigree. It was nearly an hour after his arrival at Rhodes's office before Rhodes made an appearance. Rhodes was surprised to see Giles, but invited him into his office. Giles relayed his information on John Moffat and his offer to help with Lobengula.

Rhodes said nothing for a while just starring out the window at the familiar Table Mountain. He turned to Giles and said,

"Good work, Elliott-Smith. I think I must make a move sooner than I had intended. What I am going to say now stays in this room. King Leopold of the Belgians has designs on Africa as so have the French, the Portuguese and Germans and I am determined that as much of Africa as possible must be brought into the British sphere of influence. I think we must look to getting a treaty with Lobengula for at least mining rights in Matabeleland and settler rights, if possible,"

He did not expect a reply from Giles and didn't get one. Rhodes continued, "

"I am a good judge of men and think I can trust you, so I would like Moffat to negotiate with Lobengula, but I would like you there to keep an eye on things. I know I am asking you to place heavy responsibility on your young shoulders, but I believe you are up to it. Giles, I came to Africa a sickly boy of seventeen and was a millionaire at eighteen. I see some of me in you. Will you work for me?"

"Yes sir." Said Giles.

"I am going to negotiate with John Moffat and arrange for you and he and a contingent of police to go to Bulawayo and talk to Lobengula.

I hope to arrange things for say a month's time. I will appraise Zeke of the situation and make it worth his while to let you go. I do know about your partnership with Ebrahim Agmat and will make sure that he gets help in selling your cider while you are away. Okay?"

*****

De Speville sat on the stoep nursing a mint julep. It was a hot day and he fanned himself periodically with The Cape Times he was reading. Emily was playing with Reggie, the dog, on the lawn. She seemed unaffected by the heat. He thought that he would have to speak to her about restricting the time she spent in the sun. A sun darkened skin was not an asset to a young lady in Cape Town society. As he watched his daughter, he thought how like him she was in many ways. She was as stubborn and independent in spirit as he had been and was, to an extent, still now. He thought long and hard about her chances of making a good marriage. She seemed to have no enthusiasm in this direction. His mind somehow moved onto Giles Elliott-Smith. He was young, perhaps only about nineteen or twenty, but spoke well and had had a good education. In the absence of any suitors competing for Emily's hand in marriage, he allowed himself to perhaps lower the requirements for a suitable husband for Emily. The more he thought about the matter the more he convinced himself that he should make a move to bring Emily and Giles together if only to see how they reacted together. He decided to say nothing to Molly as he knew she had set very high social standards for any suitor for her daughter.

Emily was surprised when her father invited her to join him on a trip into Cape Town to go and look at books at Mr. Goldblatt's bookshop. Emily was only moderately interested until her father suggested that there were sure to be some books on plants to be found there. He further impressed on her that it would also be a chance to be out of the harsh Cape sun. De Speville's buggy soon covered the four miles from La Mercy to the bookshop. De Speville helped his daughter down from the buggy and escorted her into the shop.

Giles was on his knees sorting some books on the lowest shelf of a rack of books. He heard the doorbell ring as de Speville and Emily entered. He jumped up and looked toward the door. He stopped and looked. He felt as if he had been punched in the solar plexus. In front of him was the most beautiful woman he had ever seen. He was unable to speak, but just took in the details of the woman who had turned her head but was also taking in every detail of the presentable young man in front of her. Giles was able to relate, sixty years later, every detail of the dress she was wearing, her fashionable white boots and the way her hair was pinned high on her head. Likewise, Emily had a picture of Giles imprinted in her mind that the years would never diminish.

It was de Speville who spoke at last. "Emily this is Giles Elliott-Smith. He helps Mr. Goldblatt and knows a lot about books. I believe he also knows Mr. Cecil Rhodes. Mr. Elliott-Smith, this is Emily my daughter." With this he looked at his pocket watch and said," Oh dear I forgot I have business at my office. Emily why don't you stay here for an hour or so and let Mr. Elliott-Smith show you some books? I will pick you up when I have finished my business." With that he left the shop.

Giles said "very pleased to meet you Miss de Speville. How can I help you?"

Emily had recovered much of her composure and said "the pleasure is mine. Do you have any books of a botanical nature?"

Giles could not take his eyes off Emily but managed to say, "We do. Come this way."

Emily followed him to a series of shelves on which were several books of a botanical nature. Giles selected and Emily read a few pages of each book Giles offered her. There was a tension in the air. The books were of no consequence. Giles plucked up courage and stated on a firm voice," Miss de Speville, you are the most beautiful woman I have ever seen.!"

Emily looked sternly at Giles and said," that is very forward of you." However, she could not keep up the pretence of disapproval and burst int laughter. She continued," You are a welcome change in this stuffy city. You are prepared to say what you think. Thank you for the compliment, good sir!"

Giles also burst into laughter and said," shall we forget about books and just get to know each other."

"Yes, to start with, call me Emily and I am going to call you Giles. How about you make us a cup of tea and we can sit and talk." Giles blessed the fates that had decreed that Zeke would be at home nursing a cold that afternoon. The tea was made, and the two young people talked.

29

De Speville arrived to collect his daughter. He could see the smiles on the faces of Emily and Giles and had a sudden feeling of doubt as to whether he had just done the right thing. Emily carried a book in her hand as she and her father left the shop, It was the white vellum bound copy of Romeo and Juliet that Giles had insisted she accept. De Speville saw the two young people say goodbye formally but saw that this formality hid another truth.

Chapter 5

Telegrams flew with regularity between Rhodes's Office and John Moffat in Francistown. Moffat did not receive the news that a Mr. Elliott-Smith would be joining him, when he set off for Bulawayo, favourably. Rhodes told Moffat that Giles would have no role to play in negotiations with Chief Lobengula. He explained that he was merely giving the young man experience in the field. Giles was scheduled to leave Cape Town in three weeks' time on the train to Kimberley and then on the Zeederberg Mail Coach to Johannesburg. From here he would be escorted on horseback by a contingent of Bechuanaland Police to Gaberone in Bechuanaland. Here he would travel on north with the same escort to Maclutsie where he would meet up with John Moffat. Giles and Moffat would then ride to Bulawayo accompanied by a well-armed detachment of police. Rhodes felt it important that Lobengula should not be under any misapprehension with regards the importance of the meeting and the power of the British Empire.

A reply to Giles's telegram to Sir Paul did eventually arrive. In brief it gave Giles the name of a senior civil servant in the Foreign Office and wished him well as he, Sir Paul, suspected that the sender of the telegram was none other than his former user of the manor house library despite the name change. Giles was slightly embarrassed by the telegram and did not show it to Rhodes. He soon forgot about it in view of his upcoming trip to Matebeleland and his twenty first birthday. He hoped that he could see Emily again before he left for might well be a considerably long period of time. Try as he might he could not get the picture of Emily standing in the bookshop doorway out of his mind. He was well aware of the social disparity between Emily and himself and feared that a direct approach to her might not be well received. In between planning for his forthcoming trip north he plotted.

Mary, the girl at the library, was pleased to see Giles but was marginally less so when he explained the reason for his visit. He requested that he be given an envelope with the library crest and address printed on it. It was his attention to use it to write to Emily in secret, working on the premise that a letter arriving at La Mercy, ostensibly from the library, would not attract attention. He left a disappointed girl at the library, but did have an envelope. That night he wrote to Emily and poured his heart out to her while sitting staring at his favourite mountain plainly visible in the moonlight. He finished his letter with a request for her to name a place and a time, preferably at the next weekend, when he could see her. The next morning, he happily placed a distinct triangular Cape of Good Hope stamp on his precious letter.

For two days Giles made notes on the forthcoming trip to Bulawayo. He learnt from his research that the name of Chief Lobengula's capitol, Bulawayo, was actually a corruption of Kobulawayo meaning "The place of killing." He had regular meetings with Rhodes and one with Ebrahim where he explained in very vague terms that he was going on a trip for Rhodes. Critically he passed on some valuable advice that had been given to him by Rhodes. This was to the effect that to purchase shares in Blue Ground Diamond Company in Kimberley could prove profitable as Rhodes's and Rudd's company, de Beers, was going to make a takeover of the said company. Giles had taken Rhodes's advice and bought shares to the value of three hundred pounds. He later learnt that Ebrahim had made a similar investment. What neither of the two young men were to know for several years, was that their investments were to produce profits the size of which they could only dream.

A letter in a mauve envelope and with the scent of a woman arrived at 76 Hout Street and caused much amusement amongst the residents of the house. A red-faced Giles took the letter to his room and tore it open. Emily had not opened up regarding any feeling she might have for Giles, but did suggest that they could meet at the huge Norfolk pine that grew on public land just to the west of her natural garden which she had already described to him. Her family were due to go to watch horse racing on Green Point Common the following Saturday. She could cry off the event with a headache and meet him at the Norfolk pine at two o'clock in the afternoon. She explained that this letter would pass through the hands of Motsephe before it reached the pillar box in Main Street in Newlands. Giles lay on his bed and just starred at the letter.

For Giles the next few days dragged. He could not wait for the weekend. During a meeting with Cecil Rhodes, his mind drifted and Rhodes had to tell him to pay attention. There was a lot to plan for the trip to Bulawayo. On Rhodes's advice, Giles bought himself some khaki trousers and shirts and a pair of calf length boots. He also found a wide brimmed hat. When he tried it on in the privacy of his room at 76 Hout Street, he saw himself in the mirror and he laughed at himself saying,"

Giles you have come long way from that schoolboy in herringbone suit and stiff collars in rainy England."

Again, on Rhodes's advice Giles consulted a pharmacist who made up a first aid box for him which included the new drug, aspirin, quinine for malaria, a morphine medication for upset stomachs and a series of creams and bandages. Giles had intended to take his leather case with him on his trip but realized he needed something more practical. He visited a saddlery not far up the road from the bookshop where he found and was pleased to purchase a pair of canvas saddle bags with leather carrying straps.

Rhodes asked Giles whether he had any experience with firearms. Giles was able to tell Rhodes that he had grown up with firearms, especially shotguns, as he was the son of a gamekeeper. Rhodes listened with interest as Giles told him about having his own 410 shotgun at the age of twelve. Rhodes encouraged Giles to tell him more about his childhood in England. He learnt that Giles was an accomplished horseman. His best friend in his teenage years was one of Sir Paul's grooms who had happily taught Giles to ride whenever Giles's school holidays coincided with Sir Paul and his family's absence from the manor house. Giles told Rhodes of many happy hours galloping full tilt across fields and over stone walls and hedges on Sir Paul's own horse, Firebrand.

Rhodes suggested to Giles that he purchase a good sidearm and rifle to take on his upcoming trip. He could charge the firearms to Rhodes's account. Accordingly, Giles took the train to Simonstown to a gun merchant known well to Rhodes. After much discussion Giles took possession of a new Webley 0.38 six shot revolver and a second hand .256 Cogswell and Harrison light sporting rifle. The revolver came with a military style holster and the rifle came with an open-ended scabbard suitable for attaching to a saddle. Giles was pleased with his purchases.

*****

Saturday dawned bright and hot to a cloudless sky. There was a slight southeasterly breeze but by the time Giles reached the outskirts of Newlands he was sweating profusely. He found La Mercy with little trouble and saw an old black man carefully watering some newly planted seedlings in what appeared to Giles to be an ordinary stretch of bush. He was surprised to find that not only did the man speak passable English but was actually waiting to direct Giles to the Norfolk pine further up the mountain slope. The old man was Motsephe who, as he was guiding Giles, was weighing up the young man who had obviously caught the attention of his young mistress. He looked a healthy young man but Motsephe reserved judgement on his moral character for the moment.

Emily was sitting on a plaid rug placed on a piece of ground where the grass was short. She was nervous and was debating as to whether she should run back down the hill home or stay and face her emotions when she saw two figures approaching. Escape was no longer possible, and she stood up. She faced Giles and gave a shy smile. Giles smiled back. Motsephe backed away and was soon out of sight. He was not too far away behind a dense protea bush, on hand to protect Emily if necessary.

A citrus swallowtail butterfly fluttered from one erica plant to another in front of the two young people who for what seemed an age said nothing, Emily broke the silence," Hello Giles. I am glad you came."

"Me too" said, Giles struggling with words.

"No, I am not just glad I came, I am in seventh heaven!" He extended his hands towards Emily. Emily cautiously took his hands in hers and squeezed them.

"Sit down. I have made a sort of picnic. Early this morning I raided the pantry and pinched some of the roast lamb from last night's dinner to make sandwiches and I also found some iced tea cakes. Hope you like what I brought. There is also a bottle of lemonade." said Emily.

"I would adore a wooden sandwich if you had made it.", said Giles in a burst of bravado.

The two young people sat and talked. They told each other about themselves, their families, their likes and dislikes. They were still talking when Emily was suddenly aware that her parents and Reggie would soon be back from the races. "

"Giles, I must go now. Please can we meet again?"

"I would like that. I would like to be able to walk out with you, but I know I am not good enough for you in your parents' eyes," said Giles.

"Damn my parents. You are my beau, but we'll keep it a secret for now. Giles, kiss me!"

Giles blushed bright red but managed a quick peck on Emily's cheek. He couldn't believe how soft her skin was and how beautiful was the perfume she was wearing.

Emily looked Giles in the eyes and said with feeling," Thank you for that lovely book you gave me. I will treasure it for the rest of my life. "

"Emily, I am going away soon for perhaps a couple of months, but I would love to have a photograph of you to take with me. Please don't ask me where I am going. I can't tell you. It is business for Mr. Rhodes.," said Giles.

The two young people packed up the picnic and then went their separate ways promising to carry on writing to each other until Giles left on the trip for Rhodes. Motsephe waited till Emily had passed him and then quietly fell in well behind her. As he walked, he said to himself "That young man is like a leopard, a shy animal that moves slowly and carefully but if annoyed will turn into a very dangerous and courageous beast,"

*****

A situation arose where Emily and Giles were able to meet without any conspiratorial manipulation. The cabinet of the Cape Colony government decide to hold a garden party in the Company Gardens next to the Parliament Building to celebrate Queen Victoria's seventieth birthday. All of Cape Town's notable citizens were invited. Giles was surprised to learn that Rhodes had insisted that his young protegee be issued with an invitation. Knowing that Emily, as the AG's daughter, was surely invited, Giles was more than happy to spend some cider money on a morning suit and elegant top hat. When he tried the new and expensive clothes on in his room, he was able to have another good laugh at himself.

May the twenty fourth dawned bright but there was a bite in the air that did nothing to diminish the enthusiasm of the crowds of the guests parading their finery in the large marquee set up in The Gardens. Giles did not know about being fashionably late and arrived in a rented trap at the time indicated on the invitation. Most invitees had yet to arrive, but Cecil Rhodes was there and happy to introduce Giles to the people who came up to greet him. He introduced him as one of 'his people'.

The faces of the people he was introduced to told an interesting story. Elderly bewhiskered men showed disapproval of his youth but their wives and particularly their daughters faces told another story.

Eventually it happened. De Speville and his family met up with Cecil Rhodes and Giles, who had been standing behind Rhodes, was introduced to them. De Speville seemed surprised to see Giles but greeted Giles with, "nice to see you again, young man."

Molly was next to be introduced. She greeted him politely but did wonder who the polite young man was. Reggie greeted Giles affably. When it came to Emily's turn, she had no idea as to handle the situation, and muttered something inaudible and Giles replied in a similar vein. For the whole if the afternoon both Emily and Giles followed each other with their eyes. Giles felt angry whenever he saw Emily being attended by one or more young men. Similarly, Emily struggled to remain composed whenever she saw any young ladies talking to Giles. The garden party was near an end before Emily and Giles managed to meet alone behind the marquee for a few precious momenta. They had just joined hands when Reggie' s strident voice, indicating that he was looking for his sister, reached Emily and Giles.

On the way home to La Mercy Molly asked Marcel," who was that young man Cecil introduced to us, Marcel. Seemed nice enough. What sort of family does he come from?"

"He is English and went to a good school, I hear. I can't give you his pedigree," said her husband.

Emily pretended to not hear the conversation and remarked that the leaves on the oaks up Newlands Avenue were starting to lose their leaves.

Reggie dug his sister in the ribs and asked," what did you think of Mr., Elliott-Smith, Sis?"

Emily ignored her brother and remarked on the beauty of the arum lilies growing on the side of the road.

Chapter 6

The train was due to leave Cape Town Station at nine o'clock in the morning. Giles was there before eight thirty. He had with him his two saddle bags and his rifle in its scabbard. He felt excited and unaware that with only a simple leather jerkin over his khaki shirt, he was not suitably clothed to face the cold north wester that was blowing. Shortly before nine o'clock, Cecil Rhodes arrived and immediately got down to business,

"Giles, I have an attaché case here that contains a letter for you to give to Moffat. I have outlined what I want him to do in his negotiations with Lobengula. There is another envelope with some ideas and suggestions for you. This attache case must stay with you all the time. Got it, Giles? The mission you are undertaking on my behalf is important to me and if all goes well you will have a place with me when hopefully I make British Empire history. In the meantime, you are now a salaried member of my staff at a salary of £20 a month."

Giles was delighted with the generous salary he had been given. "Mr. Rhodes, I will do my very best to accomplish what you want in Matabeleland."

"I know you will, young man, or I wouldn't have chosen you. You better stow your luggage and take your seat on the train," said Rhodes.

By the time Giles found his carriage and had stowed his luggage, he saw Rhodes's figure disappearing down the platform. When the train eventually left Cape Town Station over half an hour late, Giles found that he had three other companions in his compartment. Friendly talk between the occupants of the carriage revealed that one middle aged gentleman was a vicar going to take up a parish in Johannesburg. Two were young men freshly out from England on their way to seek their fortune on the Kimberly diamond fields. The vicar chatted happily about his 'calling' for about an hour before he retreated into a book on the life of Thomas Moore. His presence did however continue to moderate the language of the two young fortune seekers. They told Giles their unremarkable life stories and then pumped him for information about Africa. Giles answered their questions where he could, but was happy when conversation waned, and he was able to concentrate on the passing scenery.

The train passed through the beautiful Hex River Valley carpeted in vineyards. There was a hint of snow on the overlooking mountains. Giles took the photograph out of the top pocket of his shirt pocket and gazed at the picture of Emily that had arrived by post at No. 76 the day before he was due to leave Cape Town. 'She really was exquisitely beautiful he thought'. He also, for the first time, opened the small old metal snuff box which had come with the letter. It contained a fatty substance that Emily's letter assured him was a mosquito repellent made by Motsephe. He smiled and closed the snuff box before the unpleasant smell annoyed the other occupants of the carriage.

The further north the train travelled, the drier the countryside became. Vineyards gave way to sheep farms where there was a dearth of trees. Then there was mile after mile of dry rocky land known by the locals as The Karoo. Giles went to the saloon car for both lunch and dinner. That evening a steward worked his way down the carriages bringing bedding to those passengers who had paid for it. Giles was happy to climb on to a top bunk and go to sleep, but not before he saw that the two fortune seekers who had not afforded bedding were freezing cold. He gave them one of his blankets and a pillow which they shared. He put the attache case under his one remaining pillow for both security and to add height to his single pillow.

The next day dawned bright and cold, and the train steamed steadily northwards through a countryside distinguished by dry grass and dead looking bushes. Giles took two more meals in the saloon car, but did not eat all put in front of him. He wrapped a portion of both meals in serviettes and took them back to the two young men who were not only cold but hungry. They were very grateful. The train pulled into Kimberly station on the evening of the second day of the journey. Giles wished his three companions well on their respective journeys. It was dark, but Giles was surprised to see that the town had street lighting. The town seemed to Giles to have been thrown together in a hurry which indeed it had. As he walked through lit streets, he saw there was a preponderance of bars and what he assumed were houses of ill repute. He found a respectable hotel to stay the night

Following directions from the hotel clerk, Giles found his way to the Zeederberg Mail Service terminus. It was freezing cold and Giles shivered and wished he had bought a coat with him. The coach due to set off for Johannesbrg was large and ten mules were already inspanned.

Christian Zeederberg, founder of the coach company along with three of his brothers, was there to greet his passengers. He stowed Giles's saddle bags on the roof of the coach. Giles hung on to his rifle and the attache case. Zeederberg told Giles about the coach. It was one of many the brothers had purchased from a manufacturer in Concorde, New Hampshire in the USA. It could take up to twelve passengers but on this trip was to carry only ten. He also explained that the ten mules pulling the coach would be replaced every ten to fifteen miles and the driver twice a day. The coach would only stop for changeovers of mules. Some of the changeovers had simple food for sale and primitive but adequate ablution facilities. Giles asked Zeederrberg why horses were not used. It was explained to him that horses were more susceptible to horse sleeping sickness than mules.

When the coach seemed to Giles be overloaded, with ten passengers and their luggage, it set off. The coach was crowded but soon warner than the exterior. There were eight other men and a woman in the coach. Giles had a seat between the side of the coach and the young woman. The drive to Johannesburg was unpleasant from the start, The seats in the coach were only thinly padded and the only moderator of the bumps and holes in the dirt road was a multiple leather strap suspension arrangement.

Giles talked to the young woman next to him but said little to the other men passengers most of whom seemed to be Dutch or Afrikaans, as it was often called, speakers, The young woman was English and was going to Johannesburg to take up a post as a teacher in a girls' school. For five days the coach travelled for one and a half or two hours and then stopped for about ten minutes before setting off again. It was almost impossible for Giles to sleep being in an uncomfortable sitting position and trying not to get too close to the young woman. The young woman fell asleep on Giles's shoulder. He let her do it as he could see that she was afraid of the rough looking man on her other side. The smell of her perfume, though it was not the same as Emily's, made his heart ache for the young woman he had just got to know and had now left behind in Cape Town.

On the second day Giles changed places with the young woman much to her relief. The journey to Johannesburg took a total of five and a half days. Giles was tired and dirty. He was met at the coach station by one of Rhodes's men who took him to a good hotel where he had a large meal and bath and slept from two in the afternoon until six o'clock the following morning.

The morning was cold again. Giles was picked up in a buggy by the same Rhodes man who he persuaded to let him buy a coat on the way to the stables where he was to meet his escort to Gaberones. At the stables Giles was introduced to his ride, a large roan gelding of some seventeen hands. The owner of the stables had first satisfied himself that Giles was no mean rider before he allowed him on the magnificent beast. Giles was pleased to note that the saddle was an Australian bush saddle, with high pommel and cantle and comfortable for long rides. He stored the brief case in a saddle bag, secured the bags across the horse behind the saddle and tied his gun scabbard to the rear of the saddle. Giles was ready and happy to set off and see what the day was to bring.

He also met his Bechuanaland Police escort which consisted of a heavily built, middle aged sergeant with large moustache, sideburns and distinct Cockney accent, and six black constables. Sergeant Gulliver greeted Giles with a measure of respect in spite of Giles's youth until that is, he saw Giles adjust his stirrups prior to mounting.

"Young Sir, begging your pardon, but those stirrup leathers are too long. You best tighten them."

"Thank you, Sergeant, for your advice, but I find that the slope of the high pommel of an Australian bush saddle tends to rub on your knees if your stirrups are too short," said Giles.

The sergeant then realized that his charge was older than his years and said with a measure of respect," Yes, Sir, I see what you mean."

"Cut the Sir, Sergeant, and call me Giles," said Giles.

It did not take long for the sergeant to get his party together and ready to head for Bechuanaland. He gave Giles a canvas water bottle to hang from the rear of his saddle. He explained that the canvas allowed a slow seepage of water to the outside of the bag which cooled it and its contents. The party left the stables with the sergeant leading on a large part shire horse. Giles rode next to him followed by the mounted constables one of whom had control of two pack horses loaded with camping gear and food and water.

It took some time to leave the chaos of Johannesburg where thousands of people were milling around like a lot of ants. The all seemed fired up with gold fever. Giles did not like Johannesburg; thought it smelt of greed and discarded rubbish. Gulliver explained that they were heading for Rustenburg a small farming town a good day's ride away. The road they travelled was little more than a dirt track and singularly devoid of other travelers.

As they rode, the sun started to warm the air and Giles enjoyed being on a horse again. He and Gulliver talked to each other whilst the constables chattered to each other in a language unknown to Giles. The sergeant had served for twenty years in the British Army and had come to Africa to fight in the First Boer War. He had loved the wildness and the open expanses of Africa and joined the Bechuanaland Police instead of returning to England where he had no family worth mentioning.

Time passed quickly and Gulliver steered his party off the road to a clump of gum trees a mile or so short of Rustenburg. Here the well drilled constables erected three tents, got a fire going and brewed tea that they and the two white men drank with copious amounts of condensed milk. Giles spent a good night on a wood and canvas camp bed. It was not long after they had struck camp that Rustenburg came into sight. The party of riders passed through the small town conscious of unspoken animosity from the locals.

Just beyond the town they joined an obviously better used road that ran from Pretoria to the Bechuanaland border. Giles noticed that, as they travelled further west the dry grass plains of the Transvaal Highveld gave way gradually to a landscape characterized by trees and bushes and rocky kopjes. On the third day of their trip Gulliver announced that the party had crossed over the border into Bechuanaland. It took another day and a half to reach Fort Gaberone which consisted of little more than a collection of corrugated iron buildings fenced off with barbed wire. Gulliver delivered Giles to the office of The District Officer a young man not much older than Giles. The D.O. was obviously short of company and fed Giles on tea and then cold beers while he extracted news of Cape Town and England from Giles. He then fed Giles on kudu steaks and treacle pudding.

Travelling north along a well-defined track Giles's party covered the distance to Macloutsie in another three days of hard riding. Macloutsie was the administrative centre of Bechuanaland, but only big enough to be what would be called a small town in England. Gulliver left Giles with the District Commissioner; a crusty old man who should have been put to pasture years before. He took Giles across the road to what passed as a hotel and introduced him to John Moffat, who was a tall middle-aged man with dark hair and Lincoln style beard and large moustache. He greeted Giles affably. The D.C. took his leave. Giles and Moffat went to the hotel bar and sat in a corner with a couple of cold beers and discussed strategy for their trip to Bulawayo.

The following day Giles, Moffat and a well-armed escort left Macloutsie for Bulawayo. Giles was pleased to see that the escort was led by Gulliver and included not only ten police constables, but a detachment of ten British Army men under a corporal. Under Gulliver's direction the group of riders headed northeast on a not well-defined track through thick shrub. Gulliver assured Giles that he knew where he was going. As they rode Moffat and Giles talked. Giles was fascinated to learn from Moffat about his life as a missionary and all about David Livingstone, the missionary and explorer who had married his sister.

As they talked Moffat made it clear to Giles that though he was going to assist in getting a treaty with Lobengula, he was suspicious of Rhodes's motives and did not want to see the Matabele chief cheated or deceived. He agreed to do in principle what Rhodes requested him to do, in the letter given to him. Giles had read his letter with interest. In it was a lot of advice on how amongst other things; "how to handle a native chief; always address him from a lower position and to wait until the chief spoke first before speaking". Rhodes also outlined for Giles how getting mining concessions from Lobengula for the British to the exclusion of the Boers and the Portuguese was very important as a recent approach to Lobengula by Rudd and Maguire had failed.

Two days later the column of mounted men crested a rise and saw below them a large group of huts mostly made of grass in what could be described as a beehive design. That morning a constable had been sent ahead to appraise Lobengula of their imminent arrival. A man dressed in a skirt of animals' skins and carrying a spear and shield approached the men on horseback. He raised one arm and shouted "Sanibonani".

Moffat replied Sanibona, ninjani?"

Mofat explained that the man was one Lobengula's indunas or headmen and all communication with Lobengula would be conducted through him until such time as Lobengula condescended to speak to them personally. After a short conversation between Moffat and the induna, the visitors were led down into the kraal. A large group of men all carrying spears and shields had gathered leaving a path for the men on horseback to enter the kraal. At a signal they all shouted "Bayete."

the original royal salute of their Zulu forefathers. Giles admitted to himself that he was intimidated but got comfort from unclipping the holster of his revolver at his side. As the mounted column moved forwards the crowd of armed men closed in behind them.

The induna led Moffat's group to a separate small kraal in which there were a dozen small huts. He explained that the visiting group were to stay in the smaller kraal until Lobengula was ready to see them. They would be provided with meat and beer. Giles and Moffat moved into one of the huts. It was surprisingly clean and cool. Their escort took up residence in the other huts. In a short while large clay containers of local beer arrived along with a tin tray piled high with large chunks of roasted meat, presumably beef. Giles took a sip of the millet beer and took no more. To him it tasted like a mixture of vinegar and chalk. He went surreptitiously to where he had placed his saddle outside the hut and took the water bottle in with him. He was surprised that Moffat and the rest of the contingent had laid into the beer and by nightfall most of the constables and the soldiers were moderately drunk.

Giles lay down to sleep but was annoyed by the high-pitched whine of mosquitoes. He dug out the little snuff box and cautiously smeared a small amount of the nasty smelling unguent on both his arms and legs and neck. Within a few minutes the mosquitoes had disappeared. Moffat was also happy to make use of Motsepe's mosquito 'chaser' even though it smelt pretty foul.

The next morning more food and milk were brought to the kraal and then they waited. It was past noon when he induna of the previous day arrived to say that Lobengula would see them in his kraal. He insisted that only Moffat, Giles and Sergeant Gulliver went with him to meet Lobengula. Giles and Gulliver were uncertain about this arrangement, but Moffat assured them that it would be fine as it was not Matabele custom to kill anybody after you welcomed them with food and drink. Moffat, Gulliver and Giles followed the induna to a large kraal where he told them to sit on stools outside a large beehive hut. After a wait of about ten minutes Lobengula came out of the hut. He was a large man dressed only in a loin cloth and headdress. He raised his one arm and shouted," Bayete" and sat on a carved ebony wooden chair facing his visitors.

What followed now was a strange conversation. Moffat was capable of speaking Ndebele to Lobengula but he had to speak to the induna who then relayed what had been said. The three-way conversation went on for over two hours. Giles was bored and after a time looked around the Chief's kraal. He noted that in the chief's kraal there was a ring of smaller huts standing outside of which were only women, presumably his wives, reputed to number about twenty. He noticed that in an adjacent kraal were several more European style huts and around them a handful of white men probably, in Giles's estimation, miners and hunters enjoying the chief's patronage.

At last, the meeting, the indaba, was over, and Moffat and Giles returned to their kraal. Moffat told Giles that he had done his best with Lobengula, but the chief was undecided and would consider the matter overnight and give his answer the following day. Another uncomfortable but mosquito free night followed. The following morning back at the chief's kraal, the lengthy three-way conversation started again. Lobengula told Moffat that he was disinclined to accede to Rhodes's request but had received a letter from Dr.Leander Starr Jameson, a friend of Rhodes, asking him to sign a treaty with Rhodes. He, Lobengula, could never forget how Jameson had once treated him for gout. Before he gave a decision, Lobengula compared Rhodes and the British to a chameleon who moves very slowly and carefully until within striking distance of its prey and then shoots out his tongue and swallows the fly. He, Lobengula, was the fly. However, he was tired of all the different white people pulling him this way and that. He would sign the treaty.

Once Lobengula had made his decision and signed the treaty produced by Moffat, Lobengula announced that it was time to celebrate and a large quantity of millet beer was produced and a whole ox was slaughtered, gutted and cooked on a spit on an open fire. Drinking and eating continued for the rest of the day. Giles and Moffat made their way to their hut early in the carousing. They discussed the treaty. Giles was inclined to heap praise on Moffat for getting the treaty signed but Moffat expressed sadness,

" Giles, Lobengula has probably signed his death warrant. He is wise, bush wise that is, but he is street ignorant. Colonialism will crush him eventually."

Giles did not comment.

The signed treaty that Giles took back with him to Cape Town later became known as the Rudd Concession after Charles Rudd, business partner of Rhodes, who had done much of the early negotiating of the treaty.

Moffat and Giles battled to get their escort ready to leave Lobengula's kraal. Most of the men had massive hangovers, and some seemed likely to fall off their horses as the column rode away from Bulawayo. Giles was glad to be on his way to back what he now called home and yearned to be in the delightful presence of Miss Emily de Speville. The return journey was uneventful. In Macloutsie, Giles said goodbye to Moffat and the escort. He felt he had met a good and great man, perhaps not as famous as his brother-in-law David Livingstone. In Johannesburg Giles said goodbye to Gulliver and his smaller escort. He was sorry to see Gulliver go. To Giles, this gruff and tough man symbolized what was good in the working-class part of English society.

Before he set off on another uncomfortable coach ride, Giles went shopping in Johannesburg and bought a box of what he thought were lovely lace handkerchiefs for Emily. Again, there were ten passengers in the coach and the seats were as hard as ever, so it was with relief that Giles got onto the train in Kimberly headed for Cape Town. The grey clouds and light rain that fell over Cape Town did not diminish Giles's delight at being back in his city. He was pleased the trip had been a success for Mr. Rhodes, but he yearned to see Emily again. However, Giles had loved the wildness and lack of civilization of that country beyond Bechuanaland, a love that would last for the rest of his life. He loved the rocky characterful kopjes and the mopani and baobab trees, even the weird blue headed lizards that made the kopjes their homes and the cry of fish eagles floating hopefully over nearly dry rivers.

*****

Emily stopped what she was doing several times a day and thought about Giles. She wondered, with some concern, where exactly he was and if he was safe. She might not have spent so much time thinking of Giles if the weather had not proved to be typical of a winter in the Cape, cold and wet. Work on her garden slowed. Motsephe was too old to work in the cold and rain and he now spent most of his working day carving wooden labels on which Emily intended to put the name of indigenous plants in the garden. One day he arrived at the house with something for Emily. It was a kitten, about six weeks old apparently abandoned by its mother. Emily was delighted and happy to devote time to feeding the little black furred mite. Having established it was a little girl, she called it Erica.

Emily had managed over the past few weeks to piece together a rough idea of where Giles was and what was going on from conversation at the dinner table when on two occasions Rhodes had dined at La Mercy. She yearned to ask Rhodes where the love of her life was, but suppressed her feelings. It was therefore with great joy and excitement that she read the short note that Motsephe brought her from Giles to say he was back safely in Cape Town and couldn't wait to see her and relate his recent experiences. On questioning, Motsepe revealed that he hadn't actually spoken to Giles. Giles had hailed him from outside the natural garden and had placed the letter in the fork of a tree branch from where it had been retrieved. It thrilled her to learn that Giles had delivered the letter even before reporting to Rhodes.

*****

Giles was greeted with something almost approaching friendliness from Mrs. Van. She forgot to call him "a bloody roineck". Giles assumed that at least part of his friendly reception was due to his more than generous payment of rent in advance. He lay on his bed and reflected on the interesting weeks that had just passed. He was disappointed that he could only see his mountain through a mist of slowly falling rain.

The following day, the weather was typically wet and gloomy. Giles wore an oilskin poncho as he cycled to the Parliament Building to report to Rhodes. He did not have to wait long before Rhodes called him into his office. The treaty which he had handed over to one of Rhodes's men at the station on his arrival was lying on the desk.

"Well done, Elliott-Smith. I am very pleased with what you and Moffat have achieved. Hope you are okay and suffered no ills from your trip.?"

Giles assured Rhodes that all was fine with him. For the next hour Rhodes described in some detail what his, Giles's, role was to be over the next few months. Giles was to assist in the move for the de Beers Diamond Company's takeover of Barny Barnato's company in Kimberly. Barnato was Rhodes's biggest competitor in the diamond industry and the takeover would give de Beers more or less worldwide control of the diamond industry, He was also to assist in setting up the British South Africa Company which had just been granted a royal charter by Queen Victoria to exploit the mineral resources of both Matabeleland and Mashonaland further north. He would, in addition help in administration work associated with the formation of a substantial column of police and settlers to be sent to occupy Mashonaland. Finally, Rhodes expected him to do odd jobs associated with Rhodes's plans to be elected as Prime Minister of The Cape Colony. Giles cycled down to the bookshop to see Zeke. His mind was buzzing with all the information from Rhodes. He was however feeling proud of himself and optimistic.

He entered the bookshop and got a shock. Standing next to Zeke was Mary, the young woman from the library. Zeke was pleased to see his former assistant and explained how Mary had come into the shop about two weeks ago and impressed him with her knowledge of books. Zeke engaged her for her knowledge of books but not least to postpone his retirement. Giles gave a guarded account of his trip up north and was very much aware of the admiration it garnered from Mary.

Since Rhodes had insisted on Giles taking two days off, his next stop was to see Ebrahim. His good friend was delighted to see him and report that their stock of scrumpy was selling well and would be finished before the next apple season. Giles told Ebrahim that as far as he could see he would be so busy when the next cider making season arrived, he would be of little use to Ebrahim. The two partners of E and G Scrumpy discussed what to do about their business and decided that, having made good money out of the business so far, they should sell their company for any reasonable offer. Another relevant consideration was that Rhodes had told Giles that he could get himself a clerk to help him with administration work, and subject to Rhodes's approval he was going to put Ebrahim forward for the job. Ebrahim was shocked at the idea of having a proper job but was eventually convinced by Giles's to get his first regular job.

So it was that, two weeks later, E and G Scrumpy Company passed into the hands of a consortium made up mostly of Ebrahim's relatives, for the sum of three hundred pounds to include the orchard, equipment and remaining stock in the warehouse. Ebrahim Agmat became an administrative assistant in the Cape Colony Government. Rhodes had approved the appointment of a person of Cape Malay blood. He and Gilles celebrated Ebrahim's entry into legal employment with a tasty curry in the Malay District.

For the next few months Giles worked hard for Rhodes assisted by a very diligent and capable assistant. He had to travel for a week every month to Kimberly where he learnt a lot about diamond mining and the ruthless policies of De Beers as they swallowed up Barny Barnato's diamond company. He met Alfred Beit who was a large part of the finance behind de Beers and also Charles Rudd who was the initiator of the treaty with Lobengula. While he was in Cape Town, Giles's time was taken up the setting up of the BSA Company and the appointment of men to its newly formed para-military police force. In addition, Giles was heavily involved in the election of Rhodes as Prime Minister of The Cape Colony. His importance in the portals of parliament rose to mirror that of Rhodes.

The major flaw in Giles' s life related to his and Emily's relationship. Much as they loved each, their secret meetings on the lower slopes of Table Mountain, usually under the watchful eye of Motsepe, could not sustain a long-term relationship. Eventually it was Giles who decided that he would approach de Speville and ask permission to court his daughter. Giles suspected that de Speville was not disapproving of him but realistically realized that Mrs.de Speville would be the problem. Molly had never ceased in her efforts to find a suitable husband for her daughter. Apart from Giles's lack of so called 'breeding', he was young. On a day when the sun was shining and Emily had happily received the box of handkerchiefs, the two young people decided to take the plunge and approach her father. They decided that as long as they could see each without going behind her parents back, they would offer to not consider marriage before Emily was twenty-one.

As he walked along the corridor to de Speville's office, Giles was more terrified than he had been riding his horse down a narrow channel of armed Matabele warriors. Giles knocked and then entered the office. De Speville looked up.

Oh, it's you, Elliott -Smith. I am hearing good things about you from Rhodes. What can I do for you?"

I...I would like your permission to court your daughter, Emily." said Giles hesitatingly.

"I know you would. I saw the way you and Emily were looking at each other at Queen Victoria's birthday do. I like you, Giles, but Mrs. de Speville would never agree to it. Much as I love her, I know she is an unmitigated snob." said de Speville.

"I know I don't come from a so called 'good' family, but my family are good honest hard-working people. I have a good job and have managed to make quite a lot of money already. I have enough to keep Emily in a decent manner. Sir, if Emily and I agreed not to get formally engaged or married before she is twenty-one, would that appease Mrs. de Speville?" Giles said earnestly.

De Speville thought for a moment and then said," I think you would make a good husband for Emily. I am prepared to talk to her mother and see what I can do "

"Thank you, Sir," said Giles as he turned and left the office his heart beating like a steam engine.

That evening de Speville asked Emily and Reggie to leave the drawing room. He then told Molly what Giles had asked. Molly was adamant that her daughter had to marry well. At this point de Speville lost his temper," Molly, Giles is more of a man than all your bloody society dandies put together. He is going to amount to something and on his own efforts. If you stop him seeing Emily, you will alienate her. Let them see each other but no engagement before she is twenty-one. It might not last that long."

Molly was truly shaken by her husband's anger and backed down but only so far. "They can see each other, but only at La Mercy and at public events and with a chaperone where it is needed,

Chapter 7

1890 was a good year for Cecil John Rhodes. He became prime minister of the Cape Colony at the age of thirty-seven. His takeover of Barny Barnato's diamond interests gave him not only a virtual monopoly of world diamond trade, but made him a very rich man. He was determined to push on with his plans to expand the British Empire into Central Africa and to achieve this, a body of men was being recruited. Giles became very much involved in the setting up of the recruitment process.

Experts suggested that it would take an armed body of about two thousand odd men and a cost of about one million pounds to occupy Matabeleland and Mashonaland, the area north of Matabeleland. However, Frank Johnstone, an adventurer only twenty-three years old, offered to do the job with about two hundred and fifty men and for only £87000. Rhodes agreed. Frederick Selous, a famous hunter who knew Mashonaland well, agreed to be the guide for the column.

Giles helped Johnson set up a recruitment office in Kimberley and thousands of men volunteered. Eventually about one hundred and eighty colonists signed up and the British South Africa Police unit consisted of about two hundred men under the command of Lt. Colonel Edward Graham Pennyfather of the Inniskilling Dragoons, armed with Martini Henry bolt action rifles, seven-pound field guns and Maxim machine guns. It was agreed that each member of the Pioneer Column, as it came to be called would, on the successful occupation of Matabeleland and Mashonaland, be given a three-thousand-acre farm and sixteen mining rights to the extent of twenty-one acres.

Things were going well for Giles. The more Rhodes prospered so did he. He now earned a very respectable salary and could afford a place of his own but chose to stay at 76 Hout Street. He told himself that he liked the Mountain view from his room but in truth he found a sort of simple normality in the boarding house that contrasted with the hustle and bustle of his working life and was relaxing at the end of a busy day.

His relationship with Emily was going well. In accordance with the agreement with her parents, Giles was invited to call on Emily at La Mercy. He arrived in a suit and stiff collar and tie on a horse he had rented in Hout Street. He was greeted by Marcel de Speville on the steps up to the house.

"Let my wife dictate any conversations. Keep your tongue and good luck!" whispered de Speville.

To say that the air in the drawing room was icy would be an understatement. Giles was again introduced to Molly and Reggie. Reggie greeted Giles with a big grin, but Molly looked Giles up and down carefully before extending her hand. It angered her that the young man could not be faulted on his dress nor in his speech which Giles moderated to resemble that of his former school friends. When she considered his good looks, Molly realized that she was likely facing defeat in the contest to select a husband for her daughter.

It was de Speville who directed the conversation in any direction that aimed at getting Giles to talk about himself and the important work he did for Rhodes. Emily had very little to say but watched and listened as the love of her life was being almost interrogated. She did note that Erica the kitten, now larger than when it arrived at the house, made a beeline for Giles who was happy to scratch it behind its ears. Petit fours and Earl Grey tea was served. At last Giles was able to take his leave. Emily followed him down the steps to where the rented horse was tethered. She whispered, "Well done. Love you!"

Giles just smiled back. As he rode way from the house, he felt that the battle with Molly was, at that stage, more or less a draw. Back in the house, de Speville took Molly aside and suggested," Not such a bad lad, is he?"

"Could be worse I suppose. It won't last anyhow," replied Molly.

*****

Giles had just returned from a week in Kimberly helping Frank Johnson interviewing potential members of the Pioneer Column. He liked Johnson, a man not much older than himself, but self-assured and apparently totally in control of his adventure filled life. His love of the African bush was infections and when he suggested that Giles should join the column and get to claim three thousand acres of an Africa just waiting to be tamed, Giles gave the matter serious thought. He enjoyed working for Rhodes but did not want to spend the rest of his working life mostly tied to an office. He had loved the countryside he had seen around Lobengula's kraal and had been told that Mashonaland promised to be even better, especially for farming.

On his return to Cape Town Giles went to see Emily and, strolling with her in her natural garden, put to her the idea of going to Mashonaland and farming there. To his surprise she greeted the idea with enthusiasm,

"Can you picture us standing on the stoep of our own house and gazing out over thousands of acres of our own part of wild Africa, I love the idea.!"

"Me too. We will have enough capital to finance the farm especially if I sell my diamond shares which are worth quite a lot now," said Giles

It was there and then decided by the two young lovers that Giles would apply to join the pioneer column. He was well aware that his proposal might not be well received by Rhodes, and he avoided talking to Rhodes for several days. When he did speak to him, he was pleasantly surprised when Rhodes gave his approval for the idea saying,

" Of course, I will miss you here but, if I was in your situation, I would probably decide to do the same. Good luck to you. You can take it that you are accepted as a member of the column. I would ask one thing of you and that is that you act as my eyes and ears in Mashonaland." Giles nodded his assent.

Giles could not wait to give his news to Emily but had to wait a few days before he could smarten himself and call on her at La Mercy. He travelled to the de Speville residence by bicycle which he stood against the wall at the back of the house. The news of his acceptance as a member of the Pioneer Column was received with mixed reactions from the family. Emily was proud of Giles, but the reality of perhaps a year away from him began to sink in. Reggie was excited for Giles and wished he could go as well. De Speville admired Giles, but for the sake of peace in his family refrained from saying so. Molly had difficulty in suppressing her optimism that, in the absence of Giles, she could actively resume her quest for a suitable partner for her daughter. Giles and Emily were able to slip away from the house to her garden where they sat on a log bench made by Motsepe and talked.

Giles went to 74 Hout Street and waited for Ebrahim to return from work in Rhodes's office. When he told his friend that he was going with the Pioneer Column Ebrahim was upset,

"Do you think I could join you? Life here will become very boring without you, Giles." He said.

Giles thought for a minute and then said," You know, Eb, I am part of the enlisting team for the column. I have the right to accept you. You have to realise though that you will be the only non-white in a large group of men."

Ebrahim laughed and said," Dear Giles, do you think I would have survived so well in this city of colour and religious division if I wasn't able deal with insults and occasional offers to fight. In the bush things might be actually less divisive."

"I'll see what I can do," Giles offered.

Before Giles could do anything about Ebrahim's request to join the column, he was sent by Rhodes to Kimberley on an administrative matter. He was sitting in the Kimberley club one evening when Frank Johnson walked in. Johnson joined Giles at the polished mahogany bar. Johnson was surprised to hear that Giles had joined the column as a colonist. He impressed on Giles that taking possession of a free farm was the easy part of farming in a foreign country. He queried whether Giles had considered what he needed to take with him to establish a farm and how he was going to feed and pay the labour that would be necessary to open up a piece of wild Africa. Giles had to admit that he had let enthusiasm overlook practicalities.

That night in his hotel room Giles thought about the farming venture. He decided that as labour in Mashonaland would have no use for money in a society devoid of shops, he would take goods of all sorts with him. Thinking further on the matter he decided that he would need a wagon to take the goods he intended to purchase, and a wagon needed oxen and a driver and that was where Ebrahim could fit in. Instead of applying to be a colonist member of the column Ebrahim and possibly facing rejection, he could go as his wagon driver. Once in Mashonaland Ebrahim would be a free agent to do what he wanted.

The idea sounded good and the more he thought about it the more he liked it and saw the potential for he and Ebrahim to take more goods than they needed and set up a shop at the column's destination. He and for that matter, Ebrahim, both had more than enough money to purchase a large wagon with a team of oxen and fill it with saleable goods.

Back in Cape Town Giles was excited at the prospect of discussing the wagon and trading idea with Ebrahim. However, he decided that he couldn't wait to see Emily again. He dressed in a suit and tie and rode to La Mercy on his bicycle. Since he had not been able to warn Emily or her family of his upcoming visit, he put his bicycle behind the house and walked up the front steps with a degree of trepidation. A maid admitted him into the hallway and went to inform Mrs.de Speville of the presence of a visitor. He had to wait for ten minutes before being shepherded by the maid into the drawing room.

"Hello Giles," said Molly. "I wish you would let us know ahead of time when you are going to visit."

Giles was about to apologise when he was interrupted by the arrival of Emily, red in the face from running down from her garden,

" Mother please be reasonable. He has been away in Kimberley. How could he let us know he was coming!"

Molly said nothing and applied herself to some embroidery she had on her lap. Emily and Giles sat a modest distance apart on a sofa and Giles told Emily what he was going to do about buying a wagon and goods to take to Mashonaland. He made no mention of Ebrahim, knowing that Molly was taking in every word he said. Emily approved of Giles's plans even though she was aware that every step towards the trip to Mashonaland made her time with Giles more precious.

That evening Ebrahim joined Giles in his room. For a change Table Mountain was lit up by the evening sun. Ebrahim listened to all Giles had to say. When Giles had finished Ebrahim said, "Giles I seem to be in a situation where you are the one deciding my future all the time, but I am happy with that as long as, in this venture, I am allowed to be a proper partner and contribute half of the cost of wagon, oxen and goods. I am not short of money; I have recently sold my shares in Blue Ground Diamonds, and I am an experienced wagon driver. If you remember I was the one who brought the apples from Tokai to Cape Town in that wagon I borrowed."

The two friends celebrated the new business partnership with a couple of bottles cider Giles had in his wardrobe. Since the tentative date for the Pioneer Column to leave for Mashonaland was set for the end of June 1890, there was only two months left to buy a wagon, oxen and trade goods, the two business partners decided that Ebrahim should resign his position working for Rhodes and go to Rustenburg to buy a wagon. The Pioneer Column was scheduled to leave from Macloutsie in Bechuanaland near the border with Matabeleland.

Giles and Ebrahim felt that most of the pioneer colonists would be shopping for wagons in Kimberley and this would drive up prices and create a shortage. Ebrahim was also going to look for four 'salted' riding horses. Giles was already aware that horses raised in an area where there was horse sickness were relatively immune to the disease.

*****

Time passed quickly for Giles and now two weeks into June he faced the prospect of leaving Cape Town and Emily imminently for an unknown extended period. He said goodbye to Rhodes at his office at the Parliament building. Rhodes had wished him well and offered any help that he could provide. He said Giles could use his name but only judiciously. His goodbye at 76 Hout Street was a total contrast to his arrival two years before. Mrs. Van actually hugged him as did all her family members and the two other lodgers. Giles paid for a year's rent on the room. He justified this payment as being for storage of his meagre belongings. In truth it was probably more to preserve his connection with a very modest house and its very normal inhabitants, a place of happy memories.

Giles was in a total emotional mess on the afternoon that he went to say goodbye to Emily and her family. Giles said a formal goodbye to de Speville and Molly. De Speville wished Giles well and courted anger from his wife by telling Giles that they would look after Emily in his absence. Molly actually made an effort to be pleasant in her goodbye. Reggie was effusive and told Giles that when he was eighteen, he would go and join him in Mashonaland. At this point de Speville asked Molly and Reggie to go and help him with a problem at the stables. This left Emily and Giles alone and tearfully silent to start. Giles took Emily's hand and battled to talk,

"Emily, I don't know what to say. I will never stop loving you and I will come back for you and marry you and take you to our corner of Africa, I promise. I will try to send you a letter whenever I can. Please try to send me your news. Try through Pennyfather and the BSAP."

Emily could say nothing. She sobbed uncontrollably until Giles broke with convention and pulled Emily to him and kissed her fully on her lips. The kiss lasted and lasted. Motsepe passed the drawing room window at that moment and just smiled and moved on. Giles broke away

and rushed from the drawing room. He could just hear Emily crying out,"
I love you so much. Giles.

*****

Giles travelled by train to Kimberly and then on to Johannesburg by
the newly opened Zeederberg Coach service. He managed to find a local
coach servicing the Rustenburg area and he arrived dusty and tired there
to be met by Ebrahim. The two young men were delighted to be together
again and at the beginning of a life changing venture. Ebrahim had taken
two rooms in a small residential hotel the residents of which made it
obvious that they did not like 'Rooineks'. Giles couldn't blame them as
it was less than four years since Leander Starr Jameson had failed
miserably in an attempt to take over the Transvaal Republic.

On the outskirts of Rustenburg Ebrahim had rented a small rundown
farm. It did have a large barn and three paddocks. In the barn was a large
wooden four wheeled wagon in what appeared to be reasonable
condition. It had canvas canopy. Stacked in the same barn were boxes
and boxes of what Ebrahim explained were plates, paraffin lamps, bolts
of colourful cloth and a myriad of other things that were sure to go down
well in a basically cashless society in Mashonaland. Looking at the
merchandise Ebrahim had bought, Giles had serious doubts as to
whether it would all fit on the wagon.

Outside the barn was a stable and in the attached paddock were four
good looking 'salted' horses. In a tack room were two Australian bush
saddles as requested by Giles. In another paddock were ten oxen mostly
black and white in colour. Ebrahim explained that he had got oxen of
the Ntuli type bred by the Zulus and well adapted to the harsh conditions
of Africa. Guarding the contents of the barn and the animals were two
Tswana men who came from near Macloutsie and who were more than
happy to join Ebrahim and Giles on the trip to their hometown and
beyond. They could take it in turn to lead the oxen and do odd jobs.

It took a full day to load the wagon. By careful packing all the trade
goods fitted on the wagon along with two tents and two folding chairs.
The next day the oxen were inspanned, one horse saddled and the wagon
started to make its way slowly along the dirt road into Bechuanaland
that Giles had not so long ago travelled with Gulliver. It took four days
to reach Fort Gaberone. Here the wagon was turned north on the road

towards Macloutsie. Travelling so slowly was extremely boring for Giles and Ebrahim. At times Giles rode next to the wagon and he and Ebrahim talked of their futures and at times they just took note of the countryside that they were passing through. They saw some game, impala and eland. On one occasion a jackal scurried across the road in front of the wagon. They broke the monotony ever so often with Giles taking Ebrahim's place on the wagon. It took him many hours to learn how to crack the long whip.

It was on the seventh day after leaving Fort Gaberone as the sun was setting that they reached Macloutsie. The small town was totally overwhelmed by the host of men and horses and oxen which had descended on it. Giles and Ebrahim halted their wagon a mile short of Macloutsie next to a small almost dry stream. They tethered the oxen and horses on a patch of good grazing grass. They left their wagon and livestock in the hands of the two Tswanas and gave them each a 7mm Mauser rifle to act as guards. The two young men rode into Macloutsie. They could hardly breathe for all the dust in the air stirred up by all the men and horses on the move. Giles soon found where Featherstone was camped and renewed his acquaintance with him. He introduced Ebrahim as his business partner. Not far from Featherstone's camp Giles found a smaller camp where he found Frank Johnson. Johnson seemed genuinely pleased to see Giles and to meet Ebrahim.

"Nice to see some young men for a change," he said with a smile as he introduced Giles and Ebrahim to the older man sharing his tent. The older man was the famous Frederick Selous who was in fact only thirty-nine years old at that time. Selous was an interesting man. He came from an aristocratic family in London and was only fifteen years old when he was one of the surviving victims of the Regents Park skating disaster when about two hundred people were skating on the park lake when the ice cracked and forty people perished. At nineteen he went to the Cape and spent the next twenty years hunting in both the Cape and Matabeleland. He was well known to Lobengula and respected by him. He was a striking looking man with piercing eyes and a smart van Dyck beard.

The next two days were days of boredom for Giles and Ebrahim as there was little to do apart from feeding and watering the horses and oxen.

Chapter 8

On the twenty seventh of June the Pioneer Column left Macloutsie. It consisted of nearly four hundred men and over sixty wagons. Pennyfather and his BSAP cohort led the column followed by the wagons. Mounted colonists who were not with their wagons acted as outriders on either side of the column. Right at the front of the riders and wagons were three men, Johnson, Pennyfather and Selous. From the start progress was slow. The pace of the column was the pace of the slowest wagon. Giles and Ebrahim found themselves near the rear of the snakelike formation that wound itself along a barely defined track that led in a north easterly direction. Ebrahim drove their wagon and Giles rode close to it on one side. The dust they had to advance through stirred up by the wagons inn front of them was appalling. Luckily Ebrahim had foreseen the dust problem and had cut pieces of khaki cloth from one of their bolts of cloth for both him and Giles and their two Tswana servants. It was not long before more cloth was cut and offered to other members of the column.

From the start it was decided that the column would travel between three and six in the morning and from five thirty and nine pm in order to spare the oxen, who rested and grazed during the hottest part of the day. The area the column first travelled through was called the 'disputed territory' as this area's ownership was a matter of dispute between the Tswanas and Lobengula. Accordingly, the colonists and the members of the BSAP were on high alert. Three days after leaving Macloutsie the column crossed the Shashe River. From there on the bush was so thick that Tswana labourers were brought up to cut a road through the bush.

Giles was puzzled as to why their route was to take the column way to the south of Bulawayo and Lobengula. One afternoon he rode to the head of the now paused column and talked to Johnson. On being asked about the route they were taking, Johnston explained that Lobengula was in a state of war with various chiefs in the Mahonaland area and might think that Rhodes was going to sign treaties with the Shona chiefs to his detriment. He might try to stop the column proceeding further. Rhodes risked the ire of Lobengula by bypassing Bulawayo. Johnston confessed that he and the leaders of the column were aware that the column was being shadowed by an unknown number of Matabele warriors.

Crossing the Shashe River was difficult, and time had to be spent in digging away the riverbanks at a suitable crossing point, to provide ramps shallow enough for wagons to cross. Soil dug away from the bank was dumped in the river to make the water shallower at the crossing point. Beyond the Shashe River the column moved on slowly until the Bubye River was reached and the column paused for a suitable crossing to be constructed. The weather got hotter by the day and insects seeking moisture from mens' sweat and the clouds of flies that followed the oxen, nearly drove the men of the column mad. Mosquitoes at night were also a problem but less so for Giles and Ebrahim, who were able to dip into the large tin of unguent made by Motsepe and given to him by Emily two weeks before he left her.

Another two days and another river, the Nuanetsi, and the need to make another safe wagon crossing. Life became a succession of rivers that had little or no water flowing but with steep banks that presented problems for the wagons. Giles lost count of the names of the rivers, but it was after crossing the Tokwe River that the column halted and built a fort which was named Fort Victoria. The date was the fifteenth of August. Two days later the column turned north heading into the heart of Mashonaland. Going was slow as the oxen battled to pull heavy wagons through deep sand. Food was not a problem for the members of the column as there was plenty of game for meat and a good supply of maize meal on the wagons.

Giles noted that as they travelled north the weather became slightly warmer and the landscape changed from Msasa woodland to scattered trees on more open grassland. The air appeared thinner as the altitude increased. On the eleventh of August the column camped on the banks of the Gwebi river at a site that was originally intended to be the end of the column's trek. However, there was not enough water in the river and so the column turned round and recrossed the Makabusi River and camped near to a kopje. On the thirteenth of September the union jack was raised, in what was there and then named Cecil Square, and the town that was to grow round this spot was named Salisbury after Lord Salisbury, the then Prime Minister of Britain. Ebrahim and Giles cheered as loudly as the others as the flag was raised.

"We did it, Eb," said Giles as he shook his partners hand heartily. They each drank a couple of bottles of cider they had saved for the occasion. That afternoon they moved their wagon and horses about a mile southwest to the banks of the Makabusi River not far from the kopje which was the only prominent feature on a mostly flat plain.

Tents were soon erected, and the oxen and horses were tethered on long ropes so they could graze and drink at the river. Giles left their camp with rifle in hand and went looking for game. He soon found an impala which he dispatched with a clean shot to the heart. He dragged it back to the camp where the Tswanas gutted and dressed the carcass. That night the two young men and their servants feasted well. Under a bright moon Giles and Ebrahim lay outside their tent and gazed at the stars.

"See how clear the sky is," said Ebrahim.

"This is the place for us," replied Giles.

For another hour they talked about their journey, the difficulties the column had overcome and the people of the column they had got to know. Their fellow travelers had included men of all ages. There were farmers, carpenters, bookkeepers, teachers and even a young doctor. Giles went to sleep and dreamt of Emily and a multitude of children all of whom looked exactly like her. Ebrahim dreamt of a large shop with his name emblazoned across its front.

It was cool the following morning and crouched next to the remnants of the last nights fire was a figure wrapped in a blanket.

The figure addressed Giles and Ebrahim in passable English,

" I am Amos, and I am going to work for you,"

"Is that so and why are you going to work for us?" said Giles.

"Because you cannot talk to the people here and I can. I need a job. I am hungry," said the young man in the blanket.

"What do you think, Eb? Does he look any good to you?" said Giles.

"Looks a bit weak, but he has a point about the language problem," said Ebrahim.

"I am stronger than I look or will be after some food," offered Amos.

"First tell us where you learnt English," said Ebrahim.

"I was born far from here to the north in the land of the Bemba people. I learnt English in a school that Mr. Moffat built for my people. I came here to the land of Chief Harare with a white man, a hunter. He died many days ago and left me with nothing, no food" replied Amos.

Giles looked at Ebrahim who nodded,

"You have a job, Amos. We will see what you can do before we talk of what to pay you. Start by making a fire and cooking yourself some maize meal. You will also find some meat left over from last night."

Leaving the armed Tswanas to guard the oxen and two horses, Giles, Ebrahim and Amos headed toward Cecil Square. As they passed below the kopje Ebrahim commented to Giles,

" When Salisbury starts to grow, I think it will expand towards the Makabusi River. Here would be a good place to build our store."

Giles agreed and the two men moved on to an encampment to the north of Cecil Square where they found Johnson in a tent behind a desk.

"Morning, Frank. Happy to be here? What I want to know is firstly, is it fine with you if I build a shop near the kopje and, secondly, when can I get my three-thousand-acre farm?" asked Giles.

"Whoa, my friend. No problem at the moment as to where you put your shop, but your farm will have to wait until Mr. Rhodes sends us a surveyor. In the meantime, go and look at the area north of here near the Mazowe River. I have been there and there is some good farming land there, good rainfall and good soils, "answered Johnson.

The next day with the help of Amos, ten local men were engaged to clear a piece of land close to the Kopje and on it build a pole and daub thatched hut with two windows and a door. Ebrahim marked out the size of hut he wanted and left the rest to the locals. He felt very pleased with himself as he had put four secondhand windows and two doors on the wagon at the last moment. Amos tried to exert authority over the local hut builders without success but proved his value as a translator. Within four days, using local materials, a thirty by ten-foot thatched hut stood on a track that was being more and more used daily. Merchandise from the wagon was moved into the hut and displayed as best it could be and' E and G Traders' were in business. A sign to this effect was painted on one of the doors and erected over the other. The hut builders were paid in merchandise and went away happy.

Business flourished from the start and Ebrahim, Amos and one of the Tswanas were busy from morning to night. The other Tswana guarded the livestock at the Makabusi River. Giles had been to see Johnson again and he had offered to ride with Giles to the Mazowe River to see the farmland there. Giles was happy to leave the running of the shop to Ebrahim. It took a whole day of hard riding for Giles and

Johnson to reach the place Johnson wanted to show Giles. The last hour of riding found them on the edge of an escarpment looking down on a partly treeless plain that ran down to a river called the Mazowe River by the locals. To Giles the place looked perfect. He and Johnson rode down to the river which was still flowing strongly even though it was the dry season. They camped by the river and the next day rode along towards the northeast. It was about six miles along the river that Giles felt he had found his farm, the gods willing. The river ran wide and was full of fish that looked to be bream and way to the East was the dyke that looked like a protective barrier. To the south and north was farmland with rich looking brown loam soil. Checking landmarks in the area, Giles mentally marked his farm to be. On the third day, the two men returned to Salisbury.

Giles was surprised to find that, in his absence Ebrahim and his assistants had managed to construct a very rudimentary but usable counter out of saplings and behind it a set of similarly fashioned shelves. He complimented Ebrahim on his ingenuity. Customers came into the shop all day. Some were locals who had been paid in cash and wanted goods instead and some were colonists stocking up on things they needed while looking for farms to claim and many going to prospect for gold. Giles was amazed to see that Ebrahim had even put a small safe on the wagon and it now contained a substantial amount of money, Sterling and Transvaal Ponds and Portuguese Reals. He marveled at Ebrahim's ability to put a value on any foreign currency. There were even two small gold nuggets whose value Ebrahim had had to estimate.

Giles and Ebrahim knew that when their shop ran out of stock there trading days would be over as it would take the best part of three months to get more stock. At such time Giles was happy to go farming. It was he who suggested that Ebrahim should take over the mining leases that he was due along with the farm. Ebrahim jumped at the idea. So it was agreed that E and G Trading would soon cease to exist and from then it would be Farmer Giles and Prospector Ebrahim but still two friends.

Giles went to see Johnson who passed him on to Archibald Colquhoun who had just arrived in Salisbury as the BSA Co. administrator. Colquhoun remembered meeting Giles some time in the past in Cape Town and was aware of his connection to Rhodes. He was very helpful and suggested that in the continued absence of a survey, Giles should go to the piece of land that he wanted and put in stone cairns to demarcate the proposed farm. He should also draw a map of the proposed farm. The surveyor, when he arrived, could confirm the farm boundaries. He explained that three thousand acres would be about four and three-quarter square miles. Giles decided that he would return to the Mazowe River in two days' time to mark out his farm. That evening he sat in the shop hut and by the light of a paraffin lamp wrote a letter to Emily not knowing how he would get it to her. He wrote:

Dearest Emily,

I am sitting in a mud and stick hut in Salisbury, as it is now called, writing by the light of a lamp. Ebrahim is here with me reading a book. The journey here was slow and very dusty, but we got here. Ebrahim and I have sold most of the merchandise we brought here.

The best news is that I have found our farm. It is about thirty miles north of here. It is glorious. You will love it. The land I want for us lies between a rocky ridge and a river. The soil looks good for growing things. I am going to mark it out in a day or two.

How are your parents and Reggie and Motsepe?

I cannot tell you how much I love and miss you.

Keep well.
Your Giles.

P.S. I will find a way to get this letter to you.

The next morning Giles walked through the embryo town of Salisbury. Everywhere tents and huts and wooden buildings were springing up. He reached Colquhoun's tent and knocked on the tent pole.

"Enter," said Colquhoun, "Mr. Elliott-Smith what can I do for you?"

Sir, I have a letter for a Miss de Speville in Cape Town. Is there any way of getting it to her soon?" replied Giles.

Colquhoun took the letter from Giles and with a smile said, "can I assume that this is an important letter for a relative of The Attorney General?"

"Yes Sir, a very important letter."

"Leave it with me," said Colquhoun with a wink.

Writing to Emily had the effect of spurring him on in the search for a farm and so the next day Giles and Amos left Salisbury for the

Mazowe River. Ebrahim was to busy himself with selling the balance of their stock. Amos fell off his horse twice before he was able to stay in the saddle. Giles led the horse. On another horse Giles had packed a tent and some camping equipment. It took all day to reach the Mazowe River. On the way they had passed several locals who appeared friendly. One old man, when told by Amos where he and Giles were headed, suggested that they should pay their respects to Chief Matuswa of that area.

Giles and Amos pitched camp on the banks of the river. They ate the contents of a tin of bully beef and some hardtack biscuits. Amos sat on the riverbank and fished somewhat optimistically with a twig, some fishing line, a cork and a bent pin. Giles lay under a tree that overhung the river. He watched a malachite kingfisher sitting patiently on a branch above him. He let his gaze wander down the river from where he lay to where the water tumbled over some smooth rocks about half a mile away. What he saw was heaven except for the absence of Emily.

Bright and early next morning Giles and Amos set off riding northwards along the riverbank, heading to where the old man had said they would find the kraal of Chief Matuswa. It was not until they had covered about eight miles that they came upon a kraal of about ten huts. They were greeted by a small crowd of children with faces covered in flies. Chief Matuswa was a small elderly man dressed in skins. He had a distinct smell of acrid smoke emanating from him. He greeted Giles in a friendly manner and when Giles explained he wanted to farm about four miles away, the old man took on a serious expression and explained through Amos that the land belonged to his tribe but could be bought for a certain number of pots and pans and some material for his wives and children. He also wanted an axe and a paraffin lamp.

Though nothing had been said by the organisers of the Pioneer Column about having to buy their farms, Giles realized that for what amounted to very little he could appease the old chief. He knew that he would need the cooperation of the old man in the future when he needed labour to run his farm. He agreed to give the chief all that he had asked for. For the second time in his life Giles was then required to drink the millet beer that tasted so foul. When Giles and Amos left the chief, Giles sealed what was to be a long friendship by giving the chief his penknife and promising the other things the chief wanted as soon as possible.

The first cairn that Giles and Amos built was about a mile downstream from where they had camped the night before and on the far side of the river. The two had waded across the river with relative ease, it being near the end of the dry season. Giles sited the cairn about a hundred yards from the river and so secured a stretch of the river well within the farm boundary. The corner marker was a dead tree trunk surrounded by a pile of rocks gathered from nearby.

Giles and Amos retreated across the river and then Giles moved with measured and counted steps towards the rocky ridge. He intended to measure eighteen hundred steps but was prevented by a frightening experience. He was close to the ridge with Amos to his rear when he heard a snarl that halted him in his tracks. Not ten feet in front of him was a leopard with mouth wide open and slashing at him with her claws. Giles froze. He was tempted to draw his .38 revolver, but something stopped him. He saw that behind the leopard, crouched under a slab of rock, were two small leopard kittens. Giles withdrew backwards as slowly as he could and could sense Amos was doing the same. Gradually the leopard calmed down.

The incident with the leopard was terrifying but at the same time exciting. He longed to tell Emily that they would have their very own leopards and, there and then, decided that the farm would be called "Leopard Ridge". Because of a necessary detour, the next cairn was built on top of the ridge at an estimated mile from the river. From the second corner marker the two men turned and walked at a smart pace for exactly an hour and a quarter according to Giles's pocket watch. Assuming a pace of four miles an hour, they had covered about five miles. Another corner marker was built. Giles then headed over the ridge and down to the river, He and Amos waded the river and a hundred steps beyond built the fourth and final marker.

By the time a tired Giles and Amos returned to their campsite the sun was setting in the west. The few high clouds and the sun dipping over the ridge created a spectacular sunset. Giles rode back to Salisbury well pleased with what he had achieved over the last three days. Ebrahim was also pleased. Not only had he sold a lot more of the stock but had been befriended by an elderly prospector who having had his tongue loosened with a few bottles of the remaining cider, had given Ebrahim lots of tips on looking for gold and even had offered to teach him how to pan for gold in the nearby Makabusi.

*****

There was a certain emptiness in Emily's life. She still had her garden and a fast-growing cat and dog, but she missed Giles. Everyday she thought about him, worried about him and wondered where he was and what he was doing. She found some solace from riding the lower slopes of Table Mountain up to the Norfolk pine, the sight of which never failed to strengthen her memories of Giles. Lack of news from Giles did little to diminish her resistance to her mother's efforts to find her daughter a husband. Her father watched his daughter's sadness and he comforted her when he could without Molly's disapproval.

Marcel de Speville came home one evening with a smile for Emily as she greeted him at the top of the steps to the house. He looked to see if Molly was around, before handing Emily an envelope and whispered,

" Came to my office this morning."

Emily took the envelope in a shaking hand and then ran as fast as she could to her room where she flung herself on her bed tearing the envelope open as she did. She read the letter through three times, firstly as fast as possible in case some news escaped and then more slowly to savour every word. She was not sure whether to laugh with joy or cry with relief. Her Giles was fine and still loved her. Furthermore, he had found their farm. Giles's letter was put away in her jewelry box to be read periodically, often enough to sustain her love.

Chapter 9

Three months had passed since the Pioneer Column had raised the flag in Cecil Square. Salisbury was busy and growing fast. Buildings of a permanent nature were springing up along streets that had been carefully laid out under the supervision of Archibald Colquhoun. Wagons were now coming regularly from Bechuanaland with goods needed by the Mashonaland settlers. Ebrahim had been granted title to the piece of land on which his and Giles's shop had been built. The hut had been dismantled and replaced by a more substantial structure of sundried bricks, a shed in which Ebrahim and Giles lived when they were not occupied at Mazowe in the case of Giles or panning some river as in the case of Ebrahim.

A surveyor had arrived in Salisbury at last and at the suggestion of Colquhoun, one of the first farms he surveyed was Leopard Ridge. Giles was so happy and proud to see the four corner beacons, iron stakes in concrete, proving the extent of his farm for all to see. He had further consolidated the approval of his ownership of the farm by delivering to Chief Matuswa all the goods he had promised and more. He had been forced to drink more millet beer in the chief's hut where he almost choked on the smoke of a wood fire that explained the chief's permanent acrid smell. The chief had organized eight good strong men to go to work for Giles at an agreed wage plus a small kickback to the chief.

The first thing Giles did on Leopard's Ridge was to fence off a large pasture near the river using locally cut trees and barbed wire from the wagon stock and purposely not sold. All the oxen and two horses were put into the new pasture. Giles lived on his own in a tent erected near to the pasture and on the bank of the river. Amos had his own tent nearby. Giles had a single furrow moldboard plough stored in Salisbury. He had not been able to use it yet as the rainy season was too far advanced to start planting maize or any other crop this current season. The rains had come with a vengeance in November. Huge cumulus clouds built up each afternoon and then dropped their load of water amidst magnificent thunder and lightning storms, more spectacular than anything Giles had ever seen.

The river had risen to where it threatened to overflow its banks, Giles had to move his tent to higher ground. Not able to indulge in any farming activity as such, Giles spent many days exploring his farm. He looked for a suitable place to build a house for him and Emily. He finally chose a small almost level plateau just below the rocky ridge. There were panoramic views but perhaps the site's major asset was a small spring nearby that Giles had seen before the rains and was running then and would hopefully provide a permanent supply of clean potable water.

One day Giles was walking along just below the ridge near its southern end and thought he saw a glint in the rock above him. Further investigation revealed specks of what looked like gold. Knowing of 'fool's gold', iron pyrites, Giles did not get too excited but prized away some pieces of rock with his hunting knife and put them in his pocket and continued on his way. A week later Giles was in the shed in Salisbury with Ebrahim who had just returned from a prospecting trip with his old prospector friend. The trip had yielded, after a week of panning in the Makabuse river, a few tiny gold nuggets of virtually no value.

Giles showed Ebrahim the rock samples from the farm. Ebrahim's eyes lit up. Before Ebrahim got too excited Giles suggested that they go uptown to see the newly appointed government geologist. They showed the geologist the samples and waited. The geologist looked at the gold flecks and then using an eye dropper put a small amount of a slightly yellowish liquid on the gold flecks. He explained that the liquid was concentrated nitric acid which would dissolve iron pyrites but not gold. Ten minutes later two happy men left the geologist with their gold bearing samples.

Back at their shed Giles and Ebrahim discussed Giles's apparent good fortune. Giles however made it clear that he did not want to be a miner and suggested that he would use the sixteen mining rights he was due, to peg all along the ridge and then turn them over to Ebrahim to exploit. Ebrahim refused the offer as too generous, and the two young men argued back and forth for the time it took to drink two ciders each. Finally, Giles accepted a third ownership of E and G Mining Company, a company yet to be formed. Giles was more than happy. He had his farm and now his friend would have a gold deposit that might make them both rich.

Back on his farm Giles put his labourers to work stumping the msasa trees that were dotted over the grassland. He marked out an area of what he estimated to be about a hundred acres. He chose an area towards the northern end of the farm where he judged the soil to be good, He called on his time he had spent with Sir Paul's farm manager who told him how to judge a good loam soil taking a handful and wetting it. A handful of good loam soil would stick together but would not feel greasy like a clay soil. Giles wanted the field being stumped to be ready for ploughing and planting to maize just before the next rains.

Ebrahim had found a private geologist who had set up shop in Salisbury and hired him to go and assess the Leopard Ridge gold claims. Ebrahim and the geologist stayed with Giles who was happy to have their company. Giles walked with Ebrahim and the geologist to the ridge where he had found the traces of gold and left them there, Giles returned to what he called North Field where the labourers were working first chopping trees down, then digging round their root area and then using hand axes to chop the roots until the tree root bole could be moved. Giles intended to use oxen to move trees and roots to one side of the field where, when they were dry, they could be used for firewood.

Giles had appointed Amos as his foreman. This move had not been received well by his labourers who complained to Chief Matuswa. Giles went to see the chief and explained to him that he needed a foreman who could understand English. The chief suddenly understood the situation when Giles promised to give him six blankets. While he was with the chief Giles managed to avoid any offer of millet beer but did manage to get the chief to agree to sell him, for more blankets and goods, ten ewes and a ram from the chief's sheep flock, the choice of the sheep to be Giles's. Giles had decided to establish a flock of sheep initially of the local native breed but later to be improved by bringing in a good European ram. He saw that there was already a good market for lamb and mutton in Salisbury.

When he returned to his camp near the river, Ebrahim and the geologist were waiting for him. According to the geologist the gold deposit looked promising. It appeared to be a gold bearing stratum running at least in part along the ridge but was only visible at the place they had looked at. He suspected that the gold bearing reef could extend further but underground. He suggested that before a lot of money was spent on a rock crusher and sluice box, more of the reef should be exposed by hand and explosives to prove the extent and viability of the deposit.

Ebrahim and the geologist left for Salisbury, but not before Giles had given Ebrahim a letter for Emily to be sent on by Colquhoun, who had been passing on Giles's letters every two weeks or so. Ebrahim was to organize a miner with a blasting certificate to go to the farm and expose more of the gold bearing rock. Giles's labourers would be moved from stumping to moving broken rock using shovels.

*****

Emily lived for Giles's letters that came roughly every two weeks. She always took his letters to her room where she savoured every word he wrote. She immersed herself in his life out in the wild. She pictured him with his workers creating fences and clearing fields to be planted with some crop. She pictured him sitting outside his tent near the river watching the sun go down. She longed to hear that he had started building their house up near the ridge. When she had finished reading his letters, she put them in a jewelry box she hid under her bed. Her parents especially her father asked politely how Giles was doing. Emily always passed on good news with as little detail as possible. On her nineteenth birthday Emily was shocked to have a parcel delivered to her at La Mercy containing a set of David Livingstone's "Missionary Travels and Researches in South Africa." They were from Giles somehow ordered from Zeke. Emily was thrilled and even her family were impressed.

Emily continued to improve her wild garden with more and more indigenous plants. She discovered that, at the museum in Cape Town situated at the opposite end of the Gardens to Parliament, a collection of local plants was being collected. She went to the museum with her journal which she showed to a botanist called Ingrid van der Spuy. Ingrid was very impressed with Emily's journal and the illustrations and even more impressed on hearing about her wild garden. A mutually beneficial friendship rapidly sprang up between the two women. Ingrid and the museum collection filled, to a large extent, the gap in her life left by Giles's absence.

*****

With the aid of Giles's workers and explosives, enough of the gold bearing reef had been exposed to show that it was going to be worthwhile buying a ball mill and a trommel and sluice box to exploit the gold deposit. Giles gave Ebrahim a cheque for roughly one third of the anticipated cost of the mining equipment. Ebrahim went off with the wagon and the oxen to Kimberly to buy equipment as suggested by the geologist. The journey would take him away for nigh on four months. In Ebrahim's absence Giles devoted himself solely to his farm. He discovered that an enterprising member of the Pioneer Column had set himself up as a brick maker. He was exploiting a clay deposit near Salisbury and built a brick kiln a couple of miles south of Salisbury. Giles ordered fifty thousand bricks to be delivered to Leopard Ridge over the next three months. He regretted he couldn't collect the bricks, but Ebrahim was using the wagon and oxen.

A few months before Giles had asked Emily to put some thoughts together on her ideas for their house. With Emily's suggestions in mind, Giles made a drawing of the house that he and hopefully, Emily, wanted. The house was to face the distant river. Initially the house would consist of a large drawing room and a dining room to be Giles's bedroom for the time being, there would be a bathroom and kitchen at the back of the house. Giles planned a wide stoep to extend the whole of the front of the house.

With the help of Amos, Giles used tree branch pegs and string and a mason's square to mark the foundations of the house. Half a wagon load of lime arrived at the same time as the first of the bricks arrived from Salisbury. Using sand from a deposit just below the ridge, Giles got his workers to mix a lime mortar and proceeded to teach himself and Amos to lay bricks on the foundations of crushed stone and lime and sand. Using only a garden trowel bricklaying was slow but with experience both Amos and Giles improved as brick layers. When the starter part of the house reached roof level, Giles gave himself and his workers a week off. Giles went to spend two days in Salisbury where he gave measurements to a carpenter newly set up in business in Salisbury to make doors and windows. Amos, he left at the farm to tend to the sheep and spare horse.

Back at the farm Giles had a problem. One of his sheep had been taken. Since a blood trail led from the kraal where the sheep were put at night towards the ridge where Giles had first seen the leopards, it was reasonable to assume that the female leopard was the culprit. Giles could not blame the leopard for wanting to feed her offspring and did not want to kill it. The answer was to put close strands of barbed wire over the top of the night kraal. There were no more loses of sheep.

Work on the house progressed well over the next couple of months. Widows and doors were fitted. Rafters were erected and a roof of shiny corrugated iron soon covered the house. Giles and Amos were both proud of their work. An iron tank arrived from Salisbury along with some piping and of necessity Giles taught himself enough plumbing to link the spring above and behind the house to the bathroom and kitchen of the house. For the moment a long-drop toilet behind the house would have to suffice. He did however put in a covered way from the back door to the toilet for visits when it was raining.

Ebrahim arrived back from Kimberly, tired, dusty but happy with his purchases. He had a small ball mill, trommel and a sluice box and fittings to set up the mining operation. The purchases were expensive and both E and G Mining and the farm needed to start showing a profit within the next year or so. Ebrahim had brought Giles a present. He had bought him a young Dorset Horn ram which had been tethered to the wagon and which was glad to stop walking and be able to graze at leisure. Giles was delighted and hugged his good friend.

The next few months were busy ones for both Giles and Ebrahim. Ebrahim threw himself into the mining operation at Leopard Ridge. He paid his old prospector friend, Stanley, to come and share his mining experience and help him to install the various elements of the gold ore processing plant. He took over half of Giles's labour force that were not at that time needed on the farm. He got them breaking up rock dislodged by blasting and carrying it in wheelbarrows to the processing plant. Within a few weeks the plant was up and running powered by a stationary engine purchased in Kimberly. Water for the trommel was pumped from the river using a second stationary engine.

Meanwhile Giles concentrated on getting ready for his first maize crop. Using only the single furrow moldboard plough, untrained oxen and a willing but untrained Amos, ploughing the hundred-acre field took nearly three months. When Matuswa, the chief came to the farm to tell Giles that in his opinion the main rains were only days away and Giles was aware that that the weather was very hot and humid and black clouds were accumulating, Giles planted the field. It took a week to do by hand using five labourers. Within days the rains came and within another two weeks the hundred-acre field was dotted with regular rows of healthy young maize plants.

Giles had not ignored the livestock side of the farm. He had initially removed his old ram from his now growing flock of indigenous sheep and introduced his new Dorset Horn ram. He had to wait for five months before there was a regular supply of young cross bred lambs. Giles called these crossbreds his Dorpers, from Back Head Persians, the indigenous sheep and Dorset Horn. Giles gave the now unneeded ram to Chief Matuswa.

Work on the gold deposit went well except for when, after heavy rain, the stationary engine at the river had to be moved to higher ground. The first examination of the felt blanket in the sluice box was a day for both Ebrahim and Giles to remember. Watched by the old prospector, the blanket was lifted from the sluice box and washed and there on the blanket was gold and what appeared to be a lot of it. It was the old prospector who offered the opinion that the gold recovered could be as much as eight ounces. The last half dozen bottles of cider were finished off in no time at all.

The rains appeared to be over. A healthy crop of maize was nearly dry on the stalk and the mine was producing a steady flow of gold though it required more effort to extract the ore as the reef sloped deeper and deeper underground. One evening Ebrahim and Giles were sitting on the stoep of the house that they shared. They both smoked pipes, a habit recently acquired.

"Giles", said Ebrahim. "I am thinking of going back to Cape Town. I need to see my family and must think seriously of finding a wife. You have your Emily. I need somebody to share my life with. I can leave the running of the mine to Stanley for a while. He is old but reliable and I hope you will keep an eye on things."

"Good idea, Eb. Wish my time was up with Emily and I could go and marry her. Take your time. I will make sure that things work at the mine." replied Giles.

Before Ebrahim left for Cape Town Giles gave him a small wooden box for Emily and in it was a small bar of gold from the mine and a kernel of maize from his first crop. He wrote a short note which said:

For you Emily. The gold is to say how precious you are to me, and the mealie pip is a symbol of our future on the farm. I love you. Giles

*****

Ebrahim got off the train and paid a cab to take him to Hout Street. Nothing much had changed in nearly two years. Perhaps No. 74 needed a new coat of lime and some windows replaced. His family were happy to see him, and his mother prepared a feast of his favourite Cape Malay food. Ebrahim described his new life and the success of the mine. Up to the point when he honestly answered the question as to whether there was a mosque or not in Salisbury, he thought his family were interested in what he had to say. From there on they lost interest and Ebrahim suddenly felt that he was a foreigner in his own city. He realized that his horizons had expanded, and his family's had not. He felt a great sadness and even wished he was back at the mine and back to living in a society where ones standing was measured mostly by one's achievements.

He discussed the matter of finding a wife with his family. His parents made it quite clear that he would not find a Muslim wife of good standing as there was no mosque where he lived and no other Muslims. They suggested that he might, with all the money he had, be able to find a young woman of humble origin with limited education. Feeling depressed Ebrahim went for a walk. He found himself in Darling Street and outside the bookshop. He thought that perhaps he could buy Giles a good book for a present. He entered the shop. A young woman came up to him and asked if she could be of assistance. Ebrahim explained what he was looking for a book preferably on something to do with farming or farm animals.

The young lady busied herself looking along long stacks of books. She explained that the owner of the shop, a Mr. Goldblatt, would have known more about the books he was looking for but was off sick. Ebrahim saw in the young woman somebody who was polite and friendly and good looking. Mary saw a young man, good looking, more suntanned than most and well mannered. Neither of the two young people seemed to want to hurry the search for a book, The talked and talked. He told her of his mine and his life in the bush. She did not have lot to say about her life except that she came from a very modest home. Her father had been a wheel tapper on the railways and had died recently.

Her mother had fallen apart after the death of her husband had succumbed to an undetermined fading disease.

The more the two talked, the more the two found out that they had mutual acquaintances including Giles who she had once helped and Emily de Speville who came to the shop periodically. She did not tell Ebrahim that she had once had feelings for Giles. The afternoon passed quickly. The young couple fell in love there and then, though they both felt they had to suppress their feelings for each other in the knowledge that they came from different backgrounds and were currently in a society where the mixing of races was frowned upon. Ebrahim bought a book on sheep raising for Giles and left the shop. He was however back in less than two minutes.

"Please forgive me for what I am going to say, but I want to know you better. I know we come from different worlds but where I live now these worlds are not that far apart. Please can I see you some more?" he asked.

Mary looked him straight in the eye and in a moment of unusual daring said," Yes".

For both Ebrahim and Mary the next two weeks passed in a blur. Every weekday Ebrahim escorted Mary home after she had finished working at the bookshop. He met her mother who had little to say and was obviously very ill. On the first weekend that the young couple were together they went by train to Muizenberg and then slowly walked along the shore to St. James Bay. When they thought they were alone they held hands. It was on the second weekend and the couple had gone by train to Simonstown where they admired the ships and boats in the harbour. They were walking to the station when Ebrahim halted Mary and gently turned her to face him.

"Mary, I have been so happy the last two weeks. I know we will have problems because of our backgrounds but I want to marry you. Come with me to Mashonaland and we can hide from most of the world and be happy." said Ebrahim.

"I would marry you now, I would, but I can't leave my sick mother. I'm sorry Ebrahim," said Mary sadly.

The love affair might have ended there and then has not fate intervened. Mary and Ebrahim got back to the little house in a poorer area of Cape Town just as the sun was setting. They entered the house. There were no lights on. Mary went to her mother's bedroom and then screamed. Ebrahim rushed to see what the matter was. Mary was kneeling next to her mother's bed and crying,

"I am so sorry, Mother, I should not have left you, I shouldn't have. Please, please forgive me."

Ebrahim stood behind Mary and just waited. When Mary had exhausted her tears, Ebrahim pulled her to her feet and said," Maybe God has been good and rescued her from her suffering."

"I know you are right, but I feel guilty now that I can't even afford a proper funeral. I have failed my mother," sobbed Mary

"But I can and will," said Ebrahim earnestly. He continued, "what's more, if you want it, I will take you away from your sadness here and you can find happiness in the wide-open spaces of my new country which I will share with you."

Mary clung tightly to Ebrahim and said no more. From that point Ebrahim took over the arrangements for a funeral and paid for everything. Mary merely went along with whatever Ebrahim did. A week after the funeral Ebrahim sat Mary down in the now very empty little house and said," I must go back to the mine soon. I can leave you with some money to help you but, if you don't think I am rushing things, I am asking you to marry me and go with me back to my mine.

Mary smiled at Ebrahim and said, "you are a wonderful man, and I am ready now to marry you"

Mary and Ebrahim were married in the registry office by special licence. They had no reception. Ebrahim said goodbye to a disapproving family and the couple found themselves on a train steaming northward towards Kimberly.

Chapter 10

Marcel de Speville was walking past the closed door of Emily's bedroom. He thought he could hear crying. He retraced his steps and listened. He knocked on the door. There was no reply to start with and then a tearful voice said, "Come in."

De Speville found Emily sitting on the edge of her bed, head in hands. She had obviously been crying. Her face was tear stained and red. De Speville sat on the bed next to her and put his arms round her.

"Tell me what the matter is," he said.

Emily turned her face to look up at her father and replied,

" Father, I love him. He is a good man and he has already proved himself. Why do we have to wait? He had a good education and at the age of twenty-three has a three-thousand-acre farm, a third share in a successful gold mine and money in the bank. Why do we have to wait another year? I can't carry on living from one of his letters to the next. Please help us, Father. "

"Emily, I believe you are right about Giles, and I have come to like and respect him. Leave it with me and I will talk to your mother", replied her father.

"Thank you, dear father," said Emily as she hugged her father tightly.

After dinner that night de Speville asked Molly to go with him into his study. He closed the door behind them. He turned to Molly and said." You might as well sit down; I have a matter to discuss with you. Emily is desperately unhappy. She loves Giles and I think always will. I think it is time to accept him as a son-in-law. He will never have the so called breeding and social standing that has become an obsession with you, but in every other respect he is an ideal son in law."

Molly started to speak but de Speville got in first," He is already got more money than most of the chinless wonders that you keep trying to throw at her and certainly more guts in going to where he is and making a success of it."

Molly opened her mouth to speak, but again de Speville got in first," Molly I think time has clouded your memory. You were the daughter of a vicar and not a peer of the realm and you certainly have forgotten that you were only nineteen when I married you."

77

Molly started to cry. De Speville got up and leaning over her chair put an arm round her shoulder. He said," Molly, I love you and always try to see things your way, but this time I will go against you in what I think are your unreasonable wishes and let Emily and Giles get married."

"Marcel I am going to bow to your decision. I only hope you know what you are doing," Molly said.

"I do," said de Speville.

It was the following morning that Emily got to hear that she and Giles were going to be allowed to get married. She was shocked and could only respond by drawing both her parents into a threesome family hug that became a foursome when Reggie arrived and was appraised of the news,

Molly underwent a miraculous transformation. There and then she started plotting and planning for a wedding that could not take place for many months ahead. She spent hours making a guest list, at the top of which she put Cecil Rhodes's name followed by the names of everybody of any social standing in Cape Town society.

De Speville went out of his way to ensure that Emily's next letter to Giles was sent on its way with the whole weight of the Cape government behind it. So it was that in less than two weeks Giles got the letter.

*****

In fact, Giles got two letters on the same day. They were delivered to the farm by a messenger and had been forwarded to him by Colquhoun. When he examined the two envelopes he saw why. The one envelope had the seal of the Cape Attorney General on it and was marked urgent. Giles felt sick and didn't want to see what news would warrant the AG's seal. He steeled himself and opened the letter and relief and then extreme delight were immediately the emotions they moved in a wave over him as he read,

Dearest, Dearest Giles,

I am so happy. My parents have agreed that we can get married as soon as we like, no more twenty-one business. My father has been wonderful, and he approves of you. Even Mother has capitulated if we have a society wedding which, for the sake of peace, I have agreed to. Hope you agree and I hope you are still happy to marry me.

I love you so much Giles.

Please think about when we can get married. I know you have the farm to think about.

I can't wait to be with you again and enjoy your lovely farm with you.

Yours forever
Emily.

P.S. I loved the little box with the gold bar and mealie pip. It came in the post today. Thank you.

Giles found himself crying with both relief and happiness. He picked up the second letter which, as he read it, held another pleasant surprise,

"Dear Friend,

Be prepared for a shock. I am married. My wife you know. She is Mary, who used to work in the library and then for Mr.Goldblatt in the bookshop. She knows you and likes you. Our courting was very quick and dramatic. Her only relative, her mother died recently, and I was privileged to be able to, not only help her, but marry her in a very simple wedding. We know we come from different worlds but know our newfound love will sustain us. Hope you approve, Giles. We leave on the train tomorrow. Please organize a couple of tents for us to live in near the mine.

Sincere regards
Ebrahim.

Giles had so much to think about that he didn't know where to start. The matter of accommodation for the newlyweds was the easiest problem to solve. He would cover in one corner of the stoep at the front of the house to create a temporary bedroom for himself and let the newlyweds have his bedroom until Ebrahim was able to build a house of his own for him and his bride.

Giles had to think carefully about a wedding date. He had just recently harvested his maize. The North Field had yielded over a hundred tons that had been carted by wagon to Salisbury to be stored in the warehouse in what was now called Kopje Road. More than half of the maize had been sold for a high price as there was very little locally grown maize available for milling.

Ploughing of the North Field again was now in progress and would be ready for planting in about two months when the rains started. Immediately after planting would be a good time to leave the farm and head for Cape Town.

He then replied to Emily's letter,

Dearest Emily.

I was thrilled to get your letter. Please thank your parents for being understanding and give them my regards and to Reggie. I would love to say that we could get married tomorrow, but a farm is a demanding master and I think the earliest I can be in Cape Town for the wedding would be late October or early November, so why not plan the wedding for mid-November if that is okay with your parents.

Had a surprise letter from Ebrahim. He is on his way back here from Cape Town with his new wife, Mary, who worked in the Cape Town Library and more recently for Zeke.

Can't wait to be with you. Not long now.

Yours lovingly
Giles.

P.S. Please ask Reggie if he will be my best man. Don't know who else to ask.

Giles saddled up his horse the following day and rode to Salisbury. As he rode, he noted how the original track between Mazowe and Salisbury was, purely from wear, becoming a well-defined dirt road. He noticed that there were signs of farms being occupied along the way. The first thing he did in Salisbury was to visit Colquhoun who had become somewhat of a friend. He asked him to send the letter to Emily as he had done at least a dozen times before. He then headed to Kopje Road to check on his store of maize. He was pleased to see that since he had installed two cats in the warehouse there was no more signs of rats.

On an impulse he headed back uptown to where the surveyor had his office. He asked to see plans of the area around Mazowe and was pleased to find that the land to the west of Leopard Ridge was marked as unoccupied. He went from there back to Colquhoun's office for the second time that day. He asked Colquhoun if Ebrahim, as one of the original pioneers and who had not claimed a three-thousand-acre farm, could be allocated the land to the west of his farm. Colquhoun told Giles that pioneer allocations of farms had been closed six months ago. However, if Mr Agmat could find £500, the BSA any would be happy to sell the land in question to him.

Acting on another impulse Giles went to his bank, the newly established Standard Charter Bank, and got a draft for £500 which he took to Colquhoun and asked that the three-thousand-acre block of land to the west of Leopard Ridge be registered in Ebrahim's name. His next stop in Salisbury was to see a man, a builder newly arrived in Salisbury. Gordon Mackenzie was a rough and tough looking Scotsman who Giles took to immediately. Mackenzie admitted that he had not got much work yet and so was happy to go and see Giles on the farm and discuss the enlargement of Giles's house. As he headed back to Mazowe Giles felt pleased with his trip to Salisbury.

Only two days after getting Ebrahim's letter, Giles was sitting on his stoep drinking tea on his own, He had had a busy day choosing fat lambs from his flock to be sent to Salisbury to two butchers to slaughter and sell. Amos had gone off with them on the wagon and would be back the following day. All Giles could think about was his forthcoming wedding and being with Emily again. He let his gaze wander along the ridge, and it was then that he noticed a small cloud of dust on the horizon. As minutes past he saw a wagon approaching with three people on it.

As the wagon got closer, he couldn't believe his eyes. It was Ebrahim and Mary and a wagon driver. Giles rushed to the wagon which had come to a halt and was just in time to help Mary down from her seat. Mary spoke first," Hello Giles. This must be a big surprise for you."

"Hello Mary, it's a wonderful surprise. I couldn't be happier for you," said Giles.

Giles walked round the wagon and hugged Ebrahim,

"Welcome home friend and congratulations. I am so happy for both of you."

"It is wonderful to be home again and especially with Mary by my side" said Ebrahim as he turned and pointed to a Dorset Horn Ram tethered to the back of the wagon. "You did tell me that you needed to introduce new blood into your flock every so often. Bought it in Kimberley."

"Thanks, my friend, let's go to the house. You have my room for the moment. I have a temporary bedroom on the stoep. Your wagon driver can sleep on the stoep tonight and we will unload the wagon tomorrow." said a smiling Giles.

There were no more ciders left with which to celebrate with, but Giles found a small bottle of medicinal brandy which Giles and Ebrahim shared while Mary sipped tea. The three young people talked and talked; there was so much to talk about. Mary and Ebrahim related to Giles how they had met and subsequently got married after Mary's mother's death. They mentioned that Zeke had decided that he could no longer run the bookshop and was going to sell up and go back to the part of East London he had left nearly fifty years before.

The conversation moved from the stoep to the kitchen where Giles cooked some lamb chops with mashed potatoes. Mary and Ebrahim protested about using Giles's bedroom, but Giles would have none of it. It was then he told the newlyweds,

"You will soon have not only your own bedroom, but your own house. I have bought the farm next door to the mine. That is my wedding present to you.

Ebrahim wanted to cry, and Mary did, before giving a big wet kiss on his cheek.

"You are too good to us. Allah was great when he brought you into my life, Giles, croaked Ebrahim.

"Your Allah was good to both of us. No, to all three of us, my friend," replied Giles.

Back on the stoep conversation continued for two more hours until Giles remembered his new ram and also the wagon driver. He took the ram down to the sheep kraal and fed the wagon driver before going to sleep himself.

The wagon drove off the next morning with instructions to the driver to contact Gordon Mackenzie and ask him to come to Leopard Ridge to talk about building a house for Ebrahim and Mary and to enlarge Giles's house. Then Giles and Ebrahim rode up and over the ridge to see

Ebrahim's new farm. Mary sat on the stoep and worked at some embroidery, happy to take in the beauty of her new surroundings and to reflect on her good fortune at meeting Ebrahim. Ebrahim was pleased to find that there was a suitable place to build a house just over the ridge from the mine but on his farm and only about two hundred yards away.

Giles then led the way to the mine where Stanley was busy at work. Gold yield from the mine had been good while Ebrahim was away and there had been no major problems. However, Stanley did point out that the gold bearing reef was now dipping deeply into the earth and in the not-too-distant future surface mining would become too expensive and shafts would have to be sunk. The alternative would be to find another claim suitable for surface mining. Giles and Ebrahim felt that they had enough on their minds and decided to decide on the future of the mine when they had the time and inclination.

It was agreed that when Giles left for Cape Town and his wedding, Ebrahim would keep a watchful eye on Amos who would attend to supervising the labourers planting the maize and looking after the ever-growing sheep flock. When Mary found out about Emily's Garden, she asked Giles if she could have a labourer to help her as she would like to create a garden round his house. planting it with plants from the surrounding veld. Giles happily agreed.

Mackenzie came to the farm a few days after he was contacted by the wagon driver. Ebrahim took him to his farm and showed him the proposed site for his house and then described what he wanted built, modest to start with but open to expansion. From there Mackenzie was taken back to Giles's house and shown what Giles wanted in terms of three bedrooms, a study and a toilet with a flushing pan. Mackenzie agreed, on being offered an upfront payment, to recruit more labour and another builder in order to finish the two building jobs as soon as possible.

*****

Life was moving in a happy daze for Emily. She let herself be, at least in part, drawn into Molly's plans for the wedding. She submitted to a series of trips into Cape Town to the home of a skilled seamstress who was making her wedding dress. She did rebel enough to moderate her mother's plans for her daughter to be dressed in the fanciest wedding dress to be ever seen in the Cape Colony. During one session with the seamstress Molly went off to see a florist about flowers for the wedding. Emily took the opportunity to order from the seamstress, some practical clothes for life on the farm. She ordered two split skirts in khaki for riding, three heavy material shirts and two pairs of men's style trousers. She impressed upon the seamstress the need for secrecy as her mother would certainly disapprove.

Amidst all the joy of anticipation of her forthcoming wedding, there was one area of concern and that was her nature garden. After talking to her father, Emily went to see Ingrid van der Spuy at the museum. She offered the garden to the museum. Her father was happy to give the land to the museum. There was to be one stipulation and that was that Motsepe would be allowed to continue to work in the garden until he wanted to retire at which time, de Speville would pension him off and send him back to his Xhosa homeland. Ingrid was delighted to take over the garden on behalf of the museum and assured Emily that she would carry on her work. She tried to persuade Emily to give the museum her journals, but Emily was determined to take them with her to what people were now calling Rhodesia.

A letter from Giles gave a firm date for his proposed arrival in Cape Town, of on or about the seventh of November. Marcel and Molly were now able to go and see the Reverend Basil Mortimer of St. Paul's Church in Rondebosch and book the church for the wedding on the Saturday the twenty first of November 1891. A reception was to be held at La Mercy following the church service. It was intended that two large marquees were to be hired and erected on the lawn in front of the house. Molly decided that, because of the importance of the people on the guest list, the catering would be done by the staff of one of Cape Town's biggest and best hotels.

Emily decided that when she and Giles left for Rhodesia after the wedding, she would take Reggie the dog with her. However, in one of his letters, Giles explained to her that Reggie would be susceptible to various diseases in Mashonaland not present in Cape Town. Reggie was to stay at La Mercy with his namesake. She decided that Erica the cat would not like to be transported across Africa and she decided to leave her in Reggie's hands as well. Her horse would also remain behind largely because Giles had impressed on her the need for a 'salted' horse.

He assured her that there were good horses now available in and around Salisbury.

*****

    The time had come for Giles to leave Salisbury for Cape Town. He was to travel to Kimberly on a newly started coach service and then catch the train from there. On the farm, preparations had been made for his absence. The North Field had had a good dressing of sheep manure from the night kraal supplemented with ten wagon loads of manure purchased from Chief Matusa's village's sheep kraals. The chief was delighted that Giles would actually pay for sheep droppings. The determination of the date for planting of the field was to be left to Ebrahim and Amos to decide as and when the first rains came.

    Both Ebrahim and Giles were surprised to find how quickly Mary had settled into and fitted into life on the farm. She had brought some order approaching a garden to the wilderness round Giles's house. She cooked good meals for the two men and did their washing and mending. She found time each day to walk up and over the ridge to where her and Ebrahim's new house was rising rapidly under the sustained efforts of Gordon Mackenzie and his gang. Similarly, the extension to Giles's house was well advanced. Giles was hopeful that it would be complete when he and Emily returned late in December.

Chapter 11

The sky did not look welcoming as the train steamed its way below the Hex River Valley mountains. Rain poured down but nothing could dampen his enthusiasm, He could only think of Emily and seeing her again. He was not sure if she would be at the station to meet him. He had sent a telegram from Kimberley to tell her that he had been delayed by two days. He had hardly travelled twenty miles in the coach he had caught in Salisbury, when the heavens opened, and the rainy season began. He had initially delighted at the thought that thousands of maize seeds would be soon germinating in the North field and sheep would be delighting in the new green grass that would soon arise from the ground.

On the second day on the coach, the team of ten mules battled to pull the coach along the track wheels deep in mud. At two river crossings the coach had to wait until the water subsided enough to let the vehicle cross. From Kimberley onwards travel had been easy, boring in fact. Luckily Mary had given him a book she had brought with her from Cape town by G.A. Henty called the 'Dragon and the Raven'. Mile after mile of dry landscape passed unseen by Giles deeply absorbed in a tale of King Alfred and his fight against the Vikings.

As the train came to a halt, Giles took a quick look out of the carriage window. Some way down the platform he saw two figures who he was sure were Emily and her father. He picked up his now old and worn leather suitcase and alighted from the train. He was suddenly terrified. What if she had changed? What if she no longer loved him. His fear was not dissipated until he was a few feet away from Emily and she left her father's side and came and took his hand in hers. In deference to her father and that part of the population of Cape Town on the platform that day, she suppressed the overwhelming desire to rush to him and let him envelope her in his arms.

"Oh, Emily it is good to see you and it is good to see you too, sir. Sorry I am two days late, muttered Giles, his eyes fixed on Emily.

"It is wonderful to see you, Giles. Isn't it Father," cried Emily.

"Yes indeed, said de Speville. Let's get along. I have my buggy outside the station."

As the three of hem walked along the platform and then out of the station, de Speville told Giles that he was to stay at La Mercy but in the guest cottage for the sake of appearances. Giles tried to protest and say that he still had his room in Hout Street, but de Speville would have none of it. Giles did suspect that Molly was behind the invitation to stay at La Mercy. She would not have been able to bear the news leaking out that her future son in law was staying at some seedy address in the city.

As they drove along Cape Town's streets, Giles was surprised that he did not feel that he was undergoing a homecoming. He realized there and then that his home was now the vast open landscape of that new country, Rhodesia, and it would always be that way. As the buggy swept up the long drive and through the manicured gardens of La Mercy, Giles thought of the contrast between Emily's home and the little brick and iron farmhouse that was to be her new home.

Marcel drove directly to the guest cottage for Giles to put his suitcase down and to have a quick clean up. He looked in the mirror and was shocked to see how suntanned he was and how long and untidy was his hair. He realized that Emily would need a mirror in the farmhouse where there was not one yet. He walked a across the lawn to the main house. Motsepe appeared from nowhere even more bent than ever," Sabona, master. I am glad you have come for your wife,"

"Sabona, Madala, how are you?"

"I am well as my ancestral spirits allow, Sir. I have looked after Miss Emily as best I could," said the old man.

"Thank you. We will talk soon. I want to tell you about my piece of Africa far to the north," said Giles.

The two men parted and Giles headed for the house. On the steps the whole family was waiting. Molly looked him up and down before saying, "Hello Giles, I don't suppose they have hairdressers where you live now."

Giles gave a sickly smile," there is actually a barber in Salisbury, but I was so busy preparing for the planting season. I promise you I will have my haircut in Cape Town tomorrow".

Reggie seemed genuinely pleased to see Giles and said that he had been swatting up on a best man's duties.

De Speville guided Giles and his family into the drawing room where they had tea and sandwiches. Emily and Giles were then left to talk. Giles moved to the sofa and sat next to Emily. For the next hour the two lovers held hands tightly and talked. Emily had an exhausting need to know everything about Leopard Ridge, the farm and the mine.

That night Giles lay in bed and listened to the rain dripping off the cottage eaves. He hoped that it was raining back on the farm and that the maize crop was flourishing.

After breakfast de Speville offered Giles the use of a pony trap. Giles went on his own to Hout Street. Mrs. Van was genuinely pleased to see him to the extent that she again totally forgot to call him a rooinek! He drank coffee and ate delicious koeksisters with the van Rooyen family. Mrs. Van brought him a letter that had arrived three months before. It was from his father, as he suspected when he saw the spidery handwriting. It must be a reply to the letter he had written to his father nearly a year ago. It read:

Dear Gilly

   Got your letter. Good that you are doing well. Have you really got more land than Sir Paul? I am proud of you, boy.
   I miss you.
   Must see to the feasants.

Your Father,
Matthew.

Giles felt a genuine affection for his father but no more and he surmised that his father felt the same and probably would barely have noticed that Giles had left home.

Mrs. van Rooyen's daughter, Annelise was at home, so Giles was able to get a very respectable haircut. Annelise had cut his hair regularly during the time he had been living in Cape Town. Before he left 76 Hout Street, Giles issued Mrs. Van and her family an unofficial invitation to the wedding. He also gave her the little furniture that was in his room except for a few small personal items he took with him. As he left the house, he reflected on the happy days he had spent there especially lying on his bed staring at his favourite mountain. From Hout Street he went to Darling Street and directly to the bookshop. Here he found Zeke packing books into boxes. There was a closed sign on the window.

Zeke was delighted to see Giles and took him into his office and made tea. Giles gave Zeke all his news of his farm and his upcoming wedding to Emily.

"Lovely girl that one. You lucky man, but I suppose one makes one's luck. Good for you. Always knew you would make something of yourself," said the old man.

"Thanks Zeke you were the one that gave me my start here in Cape Town. I want you at the wedding. Now what is happening to you Zeke?" said Giles.

"I am old and tired. I have tried to sell the shop without luck, so I am going back to London. I still have a sister there. I have enough money to live on. I am leaving on the mail ship at the end of this month. If you are still here maybe you can see me off at the docks." replied Zeke.

It was nearly two hours later that Giles left Darling Street much to the relief of the horse which had stood patiently with the buggy. Molly and Marcel looked with approval at Giles sporting his new haircut. Emily went up to him and ruffled his hair and spoke.

" Almost human. I think I could get used to liking this man," and then seeing her mother's face regretted saying what she had said.

Giles had to swallow more tea in the drawing room as the wedding guest list was discussed. As it read, as Molly had made it, there was not a single name associated with himself except for Mr. Rhodes himself and a few senior officials from his office. Giles faced Molly and said," You will now want to add the names of the people I want to invite, I'm sure."

Molly looked flustered but before she could say anything he continued," just a few people, Mr. Goldblatt and the van Rooyen family and Ebrahim's cousin." Molly started to say, "We can't... "Giles finished her sentence by saying "leave out my kind landlady, can we." Molly looked shocked and said no more. Emily and her father smiled knowingly at each other.

Without further discussion Molly and Reggie sat at the dining table and filled in and addressed the wedding invitations including two to 76 and 74 Hout Street.

Later that afternoon Giles and Emily wandered through her natural garden where she introduced him to dozens of plants indigenous to the Cape. Giles just let her talk and just reveled in being close to her. He did at one stage break his silence long enough to tell her that there were different plants on the farm, but all with their own beauty. Emily declared that she would continue her plant studies, but on the plants of

Mashonaland. She said that she already had another unused journal she could use.

Dinner that night was formal as usual. Giles put on a suit and tie. As he ate and talked to the family, he blessed Sir Paul for letting him go to a good school where he had learnt manners suitable for a gentleman and even good enough to deflect any possible criticism from Molly.

The next day Giles borrowed the buggy again and went to the tailor in Adderley Street suggested by Marcel. Here he endured a session with a man with a measuring tape and tailors chalk who barely said a word. The manager of the very upmarket business told him he could have a fitting in three days' time and the morning suit would be ready in a week. Giles asked the cost of the suit and when told was shocked. It would cost more than all the clothes he had ever bought, but he was glad that the farm and the mine had been good to him, and he could afford it. He nodded to the manager and walked out of the fancy shop head held high.

That Sunday the de Speville family went to the morning service at St. Paul's Church in Rondebosch where the Reverend Basil Mortimer, an elderly man whose clerical collar was too big for his scrawny neck so he looked like a moulting chicken, showed the family to a front pew. Giles disliked the reverend's fawning and treating the de Spevilles with such reverence even though they were not regulars at his church. He sat and listened to hymns familiar from his school days and ignored the pompous spouting of the Rev. Mortimer when he delivered his version of a sermon. Giles didn't like the man but decided that it didn't matter as long as he married him to Emily on the due date.

****

Ebrahim and Mary were deliriously happy. The sadness of Mary's recent past got gradually forgotten as she got used to being a wife to the man she adored. She got deeply involved in the creation of a garden for Emily and also in the management of Giles's sheep flock. She also went over the ridge every day to watch progress on her and Ebrahim's new house. Ebrahim spent most of his days at the mine trying to find ways of making the mine still profitable as an open cast mine. He did not fancy an underground mine. In fact, he was not sure that he wanted to continue mining of any kind, especially as he now had a farm of his own. At night the young couple loved and planned their future, and they jointly came to the decision to stop mining as soon as it was no longer profitable in its current mode. Ebrahim knew Giles would agree.

The maize In the North Field looked good and healthy and the sheep flock was multiplying in leaps and bounds. On the afternoon of Saturday the 21st of November Ebrahim, Mary, Stanley and Amos stood on the stoep of Giles's house and Ebrahim opened a bottle of French champagne he had bought in Salisbury on his last visit. At the time that they guessed that Emily and Giles were leaving the church for the reception they raised their glasses and toasted the newlywed couple.

*****

Both Giles and Emily were in a daze as they left the church and were congratulated and showered with confetti. Giles did not know most of the people who were shaking his hand and didn't care. Emily was his wife and he believed that the biggest adventure in his life had begun. The last two weeks had just been a period to be endured. Giles had managed to corner the Reverend Mortimer after a Sunday service at which the bans were read. He ushered him into the vestry and firmly instructed him to cut anything he had to say at the wedding service to a minimum and to ensure that the group of Malay and black guests coming to the wedding were treated with respect. The Reverend seemed to retreat into his clerical collar like a tortoise into its shell, but nodded agreement.

Giles and Emily rode in a fancy landau, hired for the occasion to La Mercy where the two marquees had been erected next to each other with adjacent sides open to create a large space for the reception. Virtually the whole of Cape Town society filled the double marquee. Sitting at the main table Giles looked so handsome to Emily and Giles thought Emily, in her long lacy white dress and hair piled high on her head, was the most beautiful woman in the world. The reception was to be remembered in Cape Town and in the Cape for many years to come when the master of ceremonies turned out to be none other than Cecil Rhodes.

In later years neither Giles or Emily would remember the speeches and the toasts. Giles did vaguely remember making a speech toasting the bridesmaids, none of whom he had met until the day before the wedding. There were at least three photographers clicking away with cameras, the photographer doing the wedding photographs for the family album, and two from the Gazette and the Chronicle. The reception was a great success that was to provide Molly with material for conversation for months to come. Giles and Emily were pleased to see the van Rooyens, Zeke, the La Mercy staff and even old Motsepe enjoying the vast array of food.

Shortly before Giles and Emily left for their honeymoon, Rhodes approached Giles and took him aside and said,

" Well, done, Giles. You are really making it in the world. I believe it is likely that sooner or later there will be a legislative assembly set up in Mashonaland. When there is, stand for election. A new country needs strong young men like you to run it."

"Thank you, Sir, especially for being the MC today and I will think over what you have said, "Giles replied.

"Giles, when Molly wants you to do something you don't argue," quipped Rhodes. Giles just smiled to himself.

Emily and Giles changed from their wedding clothes and got into the hired landau. The landau drove away from La Mercy heading for the station. The young couple were embarrassed at the wild cheering as they left. At the railway station they caught a train to Simonstown where Giles had booked the best room at the Admiral Hotel overlooking the harbour. For four days the young couple explored the surrounds of Simonstown and each other. They walked south to a beach littered with granite boulders and watched the resident colony of penguins going about their aquatic little lives. They walked inland and high above Simonstown and Emily showed Giles the botanical beauty and diversity of fynnbos. On the last night of their honeymoon as they were lying together on the bed, Giles whispered to Emily." I love you so much Mrs. Elliott-Smith." Emily just gave a satisfied grunt and kissed him.

For the four days they had in Cape Town before catching the train to Kimberley, Emily and Giles stayed in the guest cottage at La Mercy. They had the meals with the family. Both Molly and Marcel were especially nice to the newlyweds perhaps sensing that in only a few days they would be saying goodbye to them not knowing when they would be seeing them again.

On the first day back at La Mercy, Giles borrowed the buggy again and went to see the owner of a plant nursery on the northern outskirts of Cape Town. One day of their honeymoon, sitting on a rock looking down on Simonstown Giles had told Emily that he was thinking of buying some young orange trees to take back to plant on the farm. Emily approved of the idea. At the nursery Giles spent an hour with the owner and from the information he got decided to buy a thousand young seedless Valencia trees. The small trees would be placed in perforated wooden trays to sent by train to Kimberly and then to Salisbury by wagon. With an assurance that the trees would be looked after on their journey north, Giles paid for the trees and transport on the spot. He headed back to La Mercy excited at the prospect of adding another source of income to Leopard Ridge farm even if only in years ahead.

Another thing Giles did in consultation with de Speville was to order a doctor's buggy from Concorde similar to his father in law's one. He was determined that Emily's life on the farm should be as easy as circumstances allowed, and a buggy pulled by a suitable horse would put the farm within a two and a half hour's ride of Salisbury where Emily could shop even if on a limited scale. De Speville was more and more impressed with his son in law who seemed to have more money than he had imagined, possibly enough to satisfy Molly's dreams for her daughter.

The day before their departure from Cape Town, a wagon was loaded with ten trunks, nine full of Emily's clothes and books and wedding presents and a small one with Giles's few possessions. It was as the wagon was being loaded, that Motsepe approached Emily where she stood watching the loading of the wagon. Shyly, he handed her a sapling that was planted in a bag made of some canvas material. "Missy, I want you to take this small tree with you on your journey to the north. It is what the Zulus call Umthiumtoti, the sweet tree. I do not know the Xhosa name. The English call it a Tamarind tree. This tree's ancestors come from far north in Africa and it will like to be where you are going with Master Giles. It will one day be tall and strong like he is. It will also bear fruit that is both sweet and bitter which is what life is like," said the old man.

Emily was deeply touched and surprised the old man and some staff who were watching by hugging Motsepe,

"That is the best wedding present I have been given. I will plant it near my house on our farm and every time I look at it, I will think of you and our wild garden, La Mercy and Cape Town. Thank you so much," she said with passion.

Emily and Giles sat in their own compartment and held hands as they both thought their own thoughts and said nothing. They stared out of the window and watched the landscape that flashed passed them. Goodbyes at the station had been prolonged and emotional, especially for Emily as she said her goodbyes to her family. Zeke was there as the young couple were leaving before he was due to set sail for England. Giles promised Emily's family to take care of her and after final hugging and kissing the train left Cape Town Station and steamed north.

The initial sadness felt especially by Emily, slowly dissipated as the train steamed out of the Hex River Valley and onto the harsh dry plain beyond. At Kimberly they were met by one of Rhodes's staff in that city and taken to the Kimberly Club to stay a comfortable night before getting on to the coach that would take them on a long and uncomfortable ride to their new home. Emily clutched the little tamarind tree that had never left her side since they left Cape Town. On Giles advice she had dressed in a divided skirt and khaki shirt for the dusty and sweaty coach ride. Giles let Emily have the seat next to the coach's window, the same way as he had once done before for a young lady.

It was a very tired, stiff and grubby pair who alighted from the coach. Giles left Emily at the coach station with their luggage and went and hired a wagon to take their luggage to the farm and a cab to take him and Emily to Kopje Street where, by arrangement Amos was waiting with three horses. Giles introduced Emily to his assistant and the three of them set off for Mazowe. As they rode Giles divided his time between describing to Emily where they were and questioning Amos with respect to the goings-on on the farm.

It was almost dark when the three riders crested the ridge and saw the lights of the house. The three riders dismounted and tied their horses to the tether rail at the bottom of the steps. Giles was tempted to pick Emily up and carry her into the house but restrained himself. As they reached the top step, the front door opened and out of the lamp lit house stepped Mary and Ebrahim,

"Welcome home. We took a chance on you getting back on time and came over so Mary could cook you a decent meal," said Ebrahim. He continued," Emily, this is Mary, my wife. Giles you already know Mary."

The two women hugged as did the two men. It was Emily who said," I know you, Mary; from the library."

"I know you too.," replied Mary.

Giles guided Emily into the house. He was surprised at how much the house had changed since he had left barely five weeks ago. The three bedrooms were complete as was the extension of the stoep along the entire front of the house. There was also a flushing toilet. Emily was delighted with her new home and was already picturing it with the rooms painted and curtains hung. She had not told Giles that one large trunk was full of material for curtains and her mother had given her a Singer sewing machine.

The four young people and Amos sat down to a sumptuous meal. There was the inevitable roast lamb and vegetables and a sponge pudding covered in golden treacle. After dinner Amos left for his hut down by the river. Mary and Emily sat in the drawing room and talked about the wedding and then about life on the farm. Giles and Ebrahim sat on the stoep and talked farm and mine. The mine was still producing gold but in lesser quantities, The two men decided that they would close the mining operation as soon as the yield of gold reached a level below which it was no longer profit making. Ebrahim expressed his desire to farm his three thousand acres, starting initially with vegetables for which there was a ready market in Salisbury. Giles told Ebrahim about the orange trees that were on their way. Giles was pleased to hear that the sheep were doing well and that the new ram was doing his business covering the ewes related to the older Dorset Horn ram.

It was nearly midnight when the lamps were extinguished, and Emily and Giles spent their first night in the bedroom that was to be theirs for many years to come. Mary and Ebrahim were using one of the new bedrooms.

"What do you think of your new home, sweetheart?" said Giles to Emily as they lay together in bed.

"Almost too perfect to be true, my love," replied Emily. The newly weds fell asleep in each other's arms.

The first thing that happened the next day was that Emily insisted on planting the tamarind tree. She and Giles walked the extent of the garden that had flourished under Mary's husbandry and decided that it should be planted down the slope towards the river and equidistant between the front of the house and the small kopje to the west. To Emily there was something symbolic about the planting of the Tamarind tree. It was as if she herself was being planted for once and for all in this land far from her home.

Mary helped Emily unpacking the first of the trunks. Ebrahim and Giles went over the ridge to where Mackenzie and his men were working busily on Ebrahim and Mary's almost complete house. From there the two of them went to the mine where Stanley had everything running smoothly. He was told of the possibility of closing the mine. He did not seem to be in the slightest bit upset. He explained that his wife had recently told him it was time for him to retire and join her in their little house on the outskirts of Salisbury. He had even been offered a job with the bank handling the bullion being brought in by the banks mining and prospecting customers.

Chapter 12

The summer months of 1892 were very hot, and Emily found the heat and the high humidity was draining. She discovered that, near the top of the little kopje beyond her now flourishing tamarind tree, was a place where it was cooler in the shade of a huge granite boulder and where there always seemed to be a breeze. She spent many afternoons there until chased back to the house by the impending arrival of a thunderstorm. She sometimes took her watercolour paints with her. She was ever mindful of Giles's warning about snakes and always wore her knee-high boots under her long khaki trousers. She had bought the boots on an impulse before she left Cape Town.

Before a day got too hot, Emily planned and cooked meals for Giles and then devoted her time to improving their house. She sewed curtains for all the rooms in the house. She had brought enough material with her to accomplish this and to make curtains for Ebrahim and Mary's house which was now complete and occupied. She also tended her garden and filled it with local plants, which she found did not have the diversity of the Cape fynnbos. Her journal only filled up slowly.

One hot March evening Giles and Emily were sitting on the stoep trying to stay cool when Emily said,

"Sweetheart, I have news for you which I am sure is unexpected, but I hope is good. I am going to have a baby!"

Giles jumped out of his rocking chair and knelt in front of Emily and gently patted her stomach saying," Oh that is wonderful, wonderful. Let's go and tell Ebrahim and Mary."

"Giles it's too hot, we'll have them to supper tomorrow and tell them then", said Emily.

For an hour Giles and Emily talked about their joyous news; whether they would have a boy or a girl and what they would name the child.

That night there was a massive thunderstorm. The noise of the rain on the iron roof was so loud that talking was impossible. Giles lay next to Emily with his hand on her stomach and went to sleep like that. When the news of an impending arrival was passed onto Ebrahim and Mary over dinner the following day, they both expressed their delight.

Ebrahim stood back and surreptitiously examined Mary's body profile with an air of both expectation but also trepidation.

Ebrahim's sense of trepidation returned a week later when Mary told him that she thought that she was also expecting a child. He expressed to her his delight but in truth the enormity of an impending huge responsibility bore down on him. He had never thought beyond a life with Mary and his life's mission to make her happy. Ebrahim and Mary's news was passed onto Giles and Emily at a dinner. Hearty congratulations were offered. The two men drank beer and raised a toast to forthcoming family. The two women limited themselves to a cherry cordial.

The next few months were busy ones for not only the owners of the two adjacent farms but also for the Mazowe area, Salisbury and also Rhodesia as a whole. A small village called Mazowe by its white inhabitants, started to grow about ten miles southwest of Ebrahim's and Giles's farms. Soon there was a small post office with a telegraph link to Salisbury and the outside world run by the Marconi Telegraph Company. Giles had been able to send a telegram to La Mercy with news of the unborn baby which resulted in a flurry of good wishes and from Molly especially, dire warnings of the dangers of childbirth in the wilds of Africa, A telegram to Matthew Smith in Devon elicited a two-word reply, 'well done'. Ebrahim got no reply to the telegram sent to his family.

A small general store opened to the delight of Emily and Mary who thoroughly enjoyed making a trip to the store in the new doctor's buggy about twice a month. The paucity of the store's stock did not diminish the pleasure of a chance to shop. The shop did stock wool and knitting patterns, which resulted in a flurry of knitting of baby garments supplemented by the products of the endeavors of Emily and Mary on the Singer sewing machine.

A mine called the Alice mine was started to the southwest of Mazowe village. The owners of the mine offered to buy Ebrahim's and Giles's claims adjoining their now closed mine, but the offer were rejected. Giles and Ebrahim did not want their farms disturbed by the noise and dirt of another mine. They did however secure profitable contracts to supply the mine's labour with maize meal made from Giles's second successful maize harvest and Ebrahim's first flush of vegetables.

On Giles's farm things went very well. A thousand orange trees had been planted and, in the farm's rich loam soil the trees grew well. The sheep flock continued to grow, and Giles was able to send a batch of lambs to his butcher customers on a regular basis. As the farm grew so did the need for labour and Giles was able to maintain good relations with Chief Matuswa by giving him a bonus in maize meal for every new labourer that came from his village. He had long discovered that the chief was in fact only an 'induna' or subchief or headman. Giles rather liked the old rogue, but continued to turn down offers of his beer.

Adjacent to the North Feld Giles organized the stumping of a new field of about a hundred and fifty acres which he called rather unenterprisingly, New Field. The North Field was to lie fallow for two seasons, having yielded two excellent consecutive harvests. The ever-growing labour force was housed in self built huts in a village not far from the river and close to New Field. Tree stumps from the clearing of the new field were delivered by ox wagon to the village to use as firewood. Giles had a series of 'long drop' toilets dug and enclosed to try and improve the health of the labour village. Emily, even though she had little knowledge of health matters, administered to sick and wounded labourers with a limited medical kit. She mostly dispensed aspirin and laxatives and bandaged wounds as best she could. Even Chief Matuswa came to her occasionally for treatment of real and imagined complaints. It never ceased to amuse her and Giles when he insisted, despite about fifty years seniority, in calling her 'Mummy'!

On the other side of the ridge Ebrahim's farm was going well. He had installed a large stationary engine on the banks of the river on Giles's farm. Though he did not have riparian rights, Giles had no problem with Ebrahim abstracting water from the river. Ebrahim cleared an area of about thirty acres on what Giles judged was good soil and here he established a variety of vegetables in neat beds which could be irrigated when necessary. He grew a wide variety of vegetables and even some fruits such as raspberries and strawberries. He had a ready market in Salisbury and once a week a loaded wagon of produce left what was now called Mary's Nest to Salisbury where some produce went to the newly established market and some to businesses in the food trade.

Life passed relatively uneventfully for months until the day that Amos, who was supervising labourers clearing the New Field, was bitten by a snake presumed to be a cobra of which there many on the farm. He was bitten on the leg. A labourer saw what had happened and ran as fast as he could to the orange orchard where Giles was. Giles ran quickly to where Amos was lying on the ground. Amos was already suffering badly from the neurotoxin and was battling to breathe. Giles knew that there was nothing he could do for Amos except make him comfortable. Twenty minutes after being bitten Amos passed away. Giles was distraught. Amos was a part of Leopard Ridge Farm.

Giles did not know how to get hold of Amos's family, that is if he had one. The next day, a small, sad little group of people buried Amos in a grave on the river side of the little kopje. In the wet cement that covered the grave Emily scratched:

'A sad loss of a good young man far from his home'

She scratched a floral frieze round what she had written.

Giles and Emily discussed the replacement of Amos and decided that they would advertise for an assistant farm manager in the newly established Mashonaland Herald. Over a period of two weeks seven people applied to the advert. They selected two suitable candidates and arranged to interview them in Salisbury at the warehouse in Kopje Road. One of the candidates was a young man with red hair and freckles who more or less ensured his selection with his winning smile and the fact he was the son of farmer from Bovey Tracy in Devon. He did seem intelligent. His name was William Tregaskis.

William, Bill Tregaskis, arrived at Leopard Ridge with little more than a few clothes in a well-worn canvas valise. Giles accommodated him in one of the spare bedrooms until such time as a cottage could be built by Gordon Mackenzie. From the first day he started work, Bill proved to be a likeable, bright and willing assistant with a huge appetite. Emily loved the appreciation she got for the meals she cooked, and he ate. Bill was to prove a great asset to Giles especially as he had experience in sheep farming. Within weeks he was handed the responsibility of running the sheep flock on his own.

Bill also had experience in the farming of beef cattle which was soon to prove invaluable to Ebrahim who, in a moment of either sheer madness or genius had purchased a small starter herd of North Devon cattle from a settler who had long since tired of the "wildness" of farming in Mashonaland. A quick visit to Chief Matuswa for labor, rapid dispatch of a wagonload of fence posts and barbed wire and Ebrahim was in business as a beef farmer as well as vegetable farmer. Giles agreed to Bill working for Ebrahim one day a week. Bill was aware of the many tick-borne diseases prevalent in Rhodesia and persuaded Ebrahim and Giles that a sheep dip should be built and used for both Ebrahim's cattle and Giles's sheep. A telegram was sent from Mazowe to Kimberley to expedite the sending of three drums of Coopers Dip. Mackenzie was drafted in to construct the dip on Leopard Ridge.

The first use of the dip was a disaster. Ebrahim's cattle were intended to be the first users of the dip, but they had other ideas. Despite three herders, plus Ebrahim, Giles and Bill, the fractious North Devons were soon dispersed all over Leopard Ridge farm. Dipping of the sheep did take place, but the sheep put up a good fight that resulted in six men being covered in dip and having to be hosed off. Eventually all the cattle and sheep were dipped, a process that was to be repeated every month in summer and every six weeks in winter.

There now came a period of months of relative peace on the two adjacent farms. Money was coming in regularly from vegetables for Ebrahim and from lamb and maize sales for Giles. Bill moved into a new cottage along the ridge from Giles's and Emily's house. Emily and Mary got larger and larger and did less and less. The two young couples decided that, since they could afford it, when Emily and Mary were within two weeks of their due date, they would go into a small nursing home in Selous Avenue in Salisbury where they could be attended by a midwife and a doctor if necessary. When the time came for Emily to go into the nursing home Mary decided to go into Salisbury and stay in a small boarding house in Montague Avenue not far away, so she could be with Emily over the birth. Giles and Ebrahim left their wives in good hands with the understanding that as soon as there was any sign of a forthcoming birth, a messenger would be sent post haste to Mazowe.

Ten days later a messenger arrived with news that Emily had gone into labour. Both Giles and Ebrahim set off at a fast pace in the buggy. Arriving at the nursing home they found that Emily was in the final stage of labour and within an hour a robust dark haired little boy was born. Matthew Marcel Elliott-Smith was born on the nineteenth of September 1893. Giles delighted in holding his loudly protesting little son. Placing him next to his mother he leaned over her sweat-stained face and whispered," well done. I love you. He is perfect."

Emily just looked at Giles and smiled.

Matthew had just been admired by Giles and Mary when Mary doubled over in pain and sank to the floor of Emily's room. Two nurses rushed to her and helped her to an adjacent room and put her on a bed. A midwife confirmed thar Mary had gone into labour. Ebrahim was informed. A midwife attended Mary who was in great pain to an extent that the doctor was called. For the whole of that afternoon and the night Mary called out in pain. Ebrahim could stand it no more and went for along walk in the avenues. When he got back the nursing home Mary was no longer crying out in pain. As he entered her room, he heard a small cry and saw a nurse holding a little baby wrapped in a blanket He picked the baby up and saw it was a beautiful little dark-haired girl. He turned to share his joy at the birth of his daughter with Mary and saw a sheet over her body. He lifted the sheet and kissed Mary lightly on the cheek and walked out of the room, down the corridor and out into the nursing home garden.

He knelt on the grass and with head in his hands screamed," Allah, God, whoever you are, you are evil. You give me a gift of a wonderful woman and then take her back before we can have a real life together, Go to hell!! "

Giles let Ebrahim leave Mary's room on his own but when he hard the screaming coming from the garden he went after his friend. He knelt beside Ebrahim and put his arm round his shoulder. He let Ebrahim cry until he had no more crying left in him. "Come Eb, let's go and see your daughter. She is a gift that Mary has left you.," said Giles. They found the little girl in bed with Emily and Matthew. Emily had just fed Matthew and was about to feed Ebrahim's little girl. Ebrahim looked puzzled but Emily explained that human babies need mothers first milk as it contains colostrum needed for a baby to be healthy," Ebrahim, I am going to feed your baby for as long as it takes. Go with Giles and think of a name for your lovely little girl," said Emily.

The two men sat in the garden talking for best part of an hour. They returned to Emily's room and a more composed Ebrahim was able to tell her that his daughter was to be called Mariette, meaning 'little Mary'. On either side of Emily were two small dark haired little sleeping bodies worn out from the fight to enter this world.

The Tamarind Tree

The buggy made it to Leopard ridge in just over three hours. It carried Emily, Giles Ebrahim and two little babies. It was decided that Ebrahim should stay with Giles and Emily to be near Mariette. All was well on the two farms thanks to hardworking young Bill. A wagon load of vegetables had gone to Salisbury and all the sheep and cattle had been dipped and New North Field was ready for planting with maize. Emily continued to feed the two babies who both thrived. Matthew outweighed little Mariette and grew faster but the little girl seemed to have a quiet determination about her and rarely cried.

Ebrahim went to his farm every morning after looking in on his daughter and returned for lunch and another chance to see her. In the late afternoon he came back to the house and would spend hours holding Mariette on his lap and just staring at her. One evening after supper he addressed Emily and Giles," I have done a lot of thinking especially about Mariette and her future. I am going to change my name. I am finished with Islam and Allah and as there are few Muslims in Rhodesia, I am going to change my name by deed poll to something that might sound Jewish and give my little girl certain advantages in life. How about I become Abraham Gold? I think Gold is good as most of my money has come from gold. Giles you changed your name and only good came out of it, what do you think?"

"Good thinking, Eb. I think you certainly look like a Jew. Good luck," said Giles.

"As long as changing your name doesn't change you, I think it's a good idea," said Emily.

Mary's body was laid to rest in a small grove of msasa trees near to Abraham's house. There was no formal funeral but each of Abraham, Giles and Emily said a few heartfelt words. Attending the farewell to Mary were, Bill, Gordon Mackenzie, many farm labourers and Chief Matuswa. When a gravestone eventually arrived it read,

Here lie the mortal remains of Mary Gold, born fourth February 1869, died nineteenth September 1893. Beloved wife of Abraham Gold and mother of Mariette.

Taken too soon.
Rest in peace

Chapter 13

Days after the birth of Matthew and Mariette, Giles had a telegram brought to him at Leopard Ridge asking him to make a personal visit to Salisbury to be able to talk in confidence to Rhodes via the telegraph in Colquhoun's office. Giles left Emily and Matthew in the hands of Abraham and the farming in Bill's capable hands. In Colquhoun's office Giles held a slow back and forwards telegraph conversation with Rhodes. Rhodes quickly congratulated Giles on the birth of his son and then turned to the subject of Lobengula. Giles had, often over the last three years written to Rhodes and given his assessment on how the locals were reacting to the large numbers of miners and settlers who were arriving in Rhodesia. He had passed on information he gleaned from Chief Matuswa that indicated that not only were the Shona chiefs unhappy about Europeans being given mining rights and land that they regarded as being the property of the Shona people.

Rhodes told Giles that Lobengula was unhappy that a chief in the Victoria district was refusing to pay tribute to him. Lobengula was apparently threatening to attack this chief and get his tribute. Rhodes asked Giles if he thought, having met the man, he would do what he threatened. Giles told Rhodes that it was highly likely Lobengula would carry out his threat. Rhodes then told Giles that they would have to deal with Lobengula for once and for all and asked him to join a heavily armed column that was going to be sent under a Major Forbes to join up with what amounted to mercenaries being sent from Bechuanaland. Giles declined the offer to join the column and then pleaded with Rhodes to consider negotiating with Lobengula. He had no doubt that Forbes's Maxim guns would enable him to overcome a superior number of Matabele warriors armed only with spears and a limited number of Martini-Henry rifles. Giles tried to get Rhodes to understand that the resentment of the local people in both Matabeleland and Mashonaland was real and understandable. Beating them in a military campaign would only increase resentment. Rhodes thanked Giles for his input and dismissed him. Giles went home.

What happened next, Giles got from the Mashonaland Herald. Forbes's column was attacked by about six thousand of Lobengula's men who were no match for the maxims and about one thousand five hundred were mown down. Forbes lost only four men. The column went on to Bulawayo and quickly took possession and burnt Lobengula's capital. Lobengula and remnants of his army withdrew across the Zambezi River where a scant three months later Lobengula died of smallpox. Giles had no great love for Lobengula but felt that the bringing of Matabeleland into the control of the BSA Company by armed intervention was unwise and would cause repercussions. Giles had a feeling of uneasiness about what might happen in Mashonaland and in particular the Mazowe area if an insurrection should occur. He feared for Emily and Matthew and their futures. He kept in touch with Chief Matuswa with whom he had a good relationship based on mutual respect and Emily's healing hands. What disturbed Giles most was that, according to Matuswa, insurrection was being promoted by several Shona 'spiritual mediums'. These were usually women who claimed to be in touch with the ancestral spirits. They were highly respected by the common people and what they had to say was believed.

Matthew and Mariette flourished and became inseparable friends. Mariette spent her days at Leopard ridge and nights with her father at Mary's Nest. Matthew was a good-looking little boy who looked much like a miniature of his father. Mariette was smaller than Matthew and looked much like her mother. Matthew was protective of Mariette from an early age, but happily took orders from her. Emily and Giles had been conscientious and wrote to Matthew's grandparents on a regular basis. Marcel had sent Giles a box camera and a plentiful supply of film. Emily took lots of photographs and then sent the film to Marcel who had it developed. A fair number of photographs eventually found their way back to Leopards Ridge. A few were sent on to Matthew in Devon.

Both Giles and Emily were conscious that her parents were not happy at not having seen their grandson and so, in late 1895 planned a trip with Matthew to Cape Town. A now very experienced and capable, Bill, would look after the farm under the watchful eye of Abraham. The matter of who would look after Mariette during the day was solved by hiring a live-in nanny, a good natured young Irish woman called Siobhan, who quickly got to like Mariette and never realized that she was constantly being manipulated by the strong-willed little girl.

Abraham and Mariette said goodbye to Giles, Emily and Matthew at the coach station in Salisbury. It was a tearful goodbye as Mariette and Matthew had never been parted for more than a night. Matthews tears dried quickly with the excitement of the coach trip. The weather was hot, and the coach trip was uncomfortable and long. It was relief when the three travelers reached Johannesburg to spend a day and two nights before proceeding by train to Kimberly and then on to Cape Town. Marcel de Speville was waiting at the station to pick up three tired and dusty travelers.

Matthew took to his grandfather immediately and in the days that followed became his shadow. At La Mercy, Molly and a much grown-up Reggie were waiting on the front steps. Emily looked around for Motsepe and then remembered that he had retired nearly a year before. Molly made a big fuss of Matthew which was not entirely reciprocated. He did not much like kisses and especially large wet ones. Molly had finished making himself known to her grandson and turned to Emily," Oh my God what has happened to you, my girl. You have n been too long in the sun and your hair is a mess," said Molly.

"Mother you haven't changed. When you farm you can't avoid the sun and we live thirty miles from the nearest and provably not very good hairdresser," replied Emily.

Her mother harrumphed and said, "I suppose we'll have to buy you some decent clothes if our friends are going to meet you again."

"Leave her alone, woman," said de Speville as he led his grandson in through the hall to the drawing room. Tea and iced cakes were served much to Matthew's delight. Talk bounced back and forwards mainly between Molly and Emily for nearly two hours until de Speville took Matthew by the hand and announced that they needed to go and explore.

After a sumptuous dinner that night, de Speville and Giles went and sat on the stoep while Emily and Molly and a now sleepy Matthew sat in the drawing room. Having pumped Giles for news of the farm and the fast-growing town of Salisbury, de Speville said to Giles, "You have done well young man, and you have obviously made my daughter happy. Well done! I do hear on the parliament grapevine that you had words with Rhodes. Made him sit up and think!"

"Sir, I say it as I see it, and I think Rhodes is blinding himself with his Cape to Cairo Railway dream. He has asked me to go and see him next week." replied Giles.

On the first Saturday of the family reunion, de Speville rented a carriage which took the whole family to Camps Bay, where they had a picnic on the beach. Marcel de Speville and Matthew spent the entire afternoon running in and out of the waves except for when they sat and almost ate themselves to a standstill on all the food that had come out of the La Mercy kitchen. For a little boy who had never seen the sea, the Camps Bay Beach was heaven. The company of his newfound grandson was stripping the years off de Speville.

The following week Giles took himself off to the parliament building to meet with Cecil Rhodes who seemed genuinely pleased to see Giles. He asked after both Giles and Ebrahim and expressed his sorrow at hearing of Mary's death. He then got down to business and questioned Giles about the apparent excessive influence wielded by spiritual mediums in Mashonaland. Giles did his best to get Rhodes to understand that the Shona people were very superstitious and wide open to any suggestion put forward by a so called medium. He also wanted Rhodes to understand that the Shona people had gone through years of suppression by the Matabele and were not taking kindly to being in effect suppressed by Europeans.

Rhodes listened carefully before he said, "you are probably right, but we can't back down on our colonial ambitions for your part of Africa, in the face of other colonial powers happy to take our place. Giles, there isn't much I can do to help. I am getting orders from the 'hawks 'in Westminster. When do you think we can expect an insurrection?"

"Within the next two years," said Giles with conviction.

"Just make sure that you and yours are safe. Thanks again for your advice, Giles," Rhodes said.

The following day, Giles took Emily and Matthew to 76 Hout Street to see Mrs. Van and her family. Mrs. Van was entranced by the little boy and pulled him into her ample bosom which surprisingly bought no adverse reaction from Matthew.

"Een klein rooinek", she chortled. The rest of family admired and fussed over Matthew and then produced plates of koeksisters and vetkoeks which were well received by young Matthew. Giles asked Mrs. Van if there was any point in going next door and telling Ebrahim's parents about their granddaughter. Mrs. Van said it would be time wasted as they had disowned their son when he had n married a non-believer. Before leaving Mrs. Van's, presents bought in Johannesburg during the stopover were distributed to Mrs. Van and her family. At the last-minute Giles took Emily, with Mrs. Van approval, to see what had been his room years before. He showed her the view of his mountain.

Giles and Emily left Matthew with his grandparents for a day and went by train to Simonstown. The purpose of this visit was twofold. They wanted to remind themselves of their short but happy honeymoon, but also went to see the gunsmith with whom Giles had done business before. Giles ordered two twelve-gauge shotguns with five hundred rounds of mixed buckshot and birdshot ammunition. He also ordered two Webley Scott .38 revolvers and holsters and five hundred rounds of ammunition. He explained to Emily that the firearms were for their safety back on the farm in case of an insurrection. He further explained that he was buying for Abraham as well. The gunsmith had a small target practice range under his shop and took Giles and Emily with their sidearms and some ammunition there so they, especially, Emily could get some practice. Emily didn't need any practice. She was a better shot than Giles and even the gun shop owner. She told Giles that she didn't need any practice with the shotgun as she had had plenty of practice during her last year's holidays in England.

Emily decided to have a day on her own away from the family. She spent a morning at her natural garden. It had not changed that much except that some of the small plants she remembered collecting and planting were now large shrubs and trees. One of her favorites, a bearded protea that she had found on the slopes above Simonstown was now nearly ten feet tall. There was still a feeling of wonderful, organized chaos to the garden. Motsepe and Ingrid had done well.

It was to see Ingrid that Emily went in the afternoon. She found her in a collecting room at the museum. Ingrid was pleased to see her,

"Oh, Emily, I have had such a happy time working on what I hope we can call 'our garden'. Come and have a look at the extensive specimen collection I have made of every one of the garden's species," said Ingrid.

The two young women spent a happy hour talking botany during which Ingrid showed Emily a copy of the Nature Journal in which was an article on the garden and its indigenous plant collection. "I hope you don't mind, Emily but I put you down as co-author. You aren't cross, are you?"

Emily blushed and hesitated before saying with a smile," bit late for me to disapprove, isn't it?"

Eventually, as shadows were lengthening, Emily drove her father's buggy back to La Mercy. On the buggy seat next to her was a copy of Nature. Back at La Mercy Emily could not wait to show Giles and the family the article in the journal. Giles in particular could hardly contain the pride he felt for his talented wife. At dinner that night it was de Speville who said to Molly," I hope you now see that our daughter was always too clever for those brainless pomposities you were always trying to introduce to her!" Emily blushed for the second time that day.

All good things have to come to an end and so it was that on a dull rainy day, Marcel, Molly and Reggie said their tearful farewells to Giles, Emily and Matthew at Cape Town Station. It had been a happy visit reflected in the close bond that had developed between Marcel and his grandson. Molly had softened towards Giles and even allowed him to kiss her cheek for the first time. Shortly before the train was about to leave the station, Rhodes made a surprise appearance and took Giles aside,

" Please, Giles, keep me informed of what you see is going on with the Shona and their mediums and take care of yourself and your family."

Abraham and Mariette were waiting at the coach station when the coach rolled in. Matthew and Mariette were delighted to see each other and their happy laughter and chatter from the rear of the buggy never stopped until they reached Leopard Ridge. Meanwhile on the trip to Mazowe, Abraham had been able to assure Giles and Emily that everything had gone well on the farm in their absence.

Chapter 14

Emily lay in Giles's arms. She nestled her face into the curve of his neck. It was one o'clock in the morning of January the first 1897. There had been a sort of New Year's Eve party at Leopard Ridge attended only by Giles, Emily, Bill, Abraham, Siobhan, Matt and Mariette. They had put together a good meal, had drunk a few beers in the case of the men and a bottle of Nederberg wine in the case of the two women. They had listened to music on Giles's new Edison Phonograph. The children had tired early and were asleep before ten that evening. Abraham and Siobhan were staying over for what was left of the night.

It was Giles who broke the silence," Well that is a year that is best put behind us, Emily. I was thinking just now of how to describe 1896. In Latin, courtesy of my Latin teacher at Exeter, it is best put as 'Annus Horribilis' because that is what it has been. But we have survived and so have Abraham and Siobhan. Best of all, our kids have not suffered and are flourishing. We do have a lot to be thankful for, don't we?"

Emily held him tight. "Yes, let's forget the recent past and concentrate on the coming year my sweetheart," said a now sleepy Emily.

*****

The trip to Cape Town had been good but, in many ways, both Emily and Giles were glad to be back on Leopard Ridge farm. Sitting on the stoep drinking coffee prior to getting on with farm work, they took pleasure in watching the sun rise on their little kingdom that stretched from the ridge down and then along the river for miles. It was good to see Emily's tamarind tree was now over six foot tall. It was also good to see the neat lines of orange trees down near the river which were now about to yield their first crop. They watched an augur buzzard hovering over something on one of the rocks of the kopje, probably a dassie.

While they were in Cape Town, Bill had very ably seen to the planting of nearly two hundred acres of maize and ten acres of brewer's barley for a brewery that was starting up in Salisbury. The sheep flock continued to grow and had reached two hundred in total. Sales of lambs to the now three butchers in Salisbury continued to bring in good profits.

Things were also going well on Mary's Nest. Abraham had bought another small herd of cattle at a dispersal auction. This time they were Herefords. His beef herd now numbered nearly eighty and two to three steers a month were going to the butchers in Salisbury. Sales of vegetables continued to do well as did the sales of the soft fruits he was specializing in.

One of the first things that Giles did on his return from Cape Town was to go and see Chief Matuswa. He took with him a new army style coat which he knew that old man would like. Mutasa was pleased to see Giles and especially the coat. The two men sat on wooden stools in the sun. Giles had as usual declined the offer of the chief's beer. They talked in Shona in which Giles was now quite proficient. They talked about an insurrection. Mutasa told Giles that there was talk of the people rising up against the 'Murungus', the whites. He said that most of this talk was coming from Chief Morrondela whose territory was to the east of Salisbury along the road that now ran all the way to Umtali and beyond to Beira in Portuguese territory. He said also that the insurrection was being fomented by various mediums who probably felt that their positions of importance were threatened by the Murungu and their missionaries who were trying to discourage ancestor worship.

Matuswa assured Giles that he would not be part of any insurrection. His land had not been taken from him, but fairly paid for by Giles who had always been good to him except for insulting his beer. He also mentioned the great medical treatment he got from Mommy, Emily. Giles promised to always treat the chief and his people fairly and hoped that if trouble did come to Mazowe, the chief would give him due warning. Giles was somewhat troubled by what the chief had had to say and was glad of the gun and ammunition purchases he had made in Simonstown. He had given Abraham a revolver and a shotgun and ammunition and had taken him out into the veld to learn how to handle a firearm, a skill that Abraham surprisingly did not have.

Even though it was his orange orchard's first crop, the number of ripe oranges that were being picked surprised Giles and he was happy to see a wagon load of oranges covered in grass to keep them cool, on its way to Salisbury. Part of his first crop was presold to several of Abraham's vegetable customers and the balance was taken to the market where they got excellent prices. So far, the oranges were a success and further wagon loads got good prices. It gave Giles great pleasure to walk with Emily, Siobhan and Matt and Mariette along neat rows of orange trees. It was good to pick and peel the succulent fruits for the kids to eat.

Abraham was happy with the way his little cattle empire was growing. He was aiming at breeding North Devon/ Hereford cross beef cattle with good meat characteristics and hybrid vitality. He had fenced nearly a thousand acres of good grazing into separate 'camps' so that the grazing could rotated. Regular dipping continued to protect his herd from tick borne disease.

The vegetable garden remained at about thirty acres, but productivity increased as selection of suitable varieties was improved and the vegetable beds were fertilized with cow manure of which he had plenty. The introduction of raspberry canes and strawberry plants added profitability to the enterprise. When the strawberries were in fruit they were frequently visited by the trio of Siobhan, Mariette and Matt. Abraham had also bought a thousand orange trees after seeing how well Giles's trees were doing even though he would not get a profit from them for several years to come.

Siobhan continued to work as nanny to the two children. She lived at Mary's Nest but most of the time she spent with them during the day was at Leopard Ridge. Emily turned a bedroom into a school room for the two children and she and Siobhan devoted at least two hours a day on 'activities'. Emily also took the kids on nature walks which were always the highlight of their day. It was planned that Siobhan would continue as nanny cum governess until Matt and Emily were old enough to go as boarders to school in Salisbury. Siobhan was happy to stay on at Mary's Nest as was Bill as these two young people had fallen in love. They were often to be seen in a balmy evening walking along the river hand in hand or at a weekend sharing a picnic on one of the large granite slabs on the kopje. The main impediment to the progress of their relationship was the frequent unwanted presence of two little people who loved both Bill and Siobhan.

It was Bill who called on Abe early one morning to report that something was wrong with some of the cattle. Abe went with Bill to the night kraal from which the cattle had not yet been released. Many of the beasts looked lethargic and appeared to have discharge from their noses and eyes. Abe hadn't any idea as whether there was a problem and if so, what it was. He ran to Leopard Ridge where he caught Giles just as he was heading off to the orange orchard. Giles and Abe headed to Abe's night kraal where Giles studied the obviously distressed animals.

"I don't know what it is, but I suggest you separate the obviously sick animals from the healthy ones and get a vet here as soon as possible." While Giles and Bill supervised the separation of the sick animals into another kraal, Abe readied Giles's buggy and set off for Salisbury. The sun was well past its zenith before the buggy returned with Abe and a vet. The vet, a gnarled old man, looked the cattle over for a few minutes before he pronounced in an assured voice." Ten to one its rinderpest. Saw it once in England. Not much you can do about it. It's caused by a virus and there is no cure. I suggest that you bury any animals that die and put lots of lime on their bodies before you do so."

Abe looked shattered, "will any survive?" he asked.

"Maybe ten per cent, not more. The good thing though is that it won't affect other animals like sheep and chickens. Sorry to be the bearer of bad news." said the vet.

That night after supper, Abe, Giles and Emily talked while the two children played on the stoep.

"If I lose most of my cattle, my income is going to be quite badly affected. I will still have enough to live on, but my plans will have been set back by about two years. Maybe we should sell the mining rights to the Alice Mine people." said Abe.

"We'll not rush into anything. I will pay Siobhan's salary until you are back on your feet, Abe," said Giles. Emily nodded.

Three depressed people battled to go to sleep that night. The vet stayed the night and Giles took him back to Salisbury the next morning, while Abe and Bill pitched in with some labourers to dig a huge hole in which to put dead animal carcasses. Two days later Giles and Abe went to see Chief Matuswa explain about the outbreak of rinderpest. The chief reported that some of his cows were showing the symptoms described to him. Giles impressed on the chief that any dead animals should be buried in lime as soon as possible. He promised to send some lime to the chief's village.

Over the next couple of weeks most of Abe's beef herd contracted rinderpest and most died. It took a lot of effort to pull the carcasses along the ground to the mass burial pit. Both Abe and Giles were puzzled that the seven draught oxen from the original ten that pulled their wagon in the Pioneer Column seemed unaffected by the quickly spreading disease.

They could only assume that the oxen had some sort of immunity from previous exposure to the virus in Kimberly where they were purchased.

Both Giles and Abe went to see Chief Matuswa again. They were pleased to see that he had made his people dispose of the carcasses as he had been told. The chief and all his villagers were in a sorry state. Most of their cattle were dead. The impact of this was enormous. Cattle were to the Shona people an investment and the wealth of a man was measured in the size of his cattle herd. Furthermore, cattle were needed for 'lobola', the money paid to a bride's father by the future son in law. In one fell swoop the chief and his villagers were poor. Giles and Abe assured the chief that they would do their best to help him and his people.

In the weeks that followed the rinderpest outbreak, its impact was felt across the whole population of Mashonaland. Many stock farmers went bankrupt. The man in the street in Salisbury had less money to spend and the economy dipped drastically. Abe's previously healthy sales of fruit and vegetables fell to the extent that he barely sold half a wagon load a week. Rather than throw away the produce that was not selling, Abe sent the surplus to Chief Matuswa to distribute to his suffering people. Giles and Emily were far less impacted by the rinderpest than Abe. The sheep were unaffected by the disease and with the shortage of beef, lamb sales increased sharply. Giles still had a stock of over a hundred tons of maize stored in the warehouse in Kopje Road.

Giles wrote to Rhodes and asked him to see what could be done to help not only the pioneer settlers but also the Shona tribespeople. Rhodes replied and assured Giles that the BSA Company were well aware of the situation and would do what could be done. He did contact the two banks in Salisbury with a request that they be more lenient with regard to mortgage payments in default. At least one charity set up a food distribution point in Salisbury. Giles donated five tons of maize to be ground and used to feed the poor people.

Chief Matuswa's people, apart for the ones that worked for Abe and Giles were in dire straits and desperately short of food. Giles and Emily wanted to help the chief's people and came up with a scheme. Giles had long wanted to be able to dam the river on his farm, the Bunga, a tributary of the Mazowe River. Years ago, he had found a suitable dam site on the northern end of the farm where the Bunga river ran through a small rocky gorge. Giles went to Salisbury and talked to a civil engineer who agreed to come to the farm and see if a dam was feasible.

Having established that the small gorge was a good site for a dam wall and that there was a small clay deposit to make the core of the dam wall, the engineer gave the project his blessing. Giles then went to see the chief. He proposed to him that in return for working on the dam wall any of his people would be fed a generous ration of mealie meal, surplus vegetables and a small wage. The chief readily agreed and within days a large gang of workers were wielding badzas (hoes) and pushing new wheelbarrows. Giles insisted on paying Abe for his surplus vegetables.

By April rinderpest was slowly becoming a memory. The cattle that had not died appeared to have an immunity to the disease including the seven oxen which were found a new task pulling a dam scoop built for Giles by a blacksmith in Salisbury. As life returned to a semblance of normal, Siobhan and Bill decided to get married. They decided on a civil wedding in Salisbury followed by a four-day honeymoon at a private hotel in Montague Avenue. Giles agreed to give Siobhan away and Abe agreed to be the best man. The wedding party was completed with Emily as maid of honour.

Both Giles and Abe went to Salisbury to have suits made for the wedding. Mariette and Matt went with them in order that Siobhan and Emily could concentrate on making a wedding dress They went to Solomon Cohen the Tailor in Pioneer Street. The two men entered the small shop. Behind the counter was a tubby middle-aged man and a young woman. Abe looked at the young woman and saw the most beautiful face he had ever seen. She had long black hair with a slight auburn tinge. He was transfixed and missed the initial interchange between Mariette and the young woman,

"Hello. You are a very pretty little girl, "said the young woman.

"I am nearly as big as Matt," said Mariette defensively.

"You are, but girls are always prettier," she said.

At this point she turned to Abe and said," I am Rebecca Cohen. What can I do for you?"

"A suit, I need a suit," said Abe

At this point Solomon Cohen took over the conversation. He was quick to establish that the man he was addressing was Abraham Gold and he was a widower with one young daughter.

"I haven't seen you in Schule," Cohen said to Abe.

Abe had been expecting this question or a similar one for a long time and answered," I am not a practicing Jew,"

Cohen busied himself with a tape measure and tailor's chalk. Rebeca took the two children to the back of the shop where she gave them each a sweet and a collection of empty cotton cones to play with. Half an hour later Cohen was finished his measuring. He then did the same measurement exercise on Giles. Abe and the children went to leave the shop. Rebecca came from behind the counter and Abe saw her fully for the first time. He saw that below her long skirt and strapped to her boots were two iron rods. He knew immediately that she was a polio victim. He looked her straight in the face and was again overcome with the beauty of her face.

Rebecca had seen Abe's eyes travel down and saw that he had noticed her calipers. She had waited for that look of pity that she had become used to and her heart gave a little leap of hope when the pity look never came. On the way home Giles stopped the buggy at a newly opened ice cream shop. Giles and Abe discussed the progress of the dam and the persistent rumours of a Shona rising as they made their way to Mazowe. The two children in the back of the buggy played happily with the cotton cones Rebecca had given them.

A week later Abe and Guiles went to Cohen's place for fittings. Solomon was not there but due back in half an hour, Giles went off to see his bank manager while Abraham was happy to pass time with Rebecca. They talked in generalities to start with but as time passed the two of them started to empty their hearts to each other. Abe learnt that Rebecca had contracted polio in Johannesburg at the age of six. She was lucky to survive. Two of her friends had died. Her mother had died when she was ten and it had been just her and her father since then, She complained that periodically her father tried to buy her a husband.

Abe opened up for the first time about Mary and how he had been hurt with his loss. For the first time in a long time, he found at least some of the sadness in him ebb away. The two young people were somewhat disappointed when Cohen came back to the shop. Cohen made a few minor adjustments to Abe's suit and declared that it would be completed by the end of the week. Giles had still not returned from the bank. Rebecca went into the back of the shop. On an impulse Abe turned to Cohen and said," Sir, with your permission, I would like to walk out with your daughter."

Cohen smiled and replied, "Mr. Gold, I would be delighted to have you walk out with my daughter and I will even give a dowry to..."

He never finished the sentence as Abe interrupted rudely," Mr. Cohen, don't ever insult your daughter like that again. I want to see your daughter because I like her. I don't give a damn about your money!"

Cohen did not know where to look, "I am sorry. Won't happen again. Mr.Gold."

Rebecca had been about to come into front of the shop and had heard what had been said. For the first time in her life, she felt that she had found somebody who accepted her for what she was.

Abe went up to Rebecca and said, "Miss Cohen, your father has agreed that I can walk out with you. Will you do me the honour of joining me on a walk along the Hunyani River and a picnic next Sunday. "

Rebecca looked at Abe primly but with a sly smile starting to form," I would love to Mr. Gold. Please call me Rebecca."

"And please call me Abe," said Abe.

When Giles had had his suit fitting, he and Abe left Cohen's establishment. Giles could see the 'cat with cream' look on Abe's face and had to ask," What are you so pleased about?"

"I am going to see Rebecca on Sunday and I put that silly man, her father, in his place," replied Abe.

"Good for you," said Giles.

The following Sunday, Giles took Matt and Mariette to the dam site to check on progress. Emily and Siobhan worked on the wedding dress and Abe drove the buggy to Salisbury. He stopped outside Cohen's shop. He went upstairs to where Rebecca was waiting for him. Her father sat reading the Mashonaland Herald. Abe helped Rebecca to the buggy and on to the front seat. Rebecca said to him," Abe, you mustn't pamper me. I am not a fragile doll. If I need your help, I will ask for it. Meanwhile my trusty cane will help me."

The couple drove to a place on the banks of the Hunyani that Abe had heard about. The grass was short, and he laid a blanket down. He then produced a very adequate picnic lunch made by Emily and Siobhan. After having eaten their fill and enjoyed the Leopard Ridge oranges juice, Rebecca and Abe lay on their backs and talked. The sun was hot, but they were in the shade of a large msasa tree. A pied kingfisher sat on a branch and looked for a meal and dragonflies indulged in their meaningless dances just above the surface of the water. The two young people explored each other's lives and liked what they saw. Rebecca said at one point," You're not a Jew are you, Abe.,?"

Abe laughed, "I never actually said I was, did I?" He explained why he had changed his name. Rebecca did not have a problem with what Abe had said, but did ask that her father be kept in the dark for at least the present. They both laughed when she told Abe that her father had speculated that because of his olive skin colour, he must be a Sephardic Jew of perhaps Spanish descent.

Abe was sorry when he had to take Rebecca home. Even though they had barely held hands, he felt his life was about to take an enduring turn. Abe was polite to Solomon Cohen and with his permission arranged to see Rebecca again the following weekend.

Giles was happy with progress at the dam site. The dam wall was almost twelve feet high at its highest point and the spillway was almost complete. He was pleased to see that the rocks that made up the spillway were well laid and interlocking where possible. Matt and Mariette enjoyed themselves chasing butterflies and watching the blue faced lizards the 'hohomannitjies', warming themselves on the large flat rocks by the river.

Chapter 15

The Matabele rebellion did not directly impinge on the lives of the settlers further north in Mashonaland, but when it became clear that some Shona chiefs, pushed by certain spiritual mediums were planning an insurrection, the matter became one of deep concern to Giles and Abe. They made a point of going to visit Matuswa and ask him directly what was going on in his area. Chief Matuswa was upfront with them. The Senior chief for his area, a Chief Chiweshe, had been to see him and asked for his assistance in a proposed rebellion. According to Matuswa he had told Chiweshe that he would not supply warriors from his village but would do his bit by attacking the two farms near to his village, Giles's and Abe's, and deal with the Murungus.

After a long discussion, Giles and Abe agreed to supply Matuswa with some rifles to protect himself and Abe and Giles's farms in the event that they were forced to leave the farms for their safety. Matuswa agreed to warn them in the event of an uprising in their area. Giles went further and promised the chief that if he was responsible for the protection of their farms, he would receive ten prime cattle for his and people's efforts. Both Abe and Giles agreed that there was not much more they could do to protect their families and farms.

Abe's relationship with Rebecca proceeded but at a slow pace. Not only did Abe want to be sure that he could shelve memories of Mary, but that things would go well between Rebecca and Mariette. Rebecca wanted to proceed slowly as she was moving into emotional territory totally unknown to her so far, Abe needn't have worried about Mariette and Rebecca. Abe took Rebecca to Leopard Ridge farm one weekend. Rebecca stayed the night at Emily and Giles's house but spent the best part of two days exploring Mary's Nest and the now closed mine.

Mariette took to Rebecca from the moment that Rebecca agreed happily to join Mariette and her favourite dolls for tea on a rug in the garden. Seeing Mariette wandering around with Rebecca and holding her hand most of the time he realized how much his daughter had missed having a mother. Abe was amazed at how much walking Rebecca was capable of doing in spite of her handicap. She didn't tell him how her legs ached each night until she removed the calipers.

The wedding of Siobhan and Bill took place on a Saturday afternoon in Salisbury at a small but newly built Anglican Church in Second Street. The celebrant was a young priest newly out from England whose enthusiasm more than matched his lack of experience. Rebecca was a last-minute bridesmaid. The reception was held in the Kopje Road Warehouse with catering by two large but capable Afrikaans sisters and paid for by Giles. Two happy young people went off to celebrate their union at the hotel.

Giles managed to get hold of two martini Henry bolt action rifles and two Lee-Metford rifles and a good amount of ammunition. He took them to Chief Matuswa and took his time teaching three of his sons and a couple of other young men how to shoot and how to maintain the rifles. Matuswa informed him that the 'bush telegraph' was saying that Chief Chiweshe, heavily prompted by the medium Nyanda, was planning a series of small uprisings in a crescent across Mashonaland from Hartley and Norton in the west through Mazowe and to Ruzawi and Goromonzi in the east.

Towards the end of May 1896, it became obvious that a Shona uprising was in operation. To start with isolated farmers were attacked and killed and wagon drivers on their own and even two government servants going about their business. Giles and Abe decided that, for the time being, all the occupants of the two farms should live at Leopard Ridge, and during the day farming operations would be supervised by at least two armed men. Giles and Abe made another visit to chief Matuswa who confirmed that the situation in and around Mazowe looked bad and could only get worse. Matuswa promised that as soon as he was informed of Leopard Ridge and Mary's Nest farms being evacuated, he would send his sons and some other loyal villagers with the arms that had been provided and would ostensibly take ownership of the farms in the name of Chief Matuswa. Giles believed that the chief would do what he could for Giles and Abe if for no other reason than the bad blood that existed between Matuswa and Chief Chiweshe.

In the last week of May all the residents of the Mazowe area, village occupants, miners at the Beatrice and Alice mines and local farmers had a meeting at the store in Mazowe where it was decided that, when the uprising reached their part of the world, all whites would congregate at the village store and if things got really bad, would set up a laager at the Alice Mine. Mr. Salthouse, the manager of the mine offered to lay in a store of food and water in case of a prolonged siege of the mine. He further offered to set up a lot of sticks of dynamite and short fuses to be used as extra munition.

On the fifteenth of June a messenger arrived from Matuswa's village to say that marauding tribesmen had arrived from the east, and it was time that the Murungus should move to Mazowe. His sons would soon occupy the farms. Giles got the buggy ready with two walls of sandbags along each side of the back of the buggy. Emily and Siobhan got into the front of the buggy with Matt and Mariette lying down between the sandbags. Abe, Giles and Bill mounted their horses and the party left Leopards Ridge. As they moved westwards towards Mazowe, Giles looked back at the house and prayed that it would still be there if and when they could return. As they made their way to Mazowe the evacuees could see a series of fires on the skyline, and they could hear occasional gun shots.

When Giles's party reached the village, it was to find that it had been already decided by the gathered Europeans that an easier place to defend would be Alice Mine and so the group, nine men, three women and two children moved the approximate mile and a half to the mine. Mr. Salthouse had already set up a defensive position on a kopje next to the mine but at Giles's suggestion they moved further up the kopje so they could not be overlooked from a nearby kopje. On a rocky shelf near the top of the kopje the men gathered and placed rocks in a crescent round the shelf. The women and the children got behind the rocky barrier and waited.

In the late afternoon the party on the kopje were subjected to a persistent hail of gunfire. The children huddled behind the rock wall and comforted each other. Emily took charge of one of the shotguns and fired it at any of the Shona attackers who got too close. She took her time and didn't waste ammunition. She saw several bodies fall after some of her well-directed shots. Giles, Bill and Abe moved up and round the kopje on foot looking for suitable targets of which there were many. Shortly before nightfall it was decided that the Alice Mine defenders were hopelessly outnumbered, and help would have to be requested from Salisbury. One of the men, the telegraph operator, volounteered to run for the village to the telegraph office and send a request for help from Judge Vincent, the Acting Administrator. He managed to get the message to Judge Vincent but was badly injured on

121

his run back to the mine. Emily patched up the gunshot wound in his side as best as she could and gave the man a good dose of laudanum from the mine medical supplies.

Judge Vincent was in a spot. He was short of military men as most of the BSAP Company Police were in Matabeleland dealing with trouble there. Troops were on their way from England via Beira but would be only there in several weeks. The best he could do was to send a coach which was being used as an ambulance to collect any women and children. Accordingly, the following morning he sent the ambulance to Mazowe with four armed men, all he could muster. The ambulance came under fire almost from the time it passed Mount Hampden, but did eventually reach Alice Mine. The ambulance with Mrs. Salthouse, Emily, Siobhan, the lady from the Mazowe store and the two children left Alice Mine. The men, the farmers, and miners rode their horses next the ambulance periodically moving into the bush to see where the enemy were.

Gunfire was incessant and, as the ambulance was negotiating a steep riverbed the mules slipped on the muddy bank and took fright. The ambulance tipped over and deposited the women and the children in the dry riverbed. Luckily nobody was hurt. Eventually the ambulance was righted, and the mules calmed. Two of the men accompanying the ambulance had been shot, one fatally. Giles persuaded Mr. Salthouse that to continue would be suicide and the ambulance was turned round and headed back to the mine.

Back at the mine Mr. Salthouse offered a man called Hendricks, a colored man from the Cape, £100 if he would ride to Salisbury under cover of night and appraise Judge Vincent of the desperate situation at the mine and ask again for more substantial help. Hendricks made it to Salisbury and got to see Judge Vincent who set about mustering a relief party. He put Captain Ronald Nesbitt in charge of twelve men and sent them off to Mazowe. Nesbitt's group encountered heavy opposition when they got near to Mazowe but eventually made it to the Mine.

Nesbitt organized for iron sheets to be attached to the sides of the ambulance coach and eventually all the besieged men and women were able to make their way slowly back to Salisbury. They were constantly under fire and three of Nesbitt's men were wounded. At one stage when the Shona warriors were getting close to the coach and threatening to overcome it, Giles tied his horse to the ambulance and climbed aboard.

He found the sticks of dynamite previously prepared and lit a cigar borrowed from one of Nesbitt's men. He sat at the back of the ambulance and when he saw the Shona getting too close, he lit a fuse with the cigar and tossed the bundle of dynamite in the direction of the Shona. The effect was immediate, and the armed warriors backed away. It was not until the relief party reached the open grasslands near Mount Hampden that the Shona backed off and the ambulance with the women and children and escort reached Salisbury safely. Captain Nesbitt was a hero and when months later it was announced that he had been awarded the Victoria Cross it was felt in the Elliott-Smith and Gold households that it was fully deserved. Giles, Abe and Bill and their families went to stay in a rooming house in Rhodes Avenue for a week until it was regarded as safe to go home.

The close shave with death had an immediate effect on Abe. He decided not to waste any more valuable time and he went to see Solomon Cohen to ask permission to marry his daughter. Cohen was so glad that Rebecca had secured a husband that he offered little resistance to Abe's insistence that he and Rebecca have a quiet wedding in the registrar's office in Salisbury. Rebecca was delighted and so was Mariette at the prospect of having a new mother. The reception was held in a large marquee in the park just off Jameson Avenue. Cohen went to town on the reception probably to compensate for the synagogue wedding that had never happened. There was even a band who played late into the night. Rebecca and Abe dispensed with a honeymoon, but Abe promised her that as soon as things settled on the farm, he would take her and Mariette to Cape Town.

Leopard Ridge and Mary's Nest suffered no harm over the uprising and when Giles and Abe returned to their respective farms the Chief's sons were still in effective control and Giles arranged for nine cows and a bull to be sent from Salisbury to the Chief. Life began to return back to normal on the two farms. Rebecca settled into farm life never stopping adoring her new husband. When it was discovered that Rebecca had trained as a teacher in Johannesburg before joining her father in Salisbury, she was persuaded to be teacher to Mariette and Matt.

Slowly over the whole of Mashonaland and Matabeleland peace returned. Chief Chiweshe was captured and held to account for his role in uprising which the locals called 'the Chimurenga'. He was badly manhandled by his captors. Chief Matuswa was very happy with his new cattle especially as he was overdue on a 'lobola' payment for a bride for one of his sons. The chief was showing sign of his age and asked Emily to come to his kraal to treat him as it was getting more and more difficult for him to make the journey to Leopard Ridge. Emily agreed willingly.

The dam was complete and was filling rapidly and once the rains came in late 1896, it reached its capacity and water tumbled over the spillway. It was about one hundred and forty yards wide and stretched back from the wall a distance of about eight hundred yards. Giles noted with pleasure that it soon had a healthy and ever-growing fish population mainly of tilapia. It also attracted numerous water birds and a pair of fish eagles whose characteristic calls could be heard coming from high overhead.

Giles and Abe drove in the buggy to Chief Matuswaa's village and took him somewhat reluctantly to the dam. The chief had never been on a wheeled vehicle and did not trust it. At the dam the chief saw for the first time the dam that had been created by his people. Giles informed the chief that the dam was going to be called, from that day onwards, as Nyanza Matuswa, or Lake Matuswa. Furthermore, he was granting the chiefs family and all his subjects fishing rights on the dam with the proviso that no nets would be used.

1996 passed into 1897 peacefully. Both Leopard Ridge and Mary's Nest farms were prospering. Abe was slowly, as he could afford it, buying in beef cattle. His vegetable and fruit venture had recovered and the acreage under fruit and vegetables was increased to over forty acres. Abe was even considering putting in a canning plant. Rebecca loved the farm almost as much as she loved Abe and Mariette. With her trusty cane she managed to cover considerable distances on level ground. Her father came occasionally to the farm and when with his friends in the Jewish Club, never failed to mention that his son in law had a farm of three thousand acres and a mine.

Leopard Ridge farm was also prospering. Giles now had over three thousand orange trees of different ages and sales of oranges were going well. He was considering the possibility of putting in a plant to make orange squash once he had saturated the local market for fresh oranges. His sheep flock had reached four hundred odd and needed the regular introduction of new Dorset Horn rams to avoid inbreeding. There were three hundred acres of maize already planted during the start of the rainy season. He did not plant any more barley as the last small crop had to be sold as animal feed when the brewery that wanted the initial barley crop went bankrupt.

Emily was as happy as she had ever been. Her man, Giles, was becoming a well-known person in Mashonaland and was elected as first president of the newly formed Mashonaland Agricultural Union. With Matt and Mariette in Rebecca's hands during the day, Emily could spend more time on helping Giles especially with the sheep flock. She started to devote more time to her plant collection and her journal with its watercolour paintings started to expand again. Now and again, she took a folding chair and placed it under the modicum of shade now provided by her tamarind tree and thought about Motsepe and her family and her garden in Cape Town.

Abe and Giles decided that early in 1897, Abe would take time from the farm and go and have the honeymoon he had never had.

In the latter half of that year Giles and Emily would travel to Cape Town to visit Emily's family. In Abe's absence Bill would take over the running of Mary's Nest. He has proved to be an able farm manager and was happy in his now enlarged house with Siobhan. In Giles's absence Bill would hand back management of Mary's nest to Abe and manage Leopard Nest. He was to be helped by Reggie, Emily's brother who had finished his degree in law at Cape Town University but had decided to accept an invitation to stay with Emily and Giles and get to know a part of wild Africa that was fast disappearing.

Abe and Rebecca left Salisbury on the train to Beira on a hot February afternoon. They were travelling on the quaint but slow train that crossed the grassy plains of eastern Mashonaland before climbing over a range of hills that formed the border between Rhodesia and Mozambique. The small steam engine drew its six carriages across the volcanic plain around the town of Chimoio before coasting slowly down across the Pungwe flats to Beira, a small and undistinguished town in the delta of the Pungwe River. They spent a night in Beira before boarding the S.S.Arundel Castle which steamed slowly south over four days to reach the port of Durban. It was good for Abe and Rebecca to be able to sit in steamer chairs on the deck of the ship and watch the flying fish gliding over the white crested waves and just talk and plan their future. They both missed Mariette, but had not argued with her when she said that she loved her mother and father but wanted to stay with her best friend Matt. Emily and Giles were happy to take in Mariette and Siobhan took over the childrens' education.

After a hot sweaty night in a seafront hotel in Durban, Abe and Rebecca caught the overnight train to Johannesburg where they stayed in a good hotel on the outskirts of the city. The next week was spent sightseeing, mainly places from Rebecca's past and meeting her friends from school and college. Rebecca got no end of satisfaction in introducing her successful farmer husband to friends who in the past she might have envied for their healthy bodies but none of whom had married as well as she had. Their honeymoon ended much as it started with a ship trip and a train journey back to Salisbury.

Three months later Emily and Giles went on their journey to Cape Town mainly for the de Spevilles to see their fast-growing grandson. During the planning for the trip, Giles had managed to persuade his father, now starting to feel the effects of old age to come to Cape Town. He had arranged for his father to travel first class on the S.S. Braemar Castle. Emily's father, on hearing of the plan to bring Matthew Smith to the Cape, insisted on him staying along with Giles and Emily at La Mercy. There had been a problem with Mariette who wanted to go with Matthew to Cape Town. She settled with her parents for a bribe of a Labrador puppy which she immediately called Matt.

Giles, Matt and Emily travelled by coach to Bulawayo and then caught the train that dragged itself all the way through Bechuanaland and then Kimberly to Cape Town. Marcel de Speville met them at Cape Town station. He took them to La Mercy in his buggy, arranging for their luggage to follow later, Molly was so delighted to see Emily and little Matt that she forgot to point out to Emily how her skin was getting very brown and even small wrinkles were showing. De Speville and Matt skipped the usual tea in the drawing room and escaped to the stables. Molly interrogated Giles and Emily for fully half an hour before Giles managed to slip away and join de Speville and Matt now mounted and riding round the stable yard.

Matthew Smith arrived the following day and Giles borrowed de Speville's buggy to pick him up at the docks. Giles was pleased to see that his father both looked and sounded well. He shocked Giles by actually giving him a hug, an action that had been absent in his entire childhood. Matthew Smith had thoroughly enjoyed the sea voyage and spoke of it animatedly. At La Mercy Giles introduced his father merely as Matthew and failed to mention his surname. Contrary to expectations his father and de Speville got on well. Matt and his grandfather Matthew, also got on well especially when Matthew found that his grandson liked nothing better than to be regaled with stories of foxes, pheasants and badgers. To Giles, life had reached perfection when, one morning as he stood holding hands with Emily on the front steps of La Mercy, he saw his son walking between his two grandfathers holding hands with both of them and headed for the stables.

Giles received an invitation to visit Cecil Rhodes at the Parliament Building. Rhodes seemed genuinely pleased to see Giles. He stated how happy he was that Giles and his family had survived the Mashona rebellion. He also conceded that he, Giles had been right about the poor relationship between the white people who were given land by the BSAP company and the black people who laid claim to the same land. He asked Giles what could be done to rectify the situation now. Giles suggested some sort of compensation for the land, but Rhodes shook his head, "the hawks in London will never agree. They will say," We don't pay to expand our empire. The benefits of being in the British Empire are enough."

Giles just shook his head. Rhodes switched the subject and sounded him out on his feelings about the English/ Afrikaaner situation that was raising its ugly head in southern Africa. Giles offered his opinion that the British were being very arrogant in believing that less than a century's occupation of the southern tip of Africa entitled them to take over the Orange Free State and the Transvaal from a people who had been on the southern tip of Africa for some two hundred and fifty years. Giles went on to say that in a war with the Boers, the Afrikaans farmers, British troops would come off second best. The Boers would not fight by the Marquis of Queensbury rules and would fight a low-key hit and run war against their enemy. Finally, Giles pointed out that the antagonism between the Boers and the British was largely of British making. He told Rhodes of how in Mashonaland the English speakers and the Afrikaans speakers existed happily together believing themselves to be equal citizens of the so-called Rhodesia. Rhodes did not comment further.

Emily, Giles and Matt were sad when the time came to be leaving Cape Town for home, but in a way were missing the farm and all that it stood for. Matthew senior had so enjoyed his time in Cape Town with his grandson that he proposed to retire there when he reached retirement age.

Chapter 16

The years that closed out the nineteenth century were good years for the Mazowe farming community. Produce prices rose and so did yields following a succession of good rainy seasons. Giles's oranges had eventually saturated the fresh fruit market and he had installed a small juice extractor and bottling plant on Leopard Ridge. This plant was run by Reggie who had decided that life was good in Rhodesia, and he stayed. He not only ran the bottling plant but had set up a legal office in Salisbury from where he worked for three days a week.

In January 1898 Emily gave Giles the good but unexpected news that she was pregnant. Giles had accepted that he was to have only one offspring, so he was delighted with the news. Amazingly it was on the following day that Rebecca announced to Abe that he was to be a father again. Rebecca was absolutely delighted to be having a child as somehow, she had had a terrible feeling that her polio might stop her bearing a child. Incredibly, nine months later in October, both Emily and Rebecca gave birth on the same day, Emily to a girl and Rebecca to a boy, at the nursing home in Salisbury. The little girl was named Molly Mary after her two grandmothers and the little boy was named Solomon Giles.

Mariette and Matt were only marginally put out by the arrival of their new siblings and three months later the pair of them went to board at the Dominican Convent School in Salisbury. Ostensibly a girl's school, it catered for boys up to the age of eleven. Mariette and Matt settled quickly into school life. They were in the same class and spent all their days together except for at night where they went to separate dormitories. The school was ably presided over by Sister Patrick. Matt and Mariette flourished academically and on the sports field where they spurred each other on. They became known as the Mazowe Menace and were not to be taken lightly. End of term reports most times put Mariette marginally ahead of Matt academically but Matt ahead on the sports field.

When the Second Boer War started in earnest in 1899 Giles was surprised to get a telegram from Rhodes offering him a commission and a placement as intelligence officer on the staff of General Lord Roberts. Rhodes was not surprised when Giles turned down the offer. Reggie however returned to Cape Town and enlisted in the Cape Mounted Riflemen. The Boer war did not have a major effect on the lives of Giles and Abe and their families. It did however sour a lot of relationships between English and Afrikaans speakers in Mashonaland. Financially, the needs of the large British Army fighting in South Africa ensured that crops and livestock sold by Abe and Giles continued to command good prices.

In early 1900 Reggie who was serving at Molteno in the Eastern Cape under Colonel Dalgety was killed in action. The reality of the war was brought home to Emily and Giles with a jolt. Emily grieved for her brother no less than did her mother and father. Giles, in particular, got more and more angry as the war progressed and saw the British, failing to match the Boers on the battlefield, starting to use what Giles believed were barbaric methods to crush the Boers. They instituted systemic destruction of the Boers' farms and crops and often left the Boer women and children starving. When this brutality failed to achieve the desired result, they set up internment camps where Boer women and children were placed under appalling conditions. The women and children died by the tens of thousands.

Giles read about the situation in the internment camps and wrote a letter of protest to Rhodes to hopefully pass on to the British PM. Rhodes replied that what was going on was not right but reported that, under extreme pressure from one British woman, Emily Hobhouse, the Fawcett enquiry had been set up to look into conditions in the camps. Eventually conditions in the camps were improved but not before the use of this cruel instrument had helped break an army far superior to the British army of the day.

Without Reggie to run the orange squash bottling plant Giles was overwhelmed and was happy to hand over the management of the plant to Siobhan who was still childless.

Chief Matuswa died in January 1901. He was to be sorely missed by Abe and Giles and their families. Giles suspected that the cause of his death might well have been a surfeit of millet beer. Matuswa's oldest son, Madire, one of the men that had defended Leopard Ridge during the uprising, succeeded his father. Giles and Abe and all their families attended the funeral of the chief and supplied the two steers that were butchered and then cooked on giant spits to feed the funeral guests over two days of hearty eating and drinking.

Another death occurred a year later in 1902 that affected Giles greatly. On the 26th of March Cecil John Rhodes died at his cottage at Muizenberg in the Cape. Though he had not always agreed with Rhodes, he recognized him as a great man who was at least in part responsible for his, Giles's success. He was honoured to discover that in accordance with Rhodes's wishes he was to be one of the pall bearers when Rhodes's body was to be laid in its final resting place in the Matopos, the hills south of Bulawayo. Rhodes was only forty-nine when he died. Such was the mark he had made on the history of southern Africa, that his body was sent by train all the way from Cape Town to Bulawayo stopping at every station for people to pay their respects

The two new little ones, Solly and Molly, were both healthy babies and grew fast. In the school holidays Mariette and Matt were encouraged to interact with their new siblings but found them generally an unwanted distraction. One late afternoon Mariette and Matt were catching butterflies for Matt's collection up near the ridge when they heard a loud roar coming from above them and they saw on a rocky ledge a leopard and two cubs. They stood transfixed as the leopard picked up one cub by its neck and guided the other one away from where she had stood. Matt and Mariette could not wait to tell their respective parents of their meeting with the leopards. Giles was delighted to hear that there were still leopards around as he hadn't seen any for several years.

The early years of the twentieth century were busy and productive years for Giles and Abe. Giles increased his acreage of arable land to close to four hundred acres mainly producing maize but also with a small but increasing acreage of sunflowers. With the end of the Boer War and stability returning to South Africa the demand for agricultural products was good and ever increasing. Abe decided that by canning the bulk of his vegetable and fruit crop he could get prices less affected by market variations and so installed a canning plant on Mary's Nest and marketed his canned goods under the 'Top Gold' label. Rebecca was the one who researched jam and preserve recipes which resulted in a range of jams and marmalade.

1905 was a year of memorable events for both the Elliott-Smith and Gold families. Matt and Mariette were subjected to the shock of no longer going to school together. Matt had reached the age where he had to go to a boys only school. He was sent as a boarder to Salisbury

Grammar school, whereas Mariette stayed on at the convent. Within the first week, Giles received a message urging him to see the headmaster on a matter of some urgency. It appeared that Matt could see no good reason why he could not, when he felt like it, leave the grounds of Salisbury Grammar to walk the mile or so to the Dominican Convent to see Mariette. It took considerable patience from Giles and diplomacy from Emily to convince Matt otherwise. Once he accepted the constraints of his position at the school, he settled down well and found his main strength in the game of rugby.

The same year Giles and Emily made the long journey to Cape Town to enable Marcel and Molly to see their granddaughter, Molly. Matt did not go with then as it was term time, The family spent a fortnight with the de Spevilles. La Marcy was not as happy a place as it had been. It still seemed under the cloud of Reggie's death. Little Molly hit it off straight away with her namesake grandmother with whom she most resembled. Molly senior delighted in taking Molly junior to fancy shops in the city and buying her clothes all full of lace and ribbons. Emily felt very close to her father who had aged considerably since she had last seen him and insisted that he went with her on the frequent occasions she went to her natural garden.

Giles made his usual pilgrimage to 76 Hout Street where he received a warm welcome from a rapidly ageing Mrs. Van who was so overcome with the lace shawl Giles had bought her that she forgot all about 'Rooineks'! From Hout Street Giles went into the city to walk past the shop that now sold trinkets instead of books but nevertheless was still a repository of many happy memories. Not far from there he was passing a business that was selling cars, new Ford cars. Giles lingered looking at the new marvels of the road. He went into the showroom where there was a car, black in colour with maroon upholstery that took his fancy. An hour later full of facts and figures Giles retraced his steps back to La Mercy.

Emily was surprised when Giles took her aside in the garden and started to extol the virtues of the 1905 Ford Model A four-seater 10 horsepower car. Giles explained to her how wonderful it would be to be able to get from the farm to Salisbury in little over an hour in comfort and without having to harness a horse. Emily smiled at him and said,

"My Darling, you have always put others first. You have never let your family or friends go short of anything. Treat yourself for once. Buy the car as long as you let me drive it as well." With that she flounced away with a smile on her face.

The following day Giles went with Emily to the car dealer, Emily loved the vehicle and handing over a cheque for £504 Giles took ownership of the car. It came with a tonneau cover, folding roof and tool kit. The car was to be sent by rail to Bulawayo where Giles would collect it and drive it to Salisbury. The gentleman selling the car drove Giles and Emily to an open area near Sea Point where he gave Giles the first of four lessons on driving the car.

Eventually time came for Emily, Giles and Molly to leave Cape Town. Perhaps the saddest one of the leavers was little Molly who had been thoroughly spoilt mostly by her grandmother but also by Marcel. Back in Mazowe life returned to normal. Abe and Bill had looked after Leopard Ridge well with no moments of drama. Abe couldn't wait to let Giles and Emily sees and taste his new range of jams now being marketed in glass jars under the brand name of Super Gold. He did give due credit to Rebecca for the recipes.

Giles got a telegram to say that his car was available for collection at Bulawayo Station. He and Emily caught the coach to Bulawayo. Before leaving Bulawayo Giles filled up with petrol at the only fuel outlet in the town and also filled several cans as there was reputedly no petrol available en-route to Salisbury. The road to Salisbury via Gwelo was only slightly better than a track. The car went well and at certain places on the road where it was straight and level and not too bumpy the car was able go up to twenty-five miles an hour. However, the low-level bridges and drifts through dry riverbeds slowed them down and it took the whole day to get to the small roadside town of Gatooma where they found a bed for the night. The next day they made the remaining journey to Salisbury where they arrived at about two in the afternoon. Even though they were both tired and dusty, Giles insisted on stopping off at Salisbury Grammar to let Matt have his first look at the car. Matt stared at the car, climbed in and out and then just stood and stared again. Matt had fallen for the metallic symbol of perfection that stood before him, hook line and sinker. He was speechless but was basking in the admiration being showered on him by his fellow school mates some of which had never seen and many who had never been close to a motor car.

Abe and Rebecca were also impressed with the Model A and Abe would have loved to have bought a car for himself except for a recent event that had cost him a lot of his available money. Solomon Cohen had gone broke and refusing to see that he could not compete on his own against department stores selling readymade men's clothing had persisted and ran up big debts. Abe had paid off all Solomon's debts and also paid for him to return to Johannesburg where he found a position as a tailor in one of his family's businesses. What had happened put a strain on Abe and Rebecca's relationship. Rebecca was ashamed of her father, and it took some time before she was able to accept that what Abe had done, he had done happily as it was through Solomon that he had met and fallen in love with Rebecca.

The sudden substantial outflow of funds got Abe to thinking and on a Saturday morning he took a bottle of water and a prospector's hammer and went to the original open cast mine and started to work his way along the ridge southwards looking for any signs of gold. He moved slowly and carefully stopping and chipping. After three hours he had covered about a mile. He had just stopped to straighten his body and have a much-needed drink when he spotted a puff adder sunning itself on a rock, part of the ridge. Staring at the snake he suddenly saw that the rock on which the snake was sunning itself glinted of gold. With a stick he forced the hissing snake to move off and he took samples of the rock.

Exploring further he found what he had hoped for. The reef they had worked before, and which had dipped deep into the earth had re-appeared on the surface again. His heart leapt and he couldn't wait to get to Giles's house to show him the rock samples. The next day Giles, Emily and Abe returned to the new gold bearing rocks and explored further, They then returned to Mary's Nest and joined Rebecca, The four of them decided that, if the samples they had collected did have a reasonable amount of gold, they would re-commission the ball mill, trammel and sluice box and start a new open cast mine. They decided to call it Puff Adder Mine. The following week they located Stanley who had had gone to work at the Alice Mine until the day of the uprising but had been just doing odd jobs in Salisbury since. He was more than happy to be mine manager again. Chief Madire was more than happy to provide labour for the mine along the same basis as had his father. He did not try to seal the deal with millet beer like his father.

Chapter 17

Sister Aurelia sat in her sunny art room and watched young Molly, who was proving to be the most talented child she had ever had the pleasure to teach. She had been under her tutelage now for five years and was an unusual little girl who did not socialize with the other girls. Molly was above average academically, avoided taking part in any sport but the water colour paintings that she produced for Sister Aurelia to see were, to say the least, amazing. The subject matter was either landscapes of the of the area around Mazowe or studies of local plants. The young German nun learnt that Molly's mother Emily was an accomplished artist.

Molly contrasted in nature strongly with her friend from Mazowe, young Solly, who was a highly sociable child who was very clever academically and very capable of manipulating others, including Sister Patrick, the headmistress. The only one who did not fall under Solly's spell was Molly. Consequently, Molly was the only person, young as she was, whom he respected. During the holidays Solly was happy to act as helper to Molly and carry her painting equipment all over Leopard Ridge farm.

Matt and Mariette's relationship changed rapidly. Matt had adopted the Ford Model A and the car displaced Mariette largely in his affections. Matt couldn't wait for school holidays to came so he could spend every day cleaning the car and checking that every nut and bolt was tight. He persuaded his father to let him learn to drive at the age of twelve, an operation only made possible by using a cushion behind his back so he could reach the pedals. It did not take Matt long to understand how to synchronise the speed of the engine with the speed of the road wheels and very soon he could change gear better than his father. The highlight of his young life was when his father allowed him to drive him as far as Mazowe Village. Long before he had finished school Matt had decided that he was going to the South African College in Cape Town to study engineering. He never understood how his best friend Mariette did not share his love of one Ford Model A. The strength of their friendship wavered and subsided to a level where, in the holidays they did not see each other for weeks.

Mariette loved her little brother, Solly and was happy in the holidays to take him all over Mary's nest. Sometimes for a treat she would take Solly all the way over the ridge and across Leopard Ridge to the dam where he would fish for hours while Mariette lay on her back and looked for figures in the clouds above her and sought understanding of how her Matt could have been obsessed with a piece of metal and leather and rubber.

Puff Adder Mine turned out to have much bigger ore reserves than its predecessor and would be workable as an open cast mine for the next ten years. Under the capable management of Stanley, it was to provide the means of restoring Abe's diminished bank balance. It also provided a pleasant bonus for Giles and Emily, so they did not have to worry if one year's crops did not come up to expectation. Giles put away money in a separate account for the children's further education and a fund to boost his father's pension when the time came.

Leopard Ridge farm continued to prosper to the extent that Giles felt the need for another assistant manager. Bill's time had always been more or less shared with Abe so when Bill's younger brother, Thomas arrived from England to make his way in Rhodesia, Giles was happy to install him as assistant manager. He was taller than Bill with the same red hair and freckles and happy nature.

With the income from the mine Abe was also in a position to secure an assistant. He was at first inclined to send for his cousin Adam in cape town but foresaw problems with having to explain his own apparent Jewishness and a Muslim cousin. He therefore agreed with Rebecca s suggestion to send for her cousin Aaron from Johannesburg. When Aaron arrived, he turned out to be a short dark haired and very serious young man very appreciative of being given a chance to improve himself. He stayed with Abe and Rebecca and soon became a firm favourite in their family.

Matt was only fourteen when his ability to drive the Model A was severely tested. He had driven with his father to Mazowe to look at some sheep that a local farmer was selling. They were on the way home when, with Giles driving, they went round a corner and a solitary cow stood in the middle of the road. Giles swerved the car and as he did so the right front wheel hit a rock. Giles was thrown out of the car into the road. Matt seemed to somehow remain in the car until it slowly came to a stop. Matt rushed to where his father was lying in the road. Giles tried to get up but couldn't. He had suffered a fracture of his femur. He was groaning in pain.

Matt managed to get his father into the car, and he then examined the damaged wheel. It would have to be changed for the spare. Under Matt's care the car always had a jack and spanner and Matt changed the wheel. He saw his father needed urgent medical attention. Knowing that there was no doctor in Mazowe he turned the car towards Salisbury and drove as fast as he could without endangering the car and its occupants. He drove straight to the hospital where Giles's leg was set and put in plaster. Giles was proud of his son and thankful that he had taught him to drive when many others said he was too young. Giles was soon back on the farm on crutches and surprised to find that Matt had, with his own limited toolbox, rebuilt the damaged wheel.

In 1910 Mariette and Matt finished their school education. Matt had long decided what he wanted to do, and it was easily arranged for him to enroll at The South African College to study engineering. It went without saying that he would live at La Mercy with his grandparents. Marcel had retired and was happy to spend his days in the garden or behind a newspaper on the stoep except when forced into some social event or another still very much patronized by Molly.

Mariette and her parents gave a lot of thought to what she should pursue as a career. They decided that she should also go to The South African College to study for a BA in English and language studies. She was glad that she would be with Matt again even though their friendship had cooled in recent years. The matter of where she would live was solved surprisingly easily by her being invited to stay for as long as she wanted in the gust house at La Mercy. The invitation had come about when Giles asking Molly directly, to do him a favour, and give accommodation to his friend and business partner's daughter. Molly's attitude towards Giles had undergone a major adjustment as a result of one single event. That event was when Giles was nominated to carry Rhodes coffin by the great man himself. Giles had become in a flash, 'that wealthy and well-known son in law of mine.'

Matt and Mariette had only been at the college for a few months when the four states that made up the southern tip of Africa attempted to put aside the horrors and hatred generated by the Boer War and joined together to form a single country, the Union of South Africa. Far away in the north Giles read about the event and was happy. It did not exactly mean that Rhodes's dream had been realized, but he was sure that Rhodes would approve of the creation of a country very much under the influence and control of Britain.

Matt and Mariette cycled to SAC every day together. Matt was happy to be protecting Mariette and Mariette was happy to have him by her side. The Model A Ford was more than a thousand miles away and no longer a competitor for Matt's affection. The two of them sat on the college steps each day for a lunch of Mrs. Goosen's sandwiches. Mariette was pretty enough to attract the attention of a succession of young men who rarely approached her when she was sitting with Matt, who was not only a big man but the new star of the college rugby team. When a young man did get to talk to Mariette on her own and the action was observed by Matt, he felt a jealousy rising in him which he didn't really understand.

It was in the second year of their college studies that a life changing event occurred that would affect Mariette and Matt. That particular evening Matt had been asked to attend an unplanned rugby practice. This meant that Mariette was having to cycle on her own back to La Mercy. About a quarter mile from the college, she was cycling along a quiet, heavily treed road when she found her way blocked by three young men whom she recognized from college. She was forced to stop. The young men started to taunt her and ask her where her big boyfriend was. Mariette was undaunted at this stage and verbally gave back as good as she got. This antagonized the three men who approached her closer and started to fondle her. Mariette retaliated by scratching the face of one of the men. This got the scratched young man angry enough to pull her off her bicycle and throw her to the ground.

What happened next became a bit of a blur. She later remembered fighting for her life and hitting and scratching each of the men before she was raped by each one. When it was over Mariette straightened her clothes and got back on her bicycle and rode back to La Mercy and it was only when she was back in her bedroom that the tears came. Matt came back from rugby practice and went to see Mariette and apologize for leaving her to go home on her own. He found her sobbing. Mat cradled her in his arms as she reluctantly told him of what had happened. Matt was furious and wanted to go straight away and kill Mariette's assailants. Mariette got him to calm down.

Matt eventually turned to Mariette and said, "I will have to marry you and keep you safe forever."

Mariette said in a trembling voice "How can you marry me now, Matt." His reply was, "How can I not." This simple sentence became the tie that was to bind Mariette and Matt for the foreseeable future.

Mariette and Matt decided to say nothing to her parents until Mariette had been to the police. The following day Matt went with Mariette to the police. The sergeant of police at Newlands was kind and understanding but made it quite clear that to prosecute a rape case was difficult as it was a 'she said, he said,' case and in court could be embarrassing for the accuser. As they left the police station Matt said to Mariette," don't worry I will sort things out.

Two days later a young man was admitted to the Somerset Hospital in Greenpoint with multiple injuries. He had a broken nose and broken ribs and scratched into the skin of his forehead was the letter R. He refused to tell the hospital, or subsequently the police, what had happened. A week later another young man was admitted to the same hospital with similar injuries including acute groin injury. He had an R cut into his head as well. The police were summoned and left puzzled in the absence of any explanation from the injured man. After a third young man was, three days later admitted to the Somerset, the police issued a notice to all police stations to be on the lookout for a serial attacker of young men. When the notice was read by the sergeant at the Newlands police station he smiled and consigned the notice to the waste paper basket. Mariette read what had happened to her attackers in the newspaper. Matt would not discuss the matter but just handed her three red roses and said," I have sorted the matter, Leave it at that."

Mariette was not sure that she was right in loving Matt for what he had done, but she did. Three young men never returned to continue their studies at SAC. Mariette and Matt continued their studies, but they were both changed radically. Mariette retreated into herself. She still attended lectures and made progress academically, but it was as if a fire inside her had been extinguished. Outside of lectures she avoided people, everybody except Matt. The only time she ever smiled was when she was with him.

Matt was extremely disturbed over Mariette and unreasonably blamed himself for what had happened. He devoted his every living day to looking after Mariette. They continued to cycle to college together and to lunch together. When Matt had a rugby practice Mariette would sit on the sideline and do any homework she needed to do. When Matt played in a match Mariette always went to the game and silently cheered him on from where she sat away from the college's other fans, Marcel and Molly became away of a radical change in both Matt and Mariette but were unable to get out of either of them any indication of what had happened.

Matt and Mariette travelled home to Salisbury together on the train at the end of their second academic year. Mariette felt distinct relief in the distance that had been put between her and Cape Town. She smiled more and loved her younger brother, Solly who was now at Salisbury High School, the new name of the original Salisbury Grammar School. He did well at school and was a happy boy who paid no attention to the occasional "Yid" intended insult shouted at him.

On his first day back on the farm Giles took Matt to the new garage that had sprung up near the house since he had last been home. Giles swung open the double doors to reveal a brand-new Buick Model 16 Surrey standing next to a now less impressive Model A Ford.

"My God, the mine and the farm must be doing well, father!" said a surprised Matt.

"Well enough. Things have been good recently, my boy. Use either of them over the holidays as you want," said Giles.

"Wow thanks Father. Can I go and see Mariette in the Buick, "asked Matt.

"Sure, just drive carefully on the farm roads", answered Giles.

Matt arrived at Mary's Nest with the Buick's claxon horn sounding noisily. Mariette and Solly rushed to greet him. Abe and Rebecca arrived at a more leisurely pace. After inter family greetings were complete, Matt took all of them on a drive to Mazowe and back. Young Solly was in heaven. So was Mariette but not because of the car but because Matt was again by her side.

Matt did spend a lot of time with the Buick but arranged for Marinette to be with him most of the time. He took her to Mazowe village whenever she wanted and at least once a week to Salisbury where the two of them looked at shop windows of the stores springing up all the time. They went to the Hunyani River and picnicked on its banks. It was on the banks of the Hunyani that Matt realized how much he loved Mariette seeing her lying on her back, skirt fanned out on the picnic rug. He picked up her hand and felt her tense. He continued to hold her hand and said gently "Mariette, I do love you so much and one day I will marry you. I won't rush you."

"Matt, I love you and always have. You will have to be patient with me. I am still battling to forget what happened to me. We will marry one day, "said, Mariette.

One day Mariette had walked over to Leopard Ridge to see Matt who had not yet returned from the village. Mariette found Emily sitting painting under the tamarind tree which was now thirty feet high and offered a wide circle of shade. Mariette burst into tears and sank down on to the ground in front of Emily. She couldn't stop herself from telling Emily the whole sorry story of the rape. Somehow, she wanted the hear the reaction to what had happened, of somebody other than Matt.

Emily cradled Mariette's head in her lap and when Mariette had finished, "I felt like your mother when I fed you as a baby and you are making me feel like a mother again. You must now put the matter behind you. What happened to you never changed you and Matt knows that. I have known for a long time that you two would one day be together and let me tell you that you have a good man to love you. He is very much like his father, and they are both very much like this tree, tall and strong and protective," as she said this, she ran her hand up and down the bark on the now substantial trunk of the tamarind tree. Mariette dried her tears and the two women talked until Matt came looking for Mariette.

Chapter 18

On the 28th of July 1914 war was declared and the world would not be the same for at last four years. The war did not greatly impinge on the lives of people in southern Africa, but it was a matter of fact that, even though there was no conscription in Rhodesia, that country sent more men to war in relation to its population than any other British Empire country.

Giles was inclined to volunteer to serve Britain but at a meeting with the then administrator, Chaplin, he was persuaded to play his part in the war effort by producing food and gold to pay for the war effort. Matt indicated to his grandparents that he was ready to fight but was instructed, in no uncertain terms, by Marcel, to stay at college for the few more months necessary to complete his degree. He agreed to do so to the relief of Mariette who was also within months of completing her honors degree.

Matt and Mariette travelled again together to Salisbury on the train. The three-day journey should have been a time of rejoicing at the degrees they had both been awarded and a time to plan their future together. However, the shadow of war hung over them. Matt was determined to volunteer for one of the army units being raised in Rhodesia. Mariette realized that she could not change Matts mind. She decided that she would somehow enlist as a nurse or ambulance driver.

It was good to be back at Leopard Ridge and Mary's Nest, but both Mariette and Matt were aware of a change in the everyday priorities of their parents. Both Giles and Abe had expanded their farming operations to produce more food. Abe and Rebecca's canning operation became more and more important, and they adjusted their product list to provide more canned foods needed for army rations. Giles's expanded maize producing operation was also important as part of the move to increase maize production to provide a surplus available for export to those countries where production was curtailed by the war.

Giles and Abe also joined together in another war effort. When soldiers and even some airmen started to return to Rhodesia with war injuries both physical and mental, they built a series of eight rondavels on the shore of Lake Matuswa which became available as a place for the injured to convalesce. Very soon there was a flow of young men who were able to heal their bodies and minds while they fished and played cards and fed on the good food sent down to the dam every day by either Emily or Rebecca.

As soon as Matt was back in Rhodesia, he went to army headquarters in Salisbury to find out where he could join a Rhodesian unit. He found that volounteers were being accepted for the 2nd Rhodesia Regiment. The 1st Rhodesia Regiment was formed a couple of months earlier in November 1914 and had served with distinction in German South West Africa. The 2nd regiment was partly made up of the overflow of recruits for the 1st Regiment and more recent recruits like Matt. When Matt enlisted, Mariette consoled herself with the fact that her Matt would likely serve in East Africa and would at least be on the same continent as herself. Mariette had accepted the fact that she could do more for the war effort helping her parents with the running of the farm and the cannery.

Basic training in the 2nd Rhodesia Regiment lasted for six weeks. The training took place in and around Salisbury and consisted mainly of route marching, marksmanship and parade drill for which Matt could never understand the need. At the end of the training Matt was commissioned as a second lieutenant. Giles was extremely proud of his son, but Emily feared that his officer status might make him more of a target for the enemy.

Matt was given a three-day pass to be with family prior to being sent with his regiment to East Africa. Matt spent most of his time with Mariette. They avoided talking about the present and the war and talked and planned for their future together, most likely as the next generation of farmers at Mazowe. Matt's regiment left Salisbury on the 15th of March 1915 and travelled by train to the port of Beira where they embarked on the S.S. Umzumbi. The six-day trip to Mombasa on the coast of the British colony of Kenya would have been quite pleasant if the CO had not insisted that his men have intensive PT and lessons on such things as map reading.

From Mombasa, 2 Rhodesia Regiment went by train to Makindu on the Mombasa Nairobi railway line from where they were trucked to a camp under the large and to Matt's mind, unmenacing, Mount Kilimanjaro. To him it looked like a huge round hill with a bit of snow on the top. Camp was set up only a few miles from the border of the German territory of Tanganyika. Germany did not have a lot of troops in Tanganyika but maintained enough to ensure that Britain committed men to contain the Germans, men who would not therefore be available to fight in Europe. Most of the German soldiers were native askaris but the officers were Germans.

2 Rhodesia Regiment set up camp in an area near a large wetland the locals called Amboseli. The place teamed with game and, until they made contact with the Germans, most danger came from wild animals including swarms of mosquitos that left the adjoining swamp and descended on the camp personnel every evening. Here Matt was fortunate, He had been given a tin with some foul smelling greasy brown substance by his mother to protect him against mosquitos. It came with an endorsement by his father. He used it much to the disgust of his tentmates who when they saw the efficacy of what his father had called Motsepe Muck, begged him to share it.

War with the Germans was waged on a very much hit and ran basis. When a plane was available in Nairobi it would fly over Matt and his men and signal if and when they spotted the enemy. 2 RR would either use artillery to shell the enemy or move in as quietly as possible and ambush them. One problem was that the Germans had longer range artillery. Losses on both sides were not heavy, in fact more men were removed from the battlefield due to diseases such as dysentery and malaria than due to death or wounds. The second in command of 2 RR was badly wounded in a skirmish near a place called Ting Tinga by the locals and Matt found himself promoted to Captain. Back in Mazowe Giles knew he was doing his bit for the war effort but felt he should be doing more like Matt.

Matt came back to Leopards Rock for Christmas 1915 for a month's sick leave. He had had a succession of bouts of dysentery and had lost about twenty pounds in weight. Mariette cried when she saw him. Two weeks of loving care from Mariette and good food from his mother and on occasion from Rebecca and Matt was halfway back to his normal self and was posted back to Kenya. Giles seeing his son so ravaged by disease felt guilty at being at home and well and was therefore relieved when he was summonsed to see Chaplin the Administrator in Salisbury. Chaplin explained that to help with the acute shortage of troops in Europe, there was a move to set up a Native Regiment to make use of the locals both Matebeles and Mashona who wanted to sign up to fight. The powers that be, decided that the white officers in the Native

Regiment would have to be fluent speakers of either Ndebele or Shona. He appealed to Giles as a fluent Shona speaker to join the regiment with an initial rank of Major. Giles was proud to serve his country of birth at the age of forty-seven and agreed. Emily was not pleased but knew that to argue with Giles would not help and so went about helping him to prepare for his departure.

The Rhodesia Native Regiment under Lt. Col. Tomlinson underwent extensive training in Salisbury before being sent to Zomba in Nyasaland and then on to New Langenburg in Tanganyika for further training. The regiment was then split in two. One half under Giles was sent to Songea a small town not far from Lake Nyasa that had recently been taken from the German forces. The Germans were expected to return with re-enforcements to retake the town, Giles directed his men to dig in with major defenses to be positioned on the northeast of town to face the expected direction of any German attack.

For several days all was quiet. Giles circulated from one trench to another and chatted in Shona to his men appealing to them to be vigilant all the time. He spent a lot of time with the men of the three machine gun emplacements. Giles was up early one morning and had just finished shaving when he heard a loud explosion. He ran with his Sten gun in one hand to his command trench and scanned the area round the northeast of the camp. He saw nothing until he saw a flash and another artillery shell landed amongst the trenches. He ordered the three machine guns to open up and directed his rifleman to fire on the now visible oncoming German askaris.

To Giles the engagement seemed to last for hours but in fact the sounds of battle had faded, and the dust and smoke had settled within ten minutes, During the action Giles had been aware of a pain in his foot and then a wetness in his boot but had been too busy to attend to himself. The Germans had been driven off and the RNR had gained its first modest battle colours. Giles examined his foot which now hurt like hell and saw a pool of blood was spreading along the floor of the trench. He shouted for the company medic, Lt. Ryan to come and help him.

Ryan stopped the bleeding but informed Giles that his ankle was in a mess and needed surgery. Ryan suggested that the cause of Giles's wound was shrapnel from a shell that had exploded further along the trench in which he was standing. He gave Giles a shot of morphine after Giles had checked that all his men were OK except the two wounded

Shona men and then got his number two, a Captain Darcy to search for a vehicle in Songea. An old Ford pickup was found, and Giles and the other two wounded men were placed in it which was then driven as fast as possible to New Langenburg where a British army doctor was forced to amputate Giles's one foot halfway between the knee and the ankle.

Life back on Leopards Ridge was tough on Emily. In the absence of Giles, she had assumed responsibility for all the operations, the juice plant and arable farming and the sheep flock. Thomas was a great help but lacked experience. Emily found that she had to put away her paints and it was only on rare occasions that she was able to spend time relaxing under the tamarind tree. Times were tough at Mary's Nest as well. Abe had to oversee the mine and the vegetable growing. He was ably assisted by Bill and the canning operation was managed by Rebecca who managed to put in long days of work in spite of her affliction. On many nights she was almost desperate to remove her calipers and massage her legs. On many occasions Abe massaged them for her. Rebecca never fully understood how Abe could ignore the abnormality of her thin legs but thanked God that he could.

Abe was suddenly forced to devote himself full time to the mine when Stanley suddenly dropped down dead one day from a heart attack. Aaron had to take over the vegetable growing enterprise. Stanley's funeral was held in Salisbury and all the members of the Gold and Elliott-Smith families who were not elsewhere attended the sad gathering. Abe was able to assure Stanleys wife that she would have a moderate but secure income from the ten per cent share in the mine that Stanley had been given two years before.

Ten weeks had passed, and Emily was at the station to fetch Giles. She wanted to cry when she saw him, thin and drawn and on crutches. On the way back to the farm in the Buick, Emily tried to cheer Giles up but failed. He didn't want to talk about what had happened. When they got to the farm Molly, who was on holiday, rushed up to hug her father but stopped when she saw the empty trouser leg end and the crutches. It was then that Emily saw that Giles was crying silently. Abe and Rebecca and Solly arrived to see Giles but left soon after having failed to communicate with him. Giles then poured himself a stiff whisky and went to the bedroom and shut the door.

Emily left Giles alone until it was time for the dinner she had prepared. She went to the bedroom and knocked. There was no reply. She went in. Giles was sitting on the edge of the bed staring into space,

"I am a bloody fool. I volunteered to go and get wounded and now I'm no bloody good to you or anybody else, Emily," he blurted out. Emily stood in front of him and pulled his face into her bosom," There, there, my darling. It will take time to put you right, but it will happen. Please believe that." she said.

When they went through to eat, the food was cold, bit it didn't matter. Emily knew that she and Giles had a long and rocky road ahead. Giles did not tell Emily of the DSO he had been awarded following the action at Songea.

It was late in 1916 that Matt found himself back near Mount Kilimanjaro. He was now in charge of a company of men about half of whom were recent recruits. Matt had a lieutenant and two sergeants with experience to whom he related well as they all came from farming stock in Rhodesia. The Germans were well entrenched in Arusha, a town to the southwest of where Matt and his men were based. Instructions came through ordering Matt's company to advance on Arusha and capture the town. Continued occupation of Arusha by the Germans was wasting a lot of manpower and resources.

Matt commandeered two horses from a German coffee farmer halfway between Tinga Tinga and Arusha and rode with one of his sergeants to within half a mile of Arusha. He and his sergeant then spent two days circling the town but never revealing themselves and making notes on the German defenses and the number of men committed to defending the town. They discovered that the Germans had placed most of their defenses on the northeast side of the town facing the direction from which they imagined the enemy would attack.

Back at Tinga Tinga, Matt gathered his men around him and explained his plan of to attack for Arusha. The company would march towards Arusha keeping in thick bush, circle round to the southwest and stop overnight within a mile of the town. There was to be silence and no lights, not even cigarettes overnight. And at five in the morning the company was to move as quietly as possible to within fifty yards of hopefully, a garrison of half-awake soldiers. Meanwhile the companies three machine guns were to be under cover on the northeast of town to be a reception committee for any Germans who were fleeing the town.

It was cold the next morning as Matt and his men moved, in the first light of dawn, towards the town. When Matt reached within thirty yards of the nearest German tents he stopped and listened. There was nothing to be heard except the odd cock crowing and a dog barking in the distance. Matt blew his whistle and ran toward the nearest tents firing his revolver, followed by his men firing their rifles. The enemy were caught completely by surprise. Askaris and German officers tumbled out of tents still trying to dress. The askaris ran. The German officers tried to fire back at Matt and his men but soon gave up and ran after the askaris. When the German forces reached the northeast side of town, they were subjected to deadly machine gun fire.

The German forces surrendered. Matt and his men had suffered no more serious injuries than two twisted ankles where two of his men had tripped over tent guy ropes. The Germans had had one officer killed and five askaris. There were also seven wounded men who Matt disarmed and left in the care of the nuns at a nearby mission. The rest of the Germans, four officers and seventy-two askaris were told that they were prisoners of war and were marched back to Tinga Tinga. Matt made it back to Tinga Tinga and collapsed with another bout of dysentery. Matt remembered little of the next few days until he found himself in a military hospital in Mombasa. He was linked to a saline drip and was being medicated and force fed.

As he slowly recovered Matt started to take more notice of his surroundings. The hospital was situated on the ocean front with an adjacent white beach and palm trees that rustled at night when a breeze blew. The other men around him had various injuries and sicknesses, worse than his. In a couple of weeks Matt was strong enough to join the other patients on the beach where they indulged in their favourite past time of crab racing. This involved drawing a circle in the sand with a stick and then placing up to five hermit crabs at the centre of the circle and releasing them simultaneously and betting on which crab would get to the circle first. Both cash and cigarettes were bet on the hermit crabs. Matt was not a gambler and preferred to watch the other patients playing. He often lay on his bed looking out on the sea and thought of Mariette and how lucky he was to have survived and to soon be on his way home with a permanent military discharge. The day before he was due to start the long journey home, he had a visitor. It was the Officer Commanding

British Forces in East Africa. This elderly bewhiskered grey-haired gentleman presented Matt with a DSO medal.

Homecoming for Matt was a different affair for him compared to Giles. Matt's body was weakened, and he was painfully thin, but he knew that he would get back to normal under the care of both Emily and Mariette. He was however sad to see how his father had retreated into himself, how he drank more and seemed to have no zest for life. He did get himself about on his crutches but seemed to be leaving decision making with regards to the farm to Emily. Matt lay at night and thought about his father. He came to the conclusion that if his father could be made more mobile then half his problem would have been solved.

Matt thought and sketched and the more he thought and sketched and drew on the knowledge he had gained at college the nearer he got to what he believed could be a solution for his father. He did not believe that Giles would agree to walking on a peg leg. Matt eventually decided on a plan of action for his father. Over a period of several weeks, he assembled a collection of items which included a block of vulcanite, some stainless-steel sheet an eighth of an inch thick and some plaster of Paris. After dinner one evening he collared Giles before he could escape to his bedroom and told him what he proposed to do, Giles dismissed Matt's idea without any consideration. It was then that Molly, who had been listening to Matt talking to her father shouted at her father,

" Just listen father, He's trying to help you like everybody is, but you won't accept help. Stop feeling sorry for yourself!"

Giles looked stunned, turned to Matt and said, "thank you son, please give it a go."

The next day Matt rubbed Giles' s leg stump with vaseline and then placed it hanging downwards into a large tin of plaster of Paris. When the plaster was dry, he cut the tin from around the plaster to reveal a cast of the leg stump. He then coated the inside of the cast with vaseline and filled it with another lot of plaster of Paris reinforced with gauze. When this was set, he broke the outer layer of plaster to reveal a model of Giles's stump. Matt took the stump to a saddler in Salisbury and commissioned him to make a strong leather cup with a wooden base into which the stump model could be inserted and which could be anchored to a leather collar that could be buckled above Giles's knee. Back in the workshop Matt carved a foot out of the vulcanite, the same length as Giles's remaining foot He then made a stainless-steel bracket that had a rod one end and swivel mechanism the other, that would attach the foot to the cup.

When the day came to test his new foot, Giles was apprehensive as was Matt. The leather cup fitted Giles's stump well but when he stood on it was painful. A piece of cotton wool in the cup reduced the pain. Matt had set up two parallel gum pole bars under the shade of the tamarind tree. He helped his father as far as the bars. Giles clung to the bars and walked, albeit very slowly along between the bars. There was joy in the hearts of Emily, Matt and Molly as they watched Giles making his way along on his artificial foot. He practiced every day until he was able to walk with nothing more than a walking stick to aid him. Able to walk again Giles returned to his normal self to the delight of his family and friends. With medals put away in drawers the family was able to resume a life of normality on Leopard Ridge.

Chapter 19

Solly had finished school in the last year of the war. He wanted to go and fight the Germans. It took the combined persuasive powers of both Rebecca and Abe to convince him otherwise. Abe explained that the war was nearly over. He explained to his son that he had intended to join up like Giles had done but had been told that he would not be allowed to as the canning company was classified an essential service as it made army ration products. He impressed on Solly the fact that he had already lost one dear person, Mariette's mother, and didn't want to lose another. Solly agreed to stay in Salisbury and take up an apprenticeship with a jeweler in Salisbury who had both a showroom in Union Avenue but also a workshop in the Kopje area.

Molly had also had just finished school and was sad at moving away from Sister Aurelia at the Convent. She wanted to study fine art and the obvious choice was South Africa College whose name was shortly to be changed to the University of Cape Town. Like her older brother Matt and Mariette, she was welcome to stay with her grandparents at La Mercy. Marcel and Molly were by now feeling their age but saw no problem in having their granddaughter stay in the guest cottage. Before she left for Cape Town Matt had a heart-to-heart talk with her about not moving about Cape Town on her own. He did not disclose what had happened to Mariette in the past.

As Giles got better at using his artificial foot, he was inspired to try and drive again. A bit of pain and a lot of practice later and he was able to drive as far as Salisbury and was happy to take Emily shopping on most Saturdays. The more he drove the more he wanted a more modern car. One Saturday morning while Emily was shopping and then due to meet him for tea at Meikles Hotel on Cecil Square, he was passing a motor dealer in Union Avenue and saw a superb new car. It was a Vauxhall D type Kington. It was a blue grey colour with black mudguards and running board. He mentioned the car to Emily in Meikles. Emily was delighted to see that the old Giles was slowly revealing himself and told him to buy it.

As soon as he took possession of the Vauxhall Giles gave the Buick to Matt who was delighted. This left the Ford Model A. On the spur of the moment, he gave it to Solly. Abe came to thank him for giving the car to Solly and to ask him why he had done it. Giles laughed and said," that young man is so like you and somewhere he is going to need transport to be able to wheel and deal like you!"

The Puff Adder Mine continued to produce a worthwhile amount of gold. The reef had dipped down slightly but then ran about six to eight feet below the surface for a considerable distance. Though more overburden had to be removed, the mine remained as a paying proposition in its open cast form. Abe was able to find another old miner, Maxwell Gould, a man very much in the mould of Stanley, who had come upon on hard times and was happy to take over the running of the mine. Abe had to peg and register a series of new claims running in the direction of the reef. As the mine workings became deeper and more visible, Abe and Giles decided that, even though it was to cost, they would cover in the old workings and let nature do its work in restoring the land. This move was largely prompted by pressure from Emily.

Moving overburden was made easier by the purchase of a petrol driven Ford tractor soon after the purchase of the Vauxhall car. Giles needed a faster way to plough the not inconsiderable acreage of land planted to arable crops. When the new tractor wasn't ploughing it had a blade attached to its frontend and it bull dozed overburden. Thomas Tregaskis delighted in driving the tractor.

A further development on both Leopard Ridge and Mary's Nest farms was the building of cottages, one for Thomas and one for Aaron who had for some time been sharing a rondavel on the bank of the dam. Aaron split his time between Abe's vegetable area and Giles's arable lands. Emily ran the orange squash enterprise with help from Giles who got more mobile as time passed. Matt forgot about working in the field of mechanical engineering and became a partner in Leopard Ridge. He did however make use of his mechanical knowledge looking after and maintaining the growing number of mechanical implements on both Leopard Ridge and at the mine.

Mariette grew emotionally stronger with time and was happy to help both Rebecca and her father in whatever they needed help. She and Matt grew closer together and enjoyed each other's company especially at the weekends when they would go off in the Buick and spend time at various beauty spots around Salisbury like the Hunyani river and their favourite, which was a place on a river north of Salisbury on the road to Enterprise, called by the locals, Mermaids Pool. Here the river went over a large downward sloping rock in a shallow waterfall. Matt and Mariette discovered that an inflated car tyre inner tube gave an exciting ride down the waterfall.

One Saturday afternoon Matt and Mariette had been down the water slide at least ten times and stopped to lie on a rug and dry themselves in the sun. The two were lying close to each other when Mariette suddenly turned over to face Matt. She put her arms round Matt and whispered," Matt. Take me now. I'm ready." A little later, Matt said gently to Mariette, "I guess we can get married now."

They talked about getting married on the way home and when they got home and so did all the families on Leopard Ridge and Mary's Nest for days to come. There was a party that night and champagne was produced. Standing on the stoep Giles said to Abe," I couldn't be happier that Matt and Mariette are to get married. It seems to be a fine way to cement our long and successful friendship. You do know of course that you, as father of the bride, you must pay for the wedding!"

Abe laughed and said," whoa, you are forgetting lobola. Have you any idea how many cows you will have to pay on Matt's behalf for a bride with a degree.

Emily and Rebecca both got totally caught up in the arrangements for the joyous occasion and the following day searched the trunks that had come with Emily from Cape Town those many years before. They found a bolt of white silk which was a real find as after the war, luxuries like fine materials, were in very short supply. A date for the wedding was set for Saturday the 16nth of August 1919. Solly became an important figure in the forthcoming wedding. Not only was he asked to be the best man but arranged for the making of a beautiful ring for his sister from his employer in return for an ingot of gold from Puff Adder Mine. The ring was made to a design by Molly.

The day of the wedding eventually came, non-too soon for Matt and Mariette. The service was at the little Anglican church in Mazowe and in recognition of the importance of the married couple's parents, was conducted by the Bishop of Mashonaland. The reception was held at Leopard Ridge in a large marquee that had been rented at a bargain rate by none other than the wheeler and dealer of the younger generation, Solly. The marquee was erected right next to the tamarind tree. Abe walked proudly down the aisle with Mariette on his arm. She looked stunning in her white silk dress with a headdress of small white flowers.

As he walked, he thought of how proud Mary would have been of her daughter. Matt waited for Mariette to stand next to him and knew that what was about to happen had been ordained long ago, perhaps from the time, he had been told, when he and Mariette had lain suckling on either side of Emily immediately after they were born.

The reception went well and there were many important people there including the Administrator. There was a band, the BSA Police band, organized by Solly. Speeches were made, toasts given, and the champagne flowed. The newly married couple left the reception shortly after midnight to spend one night in one of the rondavels down by the dam.

The honeymoon was planned to really start the following day when they caught the train to Durban in Natal to spend ten days at a hotel on the beach on the South Coast. As the last guest left, Giles and Emily stood on the steps of the house, holding each other tight, shared memories of a night now long ago when they committed themselves to each other. Giles and Abe took the newly weds to the Salisbury station. The two friends and now relatives by marriage watched as the train sped away carrying their precious son and daughter.

It took two days and three nights for the train to reach Durban, the city on the east coast of South Africa. The time on the train in a comfortable compartment passed quickly as Matt and Mariette really got to know each other. Meals in the dining car were good and there was a never-ending panorama passing the train's window. In Durban the newlyweds caught a taxi to take them down the South Coast Road to a small village called Ramsgate situated on both sides of a river and the lagoon where the river entered the sea. For Matt and Mariette, the days that passed were halcyon days that blended into each other until it was time to return to reality. They swam and sunbathed and walked the beaches and rocks. The return journey seemed almost a let down when the time came to go home.

Giles was in his office on the day after Matt had returned from his honeymoon. He was thinking about where to build a cottage for Matt and Mariette as life in a rondavel at the dam was not a permanent solution to their accommodation problem. There was a knock on the door and Solly came. Giles was surprised to see him as he thought that Solly was working in Salisbury.

"Please can I talk to you, Uncle, Giles", said Solly.

"Of course," replied Giles.

"I have packed it in at the jewelers. It is not the life for me. I want to do something more rewarding and exciting. I am going to go on my own. I have saved some money to help me start." said Solly.

"And where do I come into your plans," asked Giles.

"Well, the rondavels at the dam are not being used these days except for the one being used by Matt and Mariette. I would like to rent them from you. I want to offer people from Salisbury the chance of staying for a day or two or more in lovely surroundings where they can fish and walk and pay me for it" said Solly tentatively.

"No, "said Giles. "I don't want peoples' cars driving past the house on their way to and from the dam."

"I had thought of that and if you will let me rent the tractor and bulldozer blade for a few days I will put in a road from the dam away from your house to join up with the Mazowe Road." said Solly.

"Solly, I will have to think about it, and I will let you know.

Later that day, Giles drove over to Mary's Nest and was able to have a chat with Abe.

"Abe," said Giles laughing, "That young man is so like you when I first met you, that I am inclined to go along with his plan as long as it has no detrimental affect on me or the farm."

"I don't know what to say," said Abe. "I must admire his audacity."

Solly's new business began. He put in the detour road and upgraded the furnishings in the rondavels except for the one temporarily occupied by Matt and Mariette. He put an advertisement in the Mashonaland Herald and to everybody's surprise, including Solly himself, the business was an almost immediate success. Spurred on by this success, Solly wasted no time in launching his second business, his auction business. He managed to persuade his father and Giles to rent him the warehouse in Kopje Road where once a month, to start with, he held an auction. He advertised again in the Herald and sold, for a commission, anything that people brought to him. He acted as auctioneer himself and found that people liked his lighthearted banter and over the next three months paid rent to Abe and Giles but also made a good profit. Solly was on his way and Abe admitted one night to Rebecca that Solly was a chip off the old block, and he was proud of him.

Molly was happy in Cape town. She enjoyed her studies and loved everything about the Cape. She discovered the natural garden started by her mother and now curated by the Cape Town Museum. She was able to locate and identify many plants she had seen in Emily's paintings. When she could, she got Marcel to drive her to the wilder parts of the Cape Peninsular, where she walked and painted while Marcel sat in a folding chair and read a book. She endevoured to get Molly to join her and her grandfather but Molly was slowing down. She no longer took much interest in Cape Town society and left the running of the house very much to Mrs. Goosen.

One late afternoon Molly arrived back at La Mercy after a stimulating day in art classes. She went into the drawing room to find her grandmother sitting in a wingback chair facing a window. She wasn't moving. Molly had passed away quietly and peacefully. Marcel was devastated,

"God only knows we had moments of conflict, but I never stopped loving her. What am I going to do now," he asked his granddaughter who was holding him tightly?

"We are going to bury Grandmother and then sort out a new life for you, Grandfather," said Molly. "I am going to move back into the main house so I can keep an eye on you."

Giles, Emily and Matt arrived in Cape Town by train two days before the funeral which was conducted by the Bishop of Cape Town and attended by just about everybody of any importance in the Cape.

"Mother would have loved her funeral," whispered Emily to Giles as they stood by the graveside.

Molly de Speville was buried next to Reggie.

On the day after the funeral Marcel called Emily and Giles to join him in his home office.

"The sad loss of your mother has reminded me of my own mortality, and I know I am not going to be here for much longer."

Before Emily could protest, he continued," I must think about what will happen to La Mercy when I am gone. It should go to you Emily and you Giles and then eventually to young Molly."

"Father," said Emily, "Giles and I have discussed already some time ago the possibility of you leaving La Mercy to us. Sorry, father, but we had to face the day when you were to pass. Please understand, Father. I love La Mercy. It is where I grew up, but it is part of another life. For Giles and me our life is now on Leopard Ridge in the new country that we love. We wouldn't want to come back to Cape Town. Don't be hurt but we want to suggest that when the time comes and, God help it is not soon, we feel that you should leave la Mercy to the nation, the people of South Africa."

Marcel stood still and silent for some time, deep in thought and then said," I do understand. I will do, happily, what you suggest but with one proviso and that is, if young Molly doesn't want La Mercy then it can go to the nation."

Giles and Emily left Cape Town sadly but were happy to see that Molly had more or less taken over her grandfather. Before she went to the university each day, she gave an old but still capable Mrs. Goosen orders for the day.

When they got back to the farm, they got the surprising news that Siobhan and William were leaving to go to England. Bill's parents had both passed away in a boating accident on the river Exe and their farm had been left to Bill, their oldest son. Their departure had to be expedited as there were animals on the farm to be looked after and crops to be reaped. Neighbours would care for the farm for a few weeks but could not do it for longer. Everybody on Leopard Ridge and Mary's Nest were sad to see Bill and Siobhan go and threw them a party on the night before their departure. It was held on a fine warm night under the tamarind tree.

Chapter 20

1920 was to be a year of great changes on the two adjacent farms. Leopard Ridge and Mary's Nest farms were incorporated into a single proprietary limited company with shares evenly distributed between the Elliott-Smith and Gold families. Giles was to be the managing director. The canning plant on Mary's nest and the orange squash plant on Leopard's Nest were transferred to Mazowe village. A plot was purchased, and a large warehouse was built to house the two plants. A company was set up run the plants, called Mazowe Foods Pty. Ltd, shares of which were evenly distributed between the two families. Joint managing directors were Abe and Rebecca.

The two families debated for some time over the mine and eventually decided to set up yet another company with all the shares to be held by Matt and Mariette and with Matt as managing director. Chief Madire was made a minor shareholder of Puff Adder Mine Ltd. and made labour manager of Mazowe Foods on a part time basis.

Emily had been trying to get Giles to take part in politics for some time without success, but when Giles was approached directly by Sir Henry Tredgold, the then administrator, to take the place of a retiring member of the Administrative Council he agreed to consider the offer. Since the time of the Pioneer Column, Rhodesia had been governed by an administrative council. It initially consisted of four 'settler' representatives and five BSA Company nominees. The council was headed by the Administrator who had power of veto on any matter. With pressure from the pioneer public, the number of representatives of the people had risen to thirteen. Under pressure from family and the administrator, Giles agreed to stand for election to the council. He stood as a member of the Responsible Government Association later to become the Rhodesia Party. Giles was elected unopposed.

Giles joined the council at an interesting time. The RGA were pressing for Rhodesia to be accorded the same self-determination as Australia, Canada and New Zealand and the end of rule by the BSA Company. Giles had every respect for the B SA company and its officials, but agreed with the sentiment in the street that it was time for the people who had made Rhodesia their home to have sole control of their destinies. The BSA company had lost a lot of its interest in

Rhodesia when ownership of land in Rhodesia was handed over to the UK government and the company's main source of revenue, land sales, was taken away.

The BSA Company was backing a move to have Rhodesia incorporated into South Africa as a fifth province. Others including Winston Churchill, then Secretary for the Colonies, pushed for self-government. A referendum was held in 1922 and nearly sixty percent of the voters opted for self-government. The Legislative Council was replaced by an enlarged Legislative Assembly of thirty members and Southern Rhodesia came into being. Giles ran for election on the Rhodesia Party ticket and won the seat for Salisbury District by a large margin. With the re-organized farms and food factory he had more time to devote to politics and soon became a well known and respected member of the assembly.

*****

Molly completed her degree in Cape Town. She was offered a lectureship in the faculty of fine art at the University of Cape Town. She accepted the offer largely as it would allow enough time to carry on looking after her grandfather. During her years at university, she had led a very restricted social life and never met anybody who she felt prompted any more than a very limited interest on her part. One day in the first week of her job as a lecturer Molly was rushing from her modest office in the art department. She was a few minutes late for a lecture she was due to give on the history of art. She ran round the corner of the art department building straight into a man walking in the opposite direction. The substantial pile of books she was carrying went flying into the air to be joined by a more modest pile of books carried by the young man.

"Oh dammit. I am already late. Why don't you look where you are going "she threw at the young man.

The tall young blonde haired young man smiled and said calmly," I am so sorry. I will sign up for a course in looking round corners. In the meantime, please let me help you with your books.!"

With that he picked up her books, dusted them with the sleave of his jacket and handed them to her. When he had finished and recovered his own books he turned to Molly and said," I am Johan, an idiot who can't see round corners but would like to buy you tea at the union. How about it?"

Molly noticed that he spoke good English but with a distinct Afrikaans accent. "I am not sure it is good thing for a lecturer like myself to fraternize with a student."

"Thoroughly agree with you. Would it be acceptable though if I was a professor?"

Molly looked at the open-faced young man who had a wicked grin on his face and said," Are you really a prof?"

"Yes, indeed and, since I am senior to you, I expect you will not argue with my plan to have lunch with you at the union today!"

Molly gave a coquettish little smile and said," half twelve then."

As Molly rushed to deliver her lecture, she didn't like herself for agreeing to meet Johan again. She consoled herself with the thought that it was only lunch, and he did look and sound very nice. Johan on his part was thinking of the lovely girl he had crash into him and whose name he still didn't know. He wandered what he could do if she didn't turn up for the lunch date. He needn't have worried. Molly felt being drawn like a magnet to the union after delivering her third lecture.

Molly couldn't miss Johan in the crowd at the union. He stood a head taller than the mingling mass of students and more junior university staff. His thick crop of blonde hair was a beacon as well. Johan guided Molly to a table after they had collected their tea and cream scones.

"I am Johan van der Riet. I'm a sort of junior prof only because the other teaching staff in the department of chemistry think I am cleverer than I know I am. I come from Elgin where my parents have an apple farm." he said.

"I am Molly Elliott -Smith and I am from Rhodesia where my folks have a farm and a mine and a food factory. Rhodesia by the way is that wonderful country that lies to the north of the Transvaal."

Johan smiled. "I know where it is. I travel there regularly. I am assisting the department of mines in setting up a laboratory for testing mineral sample in Salisbury. It is a lovely country. No wonder you are so lovely." With this he blushed bright red.

"Wow. Carry on. You say the nicest things.! "Uttered Molly in some embarrassment.

Luckily neither Molly or Johan had to give any lectures that afternoon and so the two of them were able to dawdle and tell each other about themselves. It was Molly who took the plunge and invited Johan to Sunday lunch at La Mercy. She had a desire to have somebody in her family vet this young man as she had had very limited social contact with young men up until this time.

Molly could hardly contain herself until Sunday. Each lecture she gave, and each day dragged. Shortly after twelve on the Sunday a battered old Ford Model A drove up the drive at La Mercy leaving a trail of smoke all the way from the gate to the house. Molly heard the old car from a long way away and rushed to be on the house steps when the Johan's car came to a halt. Johan got out of the car and handed Molly a magnificent bouquet of bearded proteas." Oh beautiful, Protea Nerifolias, one of my favourites. Thank you." she said.

"Glad you like whateverthefolias are. Hello."

Molly guided Johan up the steps into the house and along to the drawing room where Marcel de Speville was sitting. He made to stand up, but Johan said," please don't get up, Sir. I am Johan van der Riet."

After introductions were complete the three of them sat and talked. From Johan's point of view, it was like an inquisition. Marcel was determined to find out everything he could about this apparently nice young man. He had to remind himself that he was behaving a bit like his dear wife would have done twenty or more years before.

Lunch was up to Mrs. Goosen's normal high standard. After lunch Marcel went to his office, in fact to have a nap on the divan in the corner. Molly showed Johan around La Mercy. She showed him the garden now run by the museum and where her mother used to spend so many happy hours She showed him the stables, now empty where her mother's Bucephalus used to be housed. As the sun was setting. Johan drove away from La Mercy sure that he was in love and Molly felt the same about the man in the departing car.

"Well grandpa, what do you think of him," said Molly sitting in Marcel's office.

"Sorry I gave him the once over. I find that I can't find fault with the young man. Please though move slowly if you are going to have a relationship with him." Said Marcel.

"I knew you would like him. He wants me to meet his parents, but I am scared. He has told me that his parents are anti-British because of family they lost in the Boer War. What can I do to make them like me, Grandpa?" asked Molly.

"Be yourself. If they bring up the subject of the Boer War, then make it clear that you are not British but Rhodesian," answered Marcel.

Molly stewed for days prior to the visit to Elgin. She decided to dress modestly and on the spur of the moment selected a watercolour painting she had done of a little white fisherman's cottage at Kommetjie, a small coastal village on the Cape Peninsula and found a frame for it. She wrapped the painting in brown paper tied it with string.

All the way to Elgin Molly clutched the wrapped painting on her lap as if it might be a magic ticket to approval by Johan's parents. The old Ford battled up the Heidelberg Mountain leaving a thicker trail of smoke than usual. Eventually the top of the mountain was reached, and the car cruised easily down to Elgin. Johan's parents house was a picture-perfect Cape Dutch cottage with ornate white gables and wide stoep along the length of the building. Surrounded by vines on lattices Molly wanted to paint the place immediately but constrained her desire.

Johan van der Riet senior was more or less a mature copy of his son. Mrs. Elise van der Riet was much shorter than her husband and dressed in a very modest long skirt and white blouse. Her greying hair was tied in a severe tight bun. Johan introduced Molly to his parents and the four of them moved into the house to a sitting room that was pleasantly cool. Elise poured coffee and a rather stilted conversation flowed slowly. Johan explained to his parents that Molly did not speak Afrikaans. Molly went on to explain that in Rhodesia the schools did not teach Afrikaans. She also went on to explain that she was not British.

At this stage in the slow-moving social interchange, Johan reminded Molly of the painting still on her lap. Molly passed the painting to Elise who carefully opened the parcel, carefully winding up the string and folding the brown paper.

She held the painting up so as her husband could see it. There was a short silence and then an excited outflow of Afrikaans. When the older couple had finished admiring the painting, Johan explained to Molly that the excitement was that the cottage in the painting was where his parents had spent their honeymoon nearly thirty years ago. From that moment on, even though language was a problem now and again, Molly was accepted by the van der Riets.

After a sumptuous lunch of roast lamb and melk tert, Molly was given a guided tour of the apple farm, all thirty acres of it. It was, to Molly so neat and organized that it was the opposite of Leopard Ridge in its vastness and wildness. Brought up on a farm Molly was able to ask all the right questions and make all the right comments and the van der Riets loved her for it. As Johan and Molly drove away from his parent's house, Johan told her that her parents had whispered to him that she was the best 'Rooinek' they had ever met.

*****

Solly's little business empire was growing. Like his father before him he liked to buy and sell anything that could yield a profit. He became known in Salisbury as the man to go to to find anything. He realized that a lot of his success in business was his persona, the character that he projected in company. He dressed well and always presented himself as a successful businessman. The old Model A Ford had long gone to be replaced with a later model T Ford. However, soon after buying the Model T, he received a telegram from a business contact in Beira, a man with whom he did business in prawns and Portuguese wines. It informed him that there was a 1920 Stutz Bearcat car going to be auctioned in Beira the following week. It belonged to a shipping company which had gone bankrupt and was probably the only one in Africa. Solly could hardly contain himself. A car like that would certainly complete his image as a successful businessman. Putting all other business aside he caught the train to Beira to arrive the day before the auction.

The car's body was bright red and the mudguards and running boards were black. It was a two-seater with a fold down top. The tyres had white walls. The car had less than a hundred miles on the clock. Before the auction Solly made himself familiar with the Portuguese/sterling exchange rate. At the auction there were a lot of bidders in the early stages. Solly did not bid until the bids reached the equivalent of six hundred pounds sterling. Solly then bid aggressively until at the equivalent of nine hundred pounds sterling the last opposition bidder dropped out. Solly found himself to be the owner of the only Stutz Bearcat in Africa.

Starting with a full tank of petrol Solly left Beira and in what was probably a record for the trip, was back in Salisbury in just less than nine hours. It was with immense pride that he drove into the town and then along the avenues to his modest rented flat in Montague Avenue. The following day he drove to Mary's Nest and then on to Leopard Ridge to show off his new car. Everybody was suitably impressed. While he was at Leopard Ridge, Solly went to see Giles about a problem regarding the fishing in the dam. Solly had had several complaints about the size of the fish in the dam. It appeared that the dam was well stocked, but the fish were all small. Giles was intrigued and promised to investigate the matter.

The good people of Salisbury were very much split on what they thought of Solly Gold. He was only of average height but with his dark hair and slightly sallow skin was regarded by the majority of the young unattached ladies of Salisbury as the town's most eligible bachelor, a title much enhanced with the purchase of the Bearcat. On the other hand, there was a large group of unattached young men who could not compete with Solly in the looks or success departments and therefore disliked him sight unseen. There was also a group of fathers of unattached young ladies who unfairly judged Solly to be a lothario and a danger to their daughters.

With regard to Solly's romantic life, it was in fact nonexistent. He had been so busy in building up his businesses that he had had no time for any romantic liaisons. That was until Solly decided that to supplement his image recently enhanced by his Stutz, he needed to buy a house at a good address. He spent a Sunday morning scanning the adverts for houses for sale in the Mashonaland Herald. He marked a few as potentially worth looking at. The following morning, he took himself to a well-known estate agents office and asked to speak to the agent dealing with a house in Salisbury's Second Street Extension. He was directed to a desk seated at which was a tall young woman with long blonde hair that cascaded down over her shoulders so different to the short hairstyles fashionable at that time.

Solly sat down and when the young woman introduced herself as Jennifer Caldicott and asked how she could help him. Solly forgot for a few seconds what his name was and why he was there. Once he had recovered his composure, he said he was interested in buying a house in a good part of Salisbury. Miss Caldicott, who was obviously not one of the young women who had heard of Solly and regarded him as highly eligible, asked him about his financial situation. Solly was not used to being questioned about business matters but answered her questions honestly. The young woman seemed surprised at some of the figures he gave her. Eventually Miss Caldicott agreed to show Solly two houses in the Second Street Extension area. Solly tried to guide her to the Stutz parked outside the real estate office, but he was firmly steered to a not so impressive Opel of fairly recent vintage. She explained that it was company policy to use company cars to transport clients, a policy that apparently had its origin that very moment.

Jennifer Caldicott knew that she was in the presence of an unusual and successful young man, but was determined not to be impressed with anything to do with him. The first house was large and impressive and in a large garden but was according to Solly not visible enough from the road. Miss Caldicott neither understood nor liked the reason for dismissing the property, but took him to see another just down the road. It was impressive with a good road frontage. It was built in quarried blue grey stone with a Broseley tiled roof. It had four bedrooms and two reception rooms. It was too big for one person, but Solly liked it. He looked directly at Jennifer and said, "I'll buy it if you will go out to dinner with me."

Jennifer looked Solly straight in the eye and said "No I won't t go out with you. I don't know you."

"How can you get to know me if you won't go out with me. I'll take the house anyway. I like it." said a shaken Solly.

Back at her desk Solly and Jennifer filled in all the forms related to the sale of the property. When they had finished Solly took his leave and shook her hand. The hand she proffered felt like a limp dead fish. Solly was not used to being rejected so directly, so he went directly to a florist and ordered a large and expensive bouquet to be delivered to the real estate office. The next morning the bouquet was lying on the step of his office at his auctioneering business in a sorry condition. Solly was not going to give up at this stage and arranged for three bouquets to be delivered to Miss Caldicott's office. The next morning the three bouquets were on the step of his office, and they had had all the blooms deadheaded.

As last resort Solly had a large cloth sign made saying,' Dinner please.' He arranged for it to be hung up outside the real estate office during the night. The following day there was no sign on the step outside his office so, full of hope, he drove to the real estate office only to see his sign still there but painted on it in large red letters 'No!'. Solly was devastated and just sat in the car outside Jennifer's firms' office. He was staring in front of him when he heard a voice to his side say. "Mr. Gold, why do you want to take me to dinner."

"I think it's because you are different to anybody I have ever known. You are the first woman I have met who isn't impressed with the outer signs of wealth and success. I really would like to know you and you are also not bad looking for an estate agent."

"Mr. Gold, I give up. Pick me up here at seven tonight. I must work a bit late tonight."

That evening Solly picked up Jennifer in his old Ford Model T, an action that was to initiate a long and lasting relationship.

Giles had not forgotten Solly's complaint about the size of the fish in the dam. He organized a meeting in the Salisbury Club with two keen fishermen, one the chairman of the Salisbury and District Fishing Club and the other the owner of a sports goods and fishing tackle business. To the two men with whom he met, the answer to the undersized fish was very simple. The dam was overstocked because of the absence of any predator species to control the prolific breeding of the tilapia in the dam. They said that the answer lay in netting and removing part of the fish population and or putting some predatory fish like tiger fish in the dam. Giles accepted their offer of some young tiger fish if and when they could be sourced from somewhere such as the Zambezi River.

Giles did further research and then acted. He ordered a fine drag net from a manufacturer in Johannesburg. He then went to see Chief Madire to whom he explained his plan. Giles's plan was for some of the women in the chief's village to make mats of reeds growing on the edge of the dam tying the reeds together with thin strips of bark from the 'mapoti' bush. The reed mats would be laid on the bank of the dam and on them would be placed small fish netted in the dam. Given a couple of weeks of sun, the little fish would dry and become a good source of protein for the people of the village. The locals called the small dry fish 'kapenta' which were produced in quantity round Lake Nyasa and imported into Southern Rhodesia.

The kapenta project was a great success and for about a week in late October every year from then on, Chief Madire's village had a good source of food. The biggest problem was encouraging the people doing the netting to return all fish over about three inches to the dam. The fish remaining in the dam grew bigger and Solly's clients were happier.

Chapter 21

It was on a warm November evening in 1924 that Mariette told Matt that she was expecting. They were sitting in the shade of the tamarind tree, Matt drinking a cold beer and Mariette a glass of chilled orange juice. Matt jumped up in excitement and hugged Mariette but not too tightly as he feared for their baby. Matt and Mariette had longed to have a child for a long time but had thought that it might not happen. When it was time for supper they walked up to the house, Mariette to take a stew off the stove and place it on the dining table and Matt to phone his parents to give them the news of a new member of the family to come. Giles and Emily were delighted. Matt made another call to Abe and Rebecca to give them the news which was also received with delight.

*****

The news of Matt and Mariette's pregnancy reached Cape Town within twenty-four hours. Marcel broke down in front of Molly when he heard that he was about to be a great grandfather. Molly heard the news with mixed emotions. She was delighted for Matt and Mariette, but it brought into focus her relationship with Johan. For over a year she and Johan had been in a steady relationship, an unusual one in that they were, character wise, two opposites. Johan was a scientist and a keen rugby player whereas Molly was an artist and had no desire to participate in any sport. Molly often reflected that perhaps their relationship was one of opposites that attracted each other. She did acknowledge a deep love between her and Johan, reflected in her attendance at every rugby match in which he played. She even found herself shouting on the sidelines when he was selected as a wing for Western Province in a game against Transvaal. It was in this match that he scored his first Currie Cup try and Molly could not help hugging both Mr. and Mrs. van der Riet who were standing next to her on the sideline, an action that was well received by Johan's parents.

Johan learned that Molly needed to commune with nature and had to escape frequently from Cape Town to the peace and tranquility of peopleless fynbos. He got used to taking a rug and a good book with him and would find a shady spot close to where Molly sketched or painted or even wandered amongst proteas and ericas and restios. He learnt how to read and carry on a desultory conversation at the same time. Molly and Johan did talk of marriage but, enjoying life as it was, avoided making the final commitment, even under pressure from Johan's parents who had decided that Molly was a special 'Rooinek' and well fit to bear them grandchildren.

*****

A thousand odd miles north of Cape Town another relationship of opposites was slowly developing. Jennifer was the daughter of a well-known Salisbury businessman, John Caldicott, He was the elected member of the Legislative assembly for Salisbury Town and knew Giles well. In fact, it was to Giles that he turned when he heard that his daughter had been seen wining and dining with the supposed Casanova of Salisbury, Solly. He asked Giles as one related to the young man in question, for an honest opinion of Solly. Giles pulled no punches and said that Solly was a young man who seemed to like the good things in life, big house flashy car, but was not guilty of being a wanton lady's man. In fact, Giles told Caldicott that, to the best of his knowledge his daughter, Jennifer was the first woman in whom Solly seemed to have ever taken an interest.

Solly became acutely aware that Jennifer reacted badly to anything that smacked of showmanism and when he persuaded her to go to dinner with him, he made sure that they dined at one of the lesser-known haunts in Salisbury more especially where he was not known by the Maître D. and not given special treatment. He discovered that Jennifer had a very real social conscience and devoted time and money to helping the poor. In this field Solly was able to put some of his wealth to good use as long as the giving did not come with obvious reward and the thing that puzzled him was, he discovered that he got a previously unknown satisfaction in helping those less fortunate than himself.

Jennifer, on the other hand could not help liking the strange young man who was so different to herself. She saw through his efforts to please her by helping her in her charity work, but accepted gratefully when she saw that he derived no obvious benefit from helping the less fortunate. Though she was not impressed by Solly's trappings of wealth, she surprised herself by finding out that she actually enjoyed the Stutz

Bearcat and being driven fast. What became a favourite outing for both her and Solly was taking a picnic and heading out of Salisbury along the Enterprise Road at a high speed to Mermaids Pool. Solly couldn't help himself and purchased a large tractor innertube so he and Jennifer could go flying down the waterslide together and faster than anybody else.

*****

Marcel de Speville was ailing fast. He was diagnosed with pancreatic cancer and given less than three months to live. Before he told the rest of the family the bad news, he called Molly to his bedside and told her. Molly was shaken and broke into tears. Marcel responded by taking her hand and stroking it gently,

"Molly Dear, I have had a good and long life. I have been surrounded by good people all my life as I am now with you here by me." He continued, "I need to talk about La Mercy. I know you are aware that unless you want it, it will be given to the nation to do with what the authorities deem is best. Giles and Emily don't want the responsibility of a large property so far from where they are. I must ask you; do you want it and what will you do with it?"

"Grandpa, Johan and I have talked about La Mercy, and we would like to do something which we think is very exciting. We want to turn it into a private school to be based on striving for excellence but with a fee structure that allows deserving students from all parts of society to attend. What do you think, Grandpa," asked Molly.

Marcel's eyes clouded over with tears. Eventually he got hold of himself and said," I can't think of a better future for La Mercy. Just hope I live long enough to see you and Johan married and in control of La Mercy's destiny."

Johan and Molly got married three weeks later in the drawing room at La Mercy. Johan's parents were understanding about the rush to get married. Giles, Emily and Solly came down from Salisbury for the wedding and there was a large cohort of guests from Johan's family. At the wedding ceremony conducted by the Anglican Bishop of Cape Town there were so many guests that they crowded out on to the stoep. The reception was held in a marquee in the grounds of La Mercy. The food was done by a catering firm supervised by Mrs. Goosen. Johan and Molly postponed their honeymoon because of Marcel's state of health.

Marcel de Speville passed away two days after the wedding. He was mourned not only by his family but many others and would go down as one of the 'good men', in the annals of the Cape of Good Hope.

When the last will and testament of Marcel de Speville was read, it turned out that he had left a considerable estate and had made cash bequests to all the members of his family. The bulk of his estate went into an educational trust to be used to finance the setting up and running of a school. The trustees were Molly, Johan and Emily. Molly now understood that the dear friend who had visited Marcel the day before the wedding may well have been a dear friend, but was obviously the lawyer who had set up the trust.

It was attending Marcel's funeral that that prompted Emily to suggest to Giles that perhaps they should consider visiting his father in England. Matthew Smith had never fulfilled his dream of retiring to the Cape. Age and ill health had caught up with him and before that could happen, Emily impressed on Giles the need to see his father until it was too late and how it would be good for the two of them to have a proper holiday, an event that had seemed to escape them so far. Once Giles had acceded to the idea of a holiday, he got excited and was happy to involve himself in the planning. The management of the family's companies was no problem as Abe, Rebecca, and senior employees could look after things for the two and a half months Giles and Emily would be away.

Their holiday started before they got on the train. Giles and Emily spent happy hours in the planning of their trip, even to getting pleasure in sticking the relevant labels on the steamer trunk and two large leather suitcases. Giles smiled to himself when he put an oval label with an E in the middle on each piece of luggage to help the shipping crew in handling them. Thirty years before it would have been an S for plain old Smith. It was Emily who suggested that they travel by BI Line as they had a better reputation than the Union Castle Line even if marginally more expensive.

Abe and Rebecca were at Salisbury station to see Giles and Emily off on the first stage of their trip. The train steamed through the night and reached Beira the following morning. A taxi took them to the unimposing and dirty harbour where they found the S.S. Modasa, a good-looking ship of a bit less than nine thousand tons. It was only a couple of years old and looked smart in its black and white colours. Their first-class cabin was spacious and well equipped. The crew of the ship were mostly Lascars from India, the stewards were all Goan and the officers British. The public rooms were well furnished with a certain degree of opulence in the gilt decorations and mirrors on the splendid staircase. The food turned out to be excellent,

The first stage of the ship's journey was from Beira to Zanzibar where Emily and Giles went ashore to stretch their legs and to admire the magnificent carved doors on many of the town's buildings. The same day the Modasa steamed northwards towards Mombasa. To Giles and Emily, it was difficult at first to have to learn to do nothing but relax on a steamer chair on deck and visit the dining room periodically. Soon sitting on deck and watching flying fish and looking down on dolphins tracking the ship, became the order of the day.

Mombasa was the ship's next stop. It was an island city on the Kenya coast. A taxi ride took them across on a ferry to the mainland where they travelled north to Nyali where they reveled in the whiteness of the beach, the stately palm trees and the colourful coral gardens just below the sea's surface. Leaving Mombasa, the Modasa steamed for several days north past the Horn of Africa and the menacing cliffs of Cape Guardafui. From there the ship headed for the Red Sea and eventually the Suez Canal. It took a whole day to traverse the canal. Emily and Giles did not go ashore. It was just too hot, but did enjoy the Gully-Gully Man, the magician who came on board and did a series of magic tricks most involving an endless stream of day-old chickens.

The last stop the Modasa made on its way to England was Genoa, where Giles and Emily hired a taxi to take them along the Italian Riviera and back through the scenic towns of Porto Fino, Rapallo and Bordighera. After over three weeks of almost constant sunshine, the rain falling slowly and persistently over Tilbury Docks was a bit of a letdown. A short taxi ride and a train trip brought Emily and Giles to Exeter where they booked into a hotel. Matthew had not been informed of their impending visit as it was meant to be a surprise. The next morning, they hired a taxi to take them to Chumleigh Waterford and to the address, the last one that had been sent to them by Mathew Smith in his now almost undecipherable writing. The taxi stopped outside a small but neat cottage. Emily stayed in the car while Giles went to the door and knocked but there was no answer. He knocked again but there was still no response.

He turned to retrace his steps to the taxi when he saw an old man was standing at the fence and staring at him. The old man spoke," He won't answer today. He's gone", he said in a broad Devon accent.

"Do you know where he's gone?" asked Giles politely.

"He's gone forever. Went yesterday," said the old man.

It then dawned on Giles that his father was dead. In a sad daze he instructed the taxi driver to take him and Emily to the police station. A kind old sergeant confirmed that Matthew Smith had passed away the day before and he could take Giles to see his father at the morgue. Giles declined. He wanted to remember his father as he was alive, and not a dead body on a mortuary slab. They went from the police station to a funeral director and arranged for a simple service and for Matthew's human remains to be placed in the village churchyard next to Giles's mother. Giles and Emily went back to the hotel where Giles sat on the bed and cried silently at first and then came a torrent of emotion. Emily held Giles tight until the sobbing stopped.

Giles dried his tears and said," We were never very close, but I did love him. He was never very close to anybody, but he was a good father in his own way. I am a part of him and always will be."

The service was simple, attended by a handful of people that Giles didn't know. Giles paid for a gravestone to be erected on his father's grave. The last thing he and Emily did in Devon was get a taxi to drive them slowly through the Grantham-Smyth estate where Giles pointed out various landmarks from his childhood.

It was almost a relief to get back on board another BI ship, the almost new SS Madura, and steam away from England. Giles never offered Emily the chance to see where she had stayed as a schoolgirl and Emily never asked. As they stepped off the train at Salisbury Station, Giles took a deep breath and said, "smells good." Emily nodded in agreement.

While Emily and Giles were away on their trip to England, Solly had managed to convince Jennifer that he was the right man for her. It had taken a long time but when she agreed to marry him, he rushed to formalize the agreement in case she changed her mind. He went to the offices of the Mashonaland Herald and placed a tasteful announcement to the effect that he Solly Gold, and Jennifer Caldicott were announcing their engagement as of that date. There was no statement stating any pleasure being expressed by Jennifer's father with regard to the event.

Solly actually hoped that her father never found out about it. However it was an unfortunate fact that on day the advert appeared in the Herald, John Caldicott had sealed a deal to sell seven tractors to a farming company, and was sinking brandy and sodas in the Salisbury Club, when he was shown the engagement announcement in the paper by a drinking companion.

As was reported in the gossip column of the Herald the following day, that Mr. Caldicott jumped up out of his chair and announced to all and sundry in the club," Over my dead body! Marry a bloody Yid!"

Solly was aware that he was not a favourite person in Caldicott's books and went to see Jennifer. She was not as upset as Solly and when she had managed to calm him down to a degree, suggested that her father would mellow in time and best leave the matter for the present. Solly went to see his father. Abe understood how his son felt but suggested that perhaps he should go and see Caldicott and explain in polite terms a few facts such as that Jennifer was over twenty-one and did not require his permission to get married and also that Solly was not a Jew. Abe mentioned to Giles what had happened over the engagement announcement and Giles went to see Caldicott. He tried to reason with the man and explained that Solly was not Jewish and had never been near a synagogue his whole life. Caldicott told Giles to mind his own business and remove himself. Caldicott refused to even speak to Solly.

Jennifer refused to consider a wedding ceremony where she was not escorted to the altar by her father, so Solly and his father got together and put into action a plan that might take time but might get Caldicott to change his mind. Solly had found out that Jennifer's father was a minority shareholder but managing director of Dewy and Company the sole agent in Rhodesia for Fordson Tractors. He instructed his broker to start buying shares in Dewy whenever they became available. He also instructed his broker to buy shares in the Rhodesia Tractor Company which was the sole agent for Massey Harris Tractors. The shares in this company were mostly held by a family trust. With added financial backing from Abe if it became necessary, Solly approached members of the family whose trust held the majority of shares in the company.

By offering a good price for the shares held by the trust and a written agreement to sell the shares back to the trust at a ten per cent discount on market price in three years, Solly took over Rhodesia Tractor Company. He attended the first shareholders meeting and introduced himself as the major shareholder in the company. At that meeting he proposed that all Massey Harris tractor prices be reduced to cost plus five percent and an intensive advertising campaign should be launched. He explained that this would push up sales immediately and that once Rhodesia Tractor had achieved a large proportion of the local market, prices could be slowly raised again. The other shareholders were shocked at Solly's proposal but had, on a vote, no option but to go along with Solly.

Sales of Massey Harris tractors soared and Caldicott saw the market share of Fordson tractors fall drastically. He was a worried man. In less than a year since Solly had launched his campaign against Caldicott, he had bought nearly thirty percent of the shares in Dewys. He now owned more shares than Caldicott and was able to call a special general meeting of the shareholders of Dewys. In his call for the special meeting, he put in the one and only item to be on the agenda and that was the removal of the managing director in the face of a severe decline in sales.

As he had expected he got a phone call from Caldicott's secretary just days before the meeting requesting a meeting with Mr.Gold as soon as possible. The meeting was held in a private room at the Salisbury Club. Solly knew he held a stacked deck of cards, but was prepared to be nice to his future father-in-law. The two men, one young and one older, faced each other across a low table. Solly broke the ice,

" Got you Mr. Caldicott. No hard feelings if you agree to me marrying your daughter and you walk her down the aisle. Oh, and also you send a donation of five hundred pounds to the local Rabbi for any charity he chooses for being so rude about Jews…" Caldicott spluttered and started to object but Solly continued "by the way I don't know the Rabbi's name as I haven't been in a synagogue in all my life!"

Caldicott was a beaten man and he asked," and what do I get out of it?"

"After the wedding I will get the price of Massey Harris tractors raised and I will withdraw the proposal to fire you and you will have the pleasure of me as your son in law. And by the way its no good appealing to Jennifer, she has worked out what I have been up to and still wants to marry me. Agreed?"

Caldicott sank lower into his chair and said," Agreed. My god you are really something!"

175

"Yes, I am Mr. Caldicott, and don't ever forget it!" said Solly with a smile.

The wedding of Miss Jennifer Caldicott and Mr. Solomon Gold may not have been the wedding of the year in Salisbury but was certainly an opulent event. The wedding service took place in the Anglican cathedral in Second Street and the reception was held at Meikles Hotel. Just about anybody of any importance was at this event. Matt was best man and Mariette was a maid of honour. Molly and Johan did not travel to Salisbury as the wedding conflicted with the opening of La Mercy School. John Caldicott did escort his daughter down the aisle to where Solly waited for her. He could not resist giving Caldicott a wicked little smile as he took Jennifer's hand. Giles, Emily, Rebecca and Abe were all seated at the main table. Solly made a brilliant speech in his toast to the bridesmaids, female relatives of Jennifer's, and when he sat down, Jennifer squeezed his hand under the table and mouthed 'well done'.

Solly kept the honeymoon destination a secret from everybody including Jennifer. The couple spent the first night at Meikles Hotel, drove in the Stutz to Bulawayo the next day and then the following day drove to the Victoria Falls Hotel where they stayed in the hotel's honeymoon suite. The couple spent an idyllic week doing little but really getting to know each other and enjoying the incredible scenery around them. Solly did leave Jennifer on her own for a couple of hours and purchased some land close to the hotel. When they returned to Salisbury Jennifer joined Solly in his lovely house in Second Street Extension. She continued with her job in real estate but found that with the publicity generated by the wedding and with a well-known husband, she was tending to be the company's preferred agent for the more up market properties.

*****

The opening of La Mercy School was attended by many of the notables of Cape Town. Marcel's will had left enough money in trust for Molly and Johan to find and employ seven highly qualified and motivated teachers for various subjects, Molly and Johan were joint Head Teachers and Johan taught science subjects and Molly art. The school opened with thirty pupils, half in the first year of high school and half in the second year. Six pupils were boarders, accommodated in what had been the guest cottage under the care of a house mother. Mrs. Goosen assisted by her daughter took over the cooking for the whole school. Johan and Molly moved into what had been the rooms occupied by the de Spevilles in a wing on their own.

The first time they had a spare moment Johan and Molly walked around La Mercy and enjoyed the sight of of boys and girls in bright green blazers and uniforms moving about the grounds of La Mercy.

Chapter 22

On a hot afternoon in late 1926, the families were gathered in the shade under the tamarind tree. In the centre of the group were two prams whose occupants were the two latest additions to the family. A few months before Mariette had given birth to twins. This was not entirely unexpected, as late in her pregnancy Dr. Wood had said that he could detect two foetal heartbeats. The occupant of the maroon pram was a baby girl now named Emily Jane. The occupant of the dark blue pram was a baby boy now named Giles Abraham. The family members who cared to proffer an opinion mostly thought Emily Jane looked like her father and Giles Abraham looked like his mother.

Emily's hair was getting quite grey and now, wearing glasses, she looked stern and studious. Next to her was Giles who was very grey, and his face was drawn. He walked with a pronounced limp even though he had had a new prosthetic device only a year ago. Abe showed no sign of growing grey in contrast to Rebecca who had a mass of silver hairs in amongst her dark hair. Jennifer sat next to Solly. She had fitted well into the family very soon after her marriage to Solly who was starting to put on weight.

There were six others under the tamarind tree. There were Matt and Mariette and Aaron and Thomas and their two recent brides, two Italian sisters, Maria and Teresa di Marco as they were before their weddings. The party under the tamarind tree was in fact being held to welcome the two sisters to the farm family and to discuss the progress of the family businesses. Giles disclosed to the family that 1926 had been a good year for them. The mine continued to show a profit and the reef seemed to extend even further at a shallow depth than they had expected. The family food operations were working to capacity and the farms had both yielded good crops despite a fairly dry season.

Giles told the others that even though things were going well, and the gold price was on the rise, it was the considered opinion of many knowledgeable businessmen, that there were signs on the horizon that the world was heading for a recession. Giles suggested that the family should consider preparing for such an eventuality and prepare for the possibility of reduced sales of both food products and farm produce. He suggested that there should be no more investment in expansion in factory capacity or crop acreage. Any investment should be geared at upgrading mine equipment to cut the cost of gold extraction.

All the family agreed with Giles and an unofficial proposal to adopt his suggestions was made with a series of head nods. Solly was asked how his little empire was growing and he was proud to announce that the auction business was flourishing, the rondavel renting produced a small but steady income and that he owned six acres of prime land next to the Victoria Falls Hotel which should grow in value as the place developed as a tourist attraction. He added that Giles had given him an idea for his next business venture which would be a pawnbroker's, a sure winner if a recession did come along. He added proudly that Jennifer had done so well selling Salisbury houses that she had been made a junior partner in the estate agent firm.

The sun was going down. Babies had been taken inside to be fed and Giles, Emily, Abe and Rebecca were left sitting in the twilight. A nightjar was calling from somewhere close. Abe raised his glass of beer and said,

"I think we have all done well, we three Capetonians and one Johannesburgian. We have got a lovely family, great kids and now great grandkids. They drank their toast and sat and talked mostly of their shared past but also of their similarly hopefully shared futures.

The more Solly thought about a recession and an apparently recession proof business such as a pawnbroker, the more he decided to do something. He had heard on the business grapevine of a pawnbroking business for sale in Bulawayo. He decided to make the trip to Bulawayo and at the least get some idea of the ins and outs of the business. He drove in the Stutz and was in Bulawayo in seven hours and booked himself into the Grand Hotel. After a hearty breakfast the following morning he went to Paul's Pawnshop in Grey Street. He introduced himself to the owner who he had spoken to on the phone two days before. Paul showed Solly round the shop and indicated what sort of objects were preferred as collateral for money lent. He explained that most money was not made on the interest charged on money lent, but on the sale of items of worth that were forfeited when interest was not paid. He was obviously a hard man, as Solly saw that he offered potential customers very low advances on objects they proffered. He gave Solly a price for the business including stock. He suggested that Solly, as a

Jew, would do very well in the business. Solly made no comment but left saying he would be in touch.

Outside the pawnshop was a bench on the pavement and on it was a middle-aged woman who had her face buried in a large handkerchief and who was obviously crying. Solly sat next her and said" Can I do anything to help?"

The woman uncovered her eyes and looked suspiciously at Solly." Not a unless you can get Scrooge in there to give me more than five pounds for all my husbands medals," With this she took a packet out of her pocket and showed Solly five medals. Solly had seem Giles's and Matt's DSO's and immediately recognized one of the other medals. He also saw one which he was sure was a Military Medal.

"Come and have a cup of tea and a cake with me and tell me about yourself. I am Solly Gold from Salisbury,

"I am Mrs. Gladys Negrini from Essexvale," said the woman.

Over tea and cake the woman told Solly about her problems. She was a widow. Her husband had never returned from the Great War and had never seen his son Ian. After her husband's death she had continued running the little chicken farm at Essexvale, a small dry little town about twenty-seven miles south of Bulawayo. Her son was doing well at school and hoped to be able to go and study medicine at Cape Town University in four years' time. He was hard working and helped his mother every weekend and evening, collecting eggs and bagging chicken manure to sell to a garden shop. She made the trip to Bulawayo every morning with eggs for the market. She dropped Ian and another boy at school and his parents collected them at the end of the school day.

Even though there were still four years to go to when Ian would be due to go to university, she had started collecting money to pay for his studies. She estimated that she needed about twelve hundred pounds. She had already sold all the silver they had, wedding presents and all, and had two hundred and eighty pounds. Solly liked this down to earth, very ordinary, but perhaps special woman. He wanted to meet her son. He persuaded her to show him her chicken farm. He followed her pick-up all the time backing away from the cloud of dust it stirred up. The house was small and in need of repair, but inside was neat and tidy. The chicken houses were clean, and the chickens looked healthy to Solly. Ian returned from school. He was a polite, fair-haired boy who obviously loved his mother.

Gladys Negrini offered Solly an evening meal of chicken, of course, and he accepted. After a good dinner Solly and Gladys sat on the stoep. Ian was doing his homework. Solly then did something which he later blamed on his association with Jennifer and her charity mindedness. He offered Gladys a loan for a thousand pounds when the time came for Ian to go to university. Gladys refused the loan on the grounds that she had no security to offer him. Solly saw that she was a proud woman and so he said he would accept a quarter share in the farm as security when the time came for Ian to go to university. As he drove away from the little chicken farm, Solly felt a warm feeling in his heart and knew he would never regret what he was going to do four years hence. He knew that Jennifer would approve and that also made him feel good.

The late nineteen twenties were a time of restricted expansion of the two family's business empire. Money was spent on the Puff Adder Mine to make it more profitable. The steel balls in the mill were replaced as they were worn, the mesh of the trammel was repaired and the matt on the sluice box was replaced. The farms continued to produce well, but planted acreages were not substantially increased though at Mary's Nest some new vegetables and fruits were tried with some success. The canning and bottling plants were running at capacity and no expansion was planned for the immediate future.

Solly, as the gambler in the family, continued to increase his business portfolio. He rented a modest shop in Union Avenue where opened a pawnbroker business modestly called just "Golds". He ran the business himself while he trained a cousin of Jennifer's. Aware of the poor opinion most people had of pawnbrokers, he set out to give his clients as good a deal as was possible, while still making a profit. He was able to raise profitability substantially by selling unclaimed items through his auction business which continued to be an ever-increasing profit generator.

Solly and Jennifer joined forces to set up a new real estate business with Solly providing the business acumen and Jennifer the knowledge of the property market. Within two years Caldicott and Gold was the number one real estate business catering to the more affluent members of the Salisbury public.

In 1929 Giles was appointed as Minister of Agriculture in prime minister Howard Moffat's cabinet. Giles was not keen on taking up the position as he was now sixty-one and starting to feel his age. Howard

Moffat pressured Giles to take the job taking advantage of Giles's friendship with his grandfather. Giles agreed to take the position on condition that he was not expected to live in Salisbury, and he would be provided with a government car and driver to carry him between his office and Leopard Ridge.

One sunny winter afternoon in 1928, Rebecca and Emily were walking slowly along the top of the ridge along the eastern boundary Mary's Rest. They moved as fast as Rebecca's legs allowed, but they were not concerned about getting anywhere fast. They were looking for a yellow Flame Lily. Emily had seen one years before and hoped to find another specimen to transplant to her garden and to paint as well. Abe and Giles were in Salisbury and had gone to watch a rugby match at the Police Sports Club with Solly and Jennifer.

It was Rebecca who called out to Emily," I've found one, I think!"

Emily walked to where Rebecca was standing looking down. Sure enough, there was a yellow Flame Lily so different to the usual red lily. She took a trowel out of the canvas bag hanging from her waist and proceeded to dig up the attractive plant. She managed to dig it up with the bulb and roots intact and placed it carefully in the bag.

Rebecca happened to look down into the hole where the flame lily had been and saw a glint of what looked like gold. She pointed it out to Emily who managed to break away some rock. Emily had been around both Leopard Ridge and Puff Adder Mines for enough years to know that the rocks probably contained gold. She put the rock samples carefully in the bag so as not to damage her precious yellow flame lily. The two women made their slow way back to Mary's Nest where Emily placed the rock samples on the drinks table on the stoep.

The sun had set by the time the men arrived back from the rugby. They were in good spirits as Rhodesia had beaten Transvaal in a closely contested match. They were shown the rock samples and immediately recognized gold bearing ore in quantities that looked promising. It was too dark to visit the place where the women had found the rock sample there and then so they decided that at first light, Abe and Giles would go on the tractor to the rock sample site in order to save Giles a long walk on his prothesis.

They found the place where Emily had been digging without a problem. Abe took a pickaxe and then a hoe and exposed more of the rock less than a foot under the surface. There was a lot more of gold flecked rock. It appeared that the men were looking at a new reef only about a hundred and fifty yards from the Puff Adder reef and running parallel to it. Putting more rock samples in a sack, Abe and Giles returned to Mary's Nest where Emily and Rebecca were waiting. Abe and Giles were all for driving straight away to Salisbury to register a series of claims running along the length of the reef and to get analysis done on the rock samples, but were restrained by Rebecca and Emily. It was Emily who said," before you go rushing off, Rebecca and I want to be joint owners of the claims and we insist that if we open a new mine, it is to be called the 'Flame Lily Mine'. Abe and Giles did not argue.

The rock samples proved to hold good levels of gold and further excavation round the Flame Lily site showed that there might be reserves of gold ore equal if not greater than Puff Adder Mine. A new ball mill, trammel and sluice box was bought and transported from Johannesburg. They also bought a new tractor for moving overburden. A new stationary engine was also purchased and sited down by the river on Leopard Ridge. The question of who to run the new mine was a problem but only for a matter of days. Giles received a visitor at his ministerial office in Salisbury. A young man possibly in his thirties politely introduced himself as Hennie van Rooyen.

Giles looked the man over and felt there was something familiar about him. He had the olive skin of a person of mixed heritage from the Cape. The young man went on to explain that he was a grandson of Mrs. van Rooyen from 76 Hout Street. He told Giles that his grandmother who had passed away some seven years ago had told him often of 'the Good Rooinek' who was a friend of Cecil John Rhodes and who was an important man in Rhodesia. Hennie explained that he had worked on a mine in Johannesburg for ten years and had risen to be a mine captain but was tired of a life, nearly half of which was spent underground and the other half spent in a dirty crowded city. He had come to Rhodesia hoping for a better life for himself wife and three-year-old child. He was hoping Giles could point him in the right direction. Giles phoned Abe and asked him to meet for lunch at the Salisbury Club as had a person he wanted him to meet,

The three men entered the club under the scrutinizing eyes of a section of the members present. Abe ignored the looks, Hennie felt somewhat embarrassed, but Giles, knowing that all the members knew he was a government minister, ignored everybody except the dining room Maître D' who steered them to a quiet table. Giles explained to Abe that Hennie was a mine captain, looking for a job and the grandson of Mrs. van Rooyen. Two hours later, three happy men left the club, Giles and Abe happy that the problem of a mine captain was solved and Hennie knowing that he had a job at a good salary and one of the lakeside rondavels to live in with his wife and child until better accommodation could be organized.

*****

La Mercy School was doing well. The total enrollment had increased to one hundred and twenty and five more teachers were engaged. The school was getting an excellent academic reputation but there was a dark cloud in the sky over Newlands. The whole world which had sailed through the nineteen twenties with gay abandon, with governments spending money that had less and less backing, was obviously heading for a recession. This was reflected in the increased number of suitable pupils wanting to be admitted to La Mercy but whose parents lacked the required funds. The percentage of full fee-paying pupils had declined. The de Speville Trust still was reasonably healthy financially, as lot of its investments were in gold and diamonds. With Giles's approval, Emily had set up three scholarships for deserving pupils.

Giles and Emily had spent a three-week holiday at La Mercy in the summer of 1929. They were happy days for both of them as the walked the grounds of La Mercy. Emily was delighted at how her natural garden had been well preserved. Giles and Emily were invited to dine at the parliament building with members of the South African Government and enjoyed talking to some members of parliament who had known Rhodes. They were invited as Giles was a minister of a neighbouring government. Emily felt so proud of her man as she sat next to him in a grand banqueting hall.

Giles decided that he would not visit Hout Street or the site of the bookshop. He explained to Emily that he thought sometimes it was best to leave certain good memories intact in one's mind. He and Emily did take a picnic to the now huge Norfolk pine where they lay on a rug and talked of days gone by. As they packed up the picnic, they both almost expected dear old Motsephe to come and join them to help carry the picnic basket.

*****

Throughout 1929 it was obvious to most people worldwide that the good days of spending and dancing and music were coming to an end, an end that would not be nice. Perhaps the one day that determined the future of the world more than any other was October the 24 th, the day that started the Wall Street crash that was to lead into the great depression. Giles and Abe and their families had fortunately seen what was coming and had planned for it as far as they could. Sales of tinned foods and orange squash declined quite rapidly as people had less and less money to spend. To start with there was still a strong demand for fresh produce and crops like maize and sunflower. However, people in desperation, started growing their own vegetables and the overseas market for maize and sunflower fell drastically as the grip of recession was felt in the rest of the world.

The number unemployed people in Salisbury increased rapidly and churches and charities worked endlessly to try and provide food for a growing b number of people. Jennifer stopped trying to sell houses to people who had no money to buy them and worked full time for a charity. It was her idea, happily accepted by all Solly's relations, that saw the setting up of a food bank in unused premises in Moffat Street. Giles organized for a large portion of the maize crop from Leopard Ridge to be milled, stored and then passed on to the people who came to the food bank. The food bank was a success giving out food to all who needed it irrespective of colour or creed. Fresh vegetables that were in excess of what the retail market wanted, was sent partly to the food bank and partly to Madire's village where there were many unemployed.

As far as the Gold and the Elliot-smith families were concerned the one trump they held compared to most people was the two functioning mines as gold remained a highly desirable commodity worldwide. The Puff Adder Mine continued to yield a good amount of gold with the reconditioned equipment and the new Flame Lily Mine under the stewardship of Hennie van Rooyen was highly profitable.

Solly, who had never amalgamated his investments with those of the rest of the family, also managed to keep his head well above water.

185

Understandably his pawnshop did big business. He kept interest rates on loans secured with items deposited as low as possible. He also had an open door to his office and was knowingly a soft touch for people who were, to his mind, in genuinely dire straits. The rondavel business went into total decline but Solly, with the approval of the rest of the family used them as accommodation of the homeless.

As 1930 came and went, for most people life was a matter of survival. For the Golds and Elliott-Smiths it was also a matter of survival but not so much for them as for the hundreds of people who depended on their generosity. The farms barely made ends meet while feeding hundreds through the food bank and handouts in Madire's village. It was the two mines that kept things going. The Puff Adder Mine continued to produce a steady flow of gold in spite of the reef dipping deeper down. The Flame Lily Mine was the real money maker. The ore continued to be of high grade and the observable reserves were greater than originally expected. Emily sometimes sat painting under the tamarind tree and stopped to look at the yellow flame lily whose success in its transplanted site, reflected to her the success of the mine with the same name.

Solly was sitting in his office at the real estate business one morning when a neatly written letter arrived from Bulawayo. It was from Gladys Negrini. Gladys politely reminded him of his offer made nearly two years before. She wrote to say that Ian had been accepted to study medicine at Cape Town University. She went on to say that she had saved another two hundred pounds and therefore would be grateful for a loan of seven hundred pounds. She enclosed a deed of indebtedness for that sum and granted Solly a lien on twenty-five percentage of the farm at Essexvale.

Solly sent a cheque for seven hundred pounds by registered post immediately. As he wrote the cheque, he had an idea. Once he had sealed the envelope, he phoned the telephone exchange and asked to be put through to a Cape Town number. Molly answered the phone and was delighted to speak to her old friend. Solly asked if there was a possibility of a spare room somewhere at La Mercy where a deserving university student could live, perhaps in exchange for some part time duties at the school. Molly said she would talk to Johan about it and get back to him. Within half an hour Molly came back with an offer of the old stable office which had a shower and toilet nearby. She and Johan would be happy if the student would supervise evening prep for two hours three nights a week. They would also throw in meals in the school dining room.

Solly couldn't wait to let Gladys know and so got her phone number at the farm and asked the exchange to connect him. Gladys burst into tears when Solly told her of the offer. When she had gathered herself, she asked why he was doing what he was,

Solly replied," because I believe he is a good kid and deserves a chance and besides when I am old, I might need my own doctor."

"You are a good man Mr. Gold.!" Said Gladys.

Solly was not surprised to get a well written letter from Ian thanking him for his generosity and promising him that he would study hard and send him a progress report on a regular basis. Jennifer said to Solly when she heard what he had done," Mr. Gold you are in dire danger of losing your hard businessman reputation, but I do love you for it!"

"It's all your fault Mrs. Gold. You must have used a magic potion on me and melted my hard core, but I still love you."

Chapter 23

Young Giles, Gilly, as he had become called after his grandfather at a similar age, and MJ as the family called Emily Jane, were suddenly deprived of their almost unfettered freedom on the farm at Mazowe. They went, as had the family generation before them, to the Convent in Salisbury. Sister Aurelia was still there and welcomed them hoping that one of them would follow in the steps of Molly and shine in the arts. However, it was not to be. Each child was blessed with above average intelligence, but it was Gilly who applied himself most to his studies. MJ was a dreamer and spent an inordinate amount of her time immersed in books.

Solly and Jennifer had not had any children by the time they had been married four years and indulged any parental feelings they might have had on Gilly and MJ. They were more than happy to pick up the two little ones from the convent at a weekend and take them to their own favourite place, Mermaids Pool, where the kids thoroughly enjoyed themselves flying down the rock slide on Uncle Solly's tractor tube. Outings usually ended at the Ice Cream Shack in Manica Road.

When Jennifer announced to Solly that he was about to be a father, he was stunned. He had never considered the possibility of being a father. The idea of sharing Jennifer with another person frightened him as did the thought of the duties and responsibilities associated with being a father. Abe and Rebecca were delighted at thought of being grandparents. Solly immediately started treating Jennifer as if she was some delicate and valuable piece of art. Jennifer reveled in the attention at first, but being attended to and helped all her waking hours started to drive her mad. She had to remind him to go to work. "Solly, I am not a precious Ming vase and certainly not an invalid. Please stop helping me. When I want help I will let you know. You go and do what you are good at and carry on keeping us safe from the problems of this terrible recession."

Solly did what he was told. The auction business continued to thrive mostly on other peoples' misfortune. Solly did not enjoy selling somebody's expensive heirloom going under the hammer that he wielded and only fetching a fraction of what it was worth. He hated seeing the disappointment and often despair on peoples' faces as they saw their possessions sold. The worst were the clearance sales where a person or family's whole life was put up for sale, usually for a pittance.

Before he acted, he talked to Jennifer one night as he lay next to her stroking her now slightly distended belly. With her approval, he subdivided the land at the Victoria Falls into acre plots and immediately sold two for several times what he had paid for the whole lot of six plots. The money he raised he put into what he called his Good Samaritan account. The money in this account he used judiciously to push up bids on items that were going to be sold for a pittance to the detriment of desperate owners of these items. He bid in the name of a phantom bidder. If he pushed the price up too far and the phantom bidder won a lot, he paid for it and put it away in a secure room behind the auction room to be sold when times improved. Jennifer was the only person who knew what he was up to and of course loved him even more for it.

*****

The La Mercy School managed to survive year after year at the expense of the de Speville trust, but became known as a centre for excellence in academia. Cape Town people of note started sending their children to La Mercy. Molly and Johan were happy with what they had created, but realized that there was something missing in their lives. This gap in their lives was very ably filled by the arrival of a little girl they called Abigail, who made her introductory appearance at the Somerset Hospital on the fourteenth of February 1933. Molly continued to teach art but relinquished all her administrative duties to Johan. She also stopped painting Cape landscapes for which she had become well known.

Johan's parents doted on their granddaughter. About every second weekend they came to La Mercy to stay in a spare room and babysit Abigail and allow Johan and Molly some time to themselves. In the Christmas school holidays in 1935, Molly, Johan and little Abigail travelled by train to Salisbury for a two week stay on the farm. Even though that Christmas was a sad time for so many people, it was a wonderful time for the Golds and the Elliott-Smiths. They held their major celebration and Christmas dinner on Christmas Eve. Children, parents, grandparents filled Leopard Ridge farmhouse with happy sounds and everybody ate well and, after they had eaten, played parlour games. Later while the younger generations danced and listened to records, Giles, Abe, Rebecca and Emily went and sat under the tamarind tree. There was desultory conversation but each of them was, at least, partially lost in memories and thankfulness for the good things that happened in the past. Emily who was nearest to the tree stroked the bark and thought of Motsephe and Reggie and her parents and days under another tree, the Norfolk Pine. Those days seemed so far away.

The following day, Christmas Day, most of the families piled into three cars and drove to Salisbury to the food bank where, with a lot of help from the public, a Christmas dinner was held for over a hundred needy people. The food was good and everybody was given a present of some kind, courtesy of Solly and Jennifer, The reward for the organisers of the event was seeing the sadness in the faces of the Christmas dinners change to smiles at least for a few hours.

A New Year's Eve's party was a happy event at Leopard Ridge. All the family were together to celebrate having survived four years of the recession. At midnight Johan who had, unusually, been a member of a pipe band while at school in Cape Town produced his bagpipes and played Auld Lang Syne as he marched slowly between the farmhouse and the tamarind tree. To the intense amusement of all, especially the children marching next to him, Johan attracted a devoted following of geese who walked solemnly behind him in single file. 1934 had ended with the strong possibility of the world slowly returning to normal in the years to come.

Solly had been receiving reports of Ian's progress at university on a regular basis. He had passed each year 'summa cum laude' and from the letters that Gladys sent regularly she was obviously very proud of her son. Ian had become a fixture at La Mercy. In spite of his relative youth, he was well respected by the pupils whose study time he supervised and there was barely a time when at least one teenage girl did not have a crush on him. He even went so far as to fill a gap in the education of some of the boys by introducing rugby to the school and becoming their coach. He had too few players under his control to produce a winning team but his team lost gracefully on a regular basis.

The market for canned goods slowly recovered and the food businesses started to generate profits again. Donations to the food bank declined as more and more people got back on their feet. Eventually the rondavels near the lake were no longer housing the homeless. The family decided that they would no longer rent them out but keep them for extra accommodation for friends and family when needed. Solly didn't mind as the money they had generated was worthwhile originally, but now he didn.t have the time to devote to them. He was expanding his business interests.

The goods won on auction as a ghost bidder were now able to be sold as the man in the street had more money to spend. What he got from this source he carefully invested in land buying up tracts of land especially in the areas north of Salisbury. He also started building up an import export business mainly with Mozambique. He travelled frequently to Beira and Lourenco Marques where he became well known in business circles. He mainly imported Portuguese wines and certain foodstuffs such as cashew nuts and exported tobacco and canned goods, many from his family's businesses. Within a year or so he became proficient in the Portuguese language

Solly was sitting in his hotel room in Beira on a very hot humid evening when reception transferred a phone call from Salisbury. It was Rebecca to tell him that Jennifer had gone into labour at the Salisbury General Hospital. Solly wasted no time in getting into his almost new Chevrolet Master car and driving through the night. He arrived tired but happy to arrive at Jennifer's bedside a mere ten minutes before she delivered a light brown haired little boy. Jennifer lay back in the hospital bed looking tired but very satisfied. She carefully handed a little bundle over to Solly who gazed in wonder at the child that he and Jennifer had made. He decided that he loved him even though he thought he did look a bit like a prune. He didn't know what to do with his son at that moment. He was terrified of dropping the precious bundle and so decided that the best thing was to hand him back to Jennifer and admire him from afar.

Jennifer and the baby were inundated with visitors the whole day, including John Caldicott and his wife who bought a large suitcase of new baby clothes. Solly was not present when Caldicott was visiting his daughter. Matt and Mariette were delighted with the new arrival. Matt said to Solly," poor little bugger. He looks like a blonder version of you. I guess he will also be a wheeler and dealer like his father. Once all visitors had gone home Jennifer and Solly had a few moments together alone and talked about a name for the baby happily suckling next to his mother. Eventually they both agreed that they would grant their little son a measure of independence and called him Marcus Henry after nobody in the family.

On his seventieth birthday Giles resigned as managing director and handed over to Matt and Abe did the same with Mariette who jointly took over the management of all the families business ventures with Matt. Matt and Mariette arranged the building of an office building in Mazowe Village and thus separated the hustle and bustle of business from the farms where the older generation could start to enjoy their retirement. It didn't work of course. Giles, Abe and Rebecca were determined to keep in touch with the family businesses and continued to interfere but on a limited level that was accepted by the younger generation. Only Emily was able to divorce herself from business and spent most of her to time wandering their six thousand acres sketching plants and landscapes which became works of art on the canvases on her easel under the tamarind tree.

Emily had her first exhibition in 1938 at Meikles Hotel and sold all of the landscapes that were on show. It was at the exhibition that she met Olive Coates Palgrave a well-known botanical illustrator whose family had come to Rhodesia in 1895. Olive and Emily became firm friends and collaborated on a number of scientific articles. While they painted, the two women talked of their families and lives and love of Rhodesian flora. Olive was entranced with the history of the large shady tree under which they painted.

Abe and Giles were encouraged by the rest of y the family to take up some sort of hobby or establish some interests outside the family businesses. They both joined The Lions Club in Salisbury a non-profit organization without political affiliations. It went well at first but the novelty soon wore off especially when they discovered that one of the moving forces in the organization was John Caldicott. They both tried golf and fishing but discovered that they were equally inadept at both sports.

It was when they joined the lawn bowls section of the Salisbury sports club that they discovered that they had found an enjoyable pastime. The two men often disappeared from Mazowe for an entire day to the relief of everybody and played bowls, lunched at the Salisbury Club and then returned to the sports club for more bowls. Within months the two were proficient bowlers and in 1938 teamed up to win the Mashonaland Men's Doubles Championship. They also enjoyed watching rugby and sometimes picked up MJ and Gilly and took them with them to watch a Currie Cup rugby match.

*****

In Cape Town Abigail was so popular with the girls at La Mercy that she became an unofficial school mascot. Johan and Molly were happy. The School had gained an excellent reputation and as the enrolment increased Ian eventually had a pool of players big enough to field a decent rugby side whose highlight of the season was only losing to SACS by ten points! Ian completed his studies and then did a two-year residency at the Somerset Hospital. In 1938. He was a fully qualified doctor. He was offered a permanent post at the Somerset, but wanted to go back to Rhodesia to be nearer to his mother who still battled her daily way through eggs and chicken manure, He applied for and got a post as a junior doctor at the Bulawayo General Hospital where he had accommodation and a salary that allowed him to make small but steady payments to Solly. He had invited Solly to his graduation but was not surprised when he did not attend, but did send him a gold watch engraved with congratulations. When his mother saw the watch, she smiled at the thought that the watch had probably cost more than the loan repayments that Ian could repay in a year.

*****

As the recession receded most thinking people became aware of Hitler and his ambitions. The dark grey cloud of the threat of war started to hang over most of the world. Solly was surprised one day when he was sitting in his office in the new building in Kopje Road. Two men, very ordinary men, dressed in very ordinary suits and ties asked if they could have a moment of his time. In truth it turned out to be much more than a moment. The men introduced themselves as working for a British Government Ministry but did not identify which one.

They asked Solly about his business in Mozambique and his proficiency in Portuguese. Having nothing to hide Solly told them of how he went quite often to both Beira and Lourenco Marques on business and knew a lot of business men in both these places, both Portuguese and foreign. He was asked if some of his business contacts were German. He answered in the affirmative. Eventually the older of the two men explained that on behalf of the British Government, they were interested in the business that the Germans were doing in Mozambique. They said that they assumed that he knew that war with Germany was a certainty in the near future and that Portugal was expected to remain neutral in the event of war.

Solly nodded and let the man continue. What he and the British government wanted was people like himself who did business in Mozambique and who travelled there frequently to become the eyes and ears there for the British Government. He explained that any offer of help in the field outlined would have to be freely given.

Solly smiled and looked the two men in the eye and said," I must be a pretty good bet to you. You will certainly know that my mother is Jewish. Even if I am not a Jew, what Hitler is doing and plans to do to Jews is dreadful. Yes, I will help you, "

The two men looked relieved at the outcome of the meeting and arranged further meetings over the next two weeks for further briefing. They ended with a request that he not tell anybody in his family or outside it. Solly sat in his office and thought about what had just transpired. He did not regret his commitment, but did question whether he had a target on his back that said "Soft Touch". He did tell Jennifer everything and she promised that all he had told her would go no further and it never did. She did make him promise that whatever he did in Mozambique would not put him or her or their son in any danger.

Chapter 24

On September the 3rd. 1939 Britain declared war on Germany following Germany's invasion of Poland. From that day on, the death knell was to be sounded continually across the world. The people of Rhodesia were generally stunned. Solly had known from his handler in the British High Commission that war would break out at any time and was not surprised. Though conscription was not introduced in Southern Rhodesia at the time and never would be, men in their thousands volunteered to fight alongside the British. It was a fact, later revealed, that Southern Rhodesia sent more men to fight in World War II for its population than any other member country of the British Commonwealth and lost proportionally as many young men.

Solly did not volunteer as he had already been asked by his handler to carry on doing business in Mozambique and to intensify his efforts to a obtain information of use to the Allies. He found himself in a difficult position. He was aware that certain people were aware that he had not volunteered, but was not able to say why. Jennifer spoke to each and every adult member of the Gold and the Elliott-Smith families and told them that Solly was doing his bit for the war effort but was unable to tell them what he was doing.

Matt made a trip to Salisbury to Army Headquarters to see Colonel Sommerville the army commander at the time. He asked Sommerville what he could do to help. Somerville knew Giles well as Giles was Honorary Colonel of the Rhodesian African Rifle regiment originally known as the Rhodesian Native Regiment. Sommerville told Matt to leave the matter with him and he would come forward with some suggestion. When Matt told Mariette what he had done she was angry. She told him in no uncertain terms, that he was no spring chicken; that he was forty-seven years old and had done his fair share in the last war as witnessed by his DSO. She did finally agree to see what Sommerville came up with.

Two days later Col. Sommerville phoned Matt to offer him a position with the RAR as Major, second in charge, to help the new CO to bring the regiment up to battle standard. He would be based in Salisbury until such time that the regiment was up to standard and ready to be deployed. Sommerville emphasized that Matt would be an asset to the regiment with his fluency in Shona. Mariette was marginally mollified by at least the continued presence of Matt in Salisbury. She decided that she would worry again when the time came for his deployment.

Ian Negrini had established himself as a highly competent and caring doctor at Bulawayo General and when news of the outbreak of war impacted on him in his busy routine of ward rounds and minor operations, he was not initially inclined to rush and enlist but when he saw many of his friends and colleagues joining up he did the same. Very quickly he was appointed an army doctor with the rank of lieutenant and made to undergo a cram course in matters military. He was then posted to Llewellin Barracks to be responsible for the health of the steady stream of volunteers passing through the barracks and then onto the various theaters of war.

Life actually continued on very much like it had at the General except that he had to wear a uniform. He never quite got the hang of saluting: how to or to whom one should salute. His uniform never looked quite neat but he assured himself, if not others, that it was sterile. He wrote to Solly to apologize that, on an army doctor's salary, he would have to reduce his debt repayments. Solly's reply was to say that he should forget the debt and get on with helping Rhodesian soldiers.

Johan was faced with conscription on the outbreak of war. As a man of Afrikaner descent and with the memory of the Boer War only just around the corner, he was not happy with the situation, but when he discussed the situation with Molly, she pointed out that Afrikaner he might be, but he now lived in an English-speaking world. Johan decided not to wait to be called up but to enlist straightaway. This was a move not entirely approved of by his parents, but he found himself commissioned as a second lieutenant and placed in the army training Corps initially based at the Castle in Cape Town. During the day he wrote training manuals on everything from camp cooking to stripping a .303 rifle. After hours he went home and was able to help Molly with the school.

When Solly was staying in Lourenco Marques he always based himself at the Polana Hotel, a hostelry of worldwide renown. It was expensive, but the British Government footed most of the bill. It was a very attractive hotel with expansive grounds and overlooked the sea.

The hotel always seemed to be full or nearly so. A stroll through the reception area and one could hear a dozen different languages: everything from French to Cantonese. On a day when Solly had spent the daylight hours doing business in the city, perhaps selling a hundred tons of tobacco and buying two hundred cases of Portuguese Fragal wine, he would have an early dinner and then sit in the corner of the bar nursing a single Laurentina beer and looking and listening.

There was one man that he saw on more than one occasion that interested him. He spoke German and obviously poor Portuguese. He looked to be in his forties. The shortness of his hair and a sort of rigidity of his body suggested to Solly that the man had a military background. This man sometimes came into the bar on his own but sometimes with another, older, also Teutonic looking man. It was several months after Solly first saw the man who was on his own approach him and say something in German.

"I am sorry I don't speak German" said Solly.

"Ah, you are English, are you?" said the man in heavily accented English.

"No, but have a drink with me. There isn't much to do after dark in LM except drink is there?" said Solly.

"Very good, we shall share a drink and talk. Are you Lebanese. You have that look. Do you do business here in Mozambique?" said the man,

Solly ignored the reference to Lebanese and admitted that he was a business man. He described what he sold and what he bought. When he asked his new drinking companion what he did, the man knocked over his drink and went to get another drink without answering the question. A very stilted conversation continued between Solly and his new friend. When he reflected on what had been said, when he retired to his room, he had to admit that the conversation was more like a fencing match and he hadn't a clue as to what the man was up to. He did ascertain that his name was Otto. He had told Otto that he was Solomon.

Solly rather looked forward to having dinner with his German the following day. He was determined to find out what the man was up to. They met in the hotel's a la carte restaurant They both ordered prawn cocktails to be followed by crayfish thermidor. To accompany the food Otto ordered a bottle of chilled Lagosta wine. It was only when the two men had moved on to the hotel verandah to enjoy coffee while being cooled by the steady sea breeze that blew across Delagoa Bay, that conversation changed from being just an exchange of niceties. Otto asked Solly if he had any English friends in LM. Knowing that he was often in the company of some of the senior staff of the British Consulate who might well be known to Otto he admitted that he did. Solly immediately turned the conversation round and asked Otto about his German friends. Otto admitted that he had some German business acquaintances in the city. Solly felt that Otto was about to say something that might reveal what he was up to when Otto suddenly asked," Solly, if you had some information to sell who would you sell it to?!

Solly's mind went into overdrive and he answered," who ever offered the better deal". At this Otto declared that he was tired and had a busy day the next day and took his leave. Before he went he suggested that they have dinner again the next night, but not at the Polona. They agreed to meet at the Cardosa at eight. Solly battled to get to sleep wondering what surprise Otto might spring on him.

Otto steered Solly to a quiet corner of the bar at the Cardosa. The bar was not as busy as the bar at the Polona always was and the few customers seemed to ignore the trio who played fado music in the one corner. Having brought two Laurentina beers to the table, Otto looked Solly straight in the face and said," I have client here in LM who wants some information on the strength of the Rhodesian Army and how many British soldiers are currently in Rhodesia. For a good fee, can you help me?"

Solly was caught off guard, but only hesitated for a split second before saying," Not a problem. When do you need the info? I expect a hefty payment."

Otto smiled at Solly and said," Thank God you are the man I need. You are working for the British. I saw that in your face when I asked you to betray the British. I want a deal with your people."

Solly said nothing and just listened. Otto continued," I have some valuable information on a scheme here in Mozambique involving the Germans. I am willing to trade this information in exchange for the release of my wife from an high security internment camp in England. She was a lecturer in German at Cambridge University but because, I think, the British know I am involved in a military operation here, are holding my wife. I am quite happy to betray Germany if I can be allowed to live in England with my wife. I am not a Nazi and despise Hitler. That' s the deal."

Solly finished his beer. " I am not admitting to anything but I will think about what you have said and I will meet you right here in exactly a week's time. He shook hands with Otto and the two men left the bar separately.

Solly was back in Salisbury the following day. He sat with his handler, a mild looking grey-haired man who said his name was Smith in the public lounge in Meikles Hotel. Solly related what had been said at the meeting in the Cardosa. Smith listened carefully and then asked Solly to return to LM the following week and attend the planned meeting with Otto. He said that he could offer Otto a deal if, what he was about to reveal was in Solly's opinion, of importance to the Allies war effort.

Solly was at the Cardosa at the appointed time. Otto was already there. He looked very uncomfortable and was sweating profusely. He kept looking around the room.

"Relax, "said Solly. "You have a deal if what you tell me is important enough."

Otto looked relieved and told Solly of the details of a submarine refueling base being built by the Germans on a small uninhabited island about fifteen miles off the coast of Mozambique roughly halfway between Beira and Lourenco Marques. The Portuguese were not aware of what was going on. He explained that he was in charge of the acquisition and transport of material to the site. He explained that this island, called Magaroque, had been selected because on its eastern side there was a gap in the surrounding reef where within yards of the shore the sea was deep enough for a submarine to dock and take on fuel. Large fuel tanks were being constructed. The construction was not obvious from the air as a series of large nets coloured to mimic the colour of sea and adjoining shore were draped over the construction site at all times.

Solly listened fascinated. Following Smith's instructions, he told Otto that as far as he was concerned the deal was on. He instructed Otto to remain in LM and continue to do what he was expected to do. In the meantime, his British contacts in Salisbury would decide what to do about the supposed submarine base. Once plans had been made, he would be taken to Salisbury to be de-briefed and once the submarine base had been neutralized, he would be flown to the UK where his wife would be released from internment and Otto and his wife would be helped to start a new life in England.

Back in Salisbury Solly gave Smith a full report on what had been said in LM. When he had finished Smith complimented Solly on how he had handled the matter and arranged another meeting at Meikles the following day. In the meantime, he told Solly a small civilian aircraft would be flown over Magarouque Island and photographs would be taken. That night Solly took Jennifer out to dinner where the two of them ate well and lingered over their coffees. They did not have to rush home as young Marcus was spending the night with his doting grandparents. Solly longed to be able to tell Jennifer what he had been up to.

At the meeting the following day, Smith revealed to Solly that a civilian Auster aircraft had flown over the island and it would appear that there was evidence that some construction was going on on the east d side of the island. Two large circular shapes could be seen under what appeared to a net of sorts. There also appeared to be some rectangular shapes just south of the large round shapes that might be tents for workers. Smith asked Solly to make himself available the following day for a meeting with some local military men who would be involved in a plan to destroy the submarine fueling base.

Matt was surprised when Col. Sommerville walked into his office that afternoon. For a few minutes they discussed the rugby match the previous Saturday and then Sommerville came straight to the point," Matt, you are bored stiff here doing what you are doing and I have an offer of a small operation for you to get your teeth into. It won't take long but will give you a nice interesting break. Oh, and by the way you will be working with that fascinating relative of yours, Solly Gold. This operation will need a small group of your Shona troops and yourself of course".

The meeting took place at Army Headquarters. Those present were Solly, Sommerville and Smith and another man from the British High commission who was not introduced to the others. The nameless man opened the meeting. He laid out a plan for the destruction of the submarine base. He asked for comments as he laid out the plan which called for a small group of local military to travel as civilians through Mozambique down to a small village on the coast well south of Beira, called Vilanculos, where they would get into a rubber dinghy at night and travel east and round the north end of Magarouque. They would land as quietly as possible and then follow the beach south to the base where they would lay explosive charges in and around the tanks and what might be a newly constructed wharf. The operation would involve Matt and four of his men who would carry the explosives, Solly was to go, if he agreed, as a Portuguese speaker in case of things going wrong. A sapper, to lay and explode the charges would complete the team

In the discussion it was Matt who insisted that the op took place when there was at least some light in which to find the small island. This was agreed and the launch date for the operation was set for a week hence. As they left the meeting Matt gave Solly a friendly punch on his shoulder and said," My God you are always get mixed up in something devious. "

"That's the way I like it," said Solly grinning widely.

The journey from Salisbury to Vilanculos took two days. About thirty miles short of Beira, the civilian three-ton truck turned south and struggled along a dirt road in places almost impassable in deep sand. On the way Matt tried to strike up a conversation with Sapper Digby Trench without success. At Vilanculos the party camped in a coconut grove right on the beach. Solly told inquisitive locals that they had come to catch fish. The next day dragged for all the men. Matt and Solly walked up the beach and back stopping every so often to jump in to the sea and cool off.

At sunset the large rubber dinghy was inflated with a hand pump. This took the best part of an hour. Matt attached the small Seagull outboard to the transom, started it and then steered towards the open sea. On board were Solly, Matt, Trench and three of Matt's men. One man was left to guard the truck. There was a partial moon and the sea was calm. Fifty pounds of high explosive were placed in the dinghy. Matt steered the boat using a compass. After nearly five hours of slow travel Matt cut the motor and scanned the horizon with his binoculars. On the horizon was a low dark shape and it was towards this he headed the dinghy. Nearer to the island Matt turned slightly north to pass along the north of the island. He cut the motor again and signaled to Solly and the three Shonas to start paddling quietly. The dinghy travelled slowly southwards until the sound of breakers could be heard signaling a break in the reef. Matt ran the dinghy onto the beach and tied the painter to a fallen coconut tree.

Matt led his party quietly along the beach keeping close to the vegetation above the beach. The three Shona men and Solly carried the explosives in rucksacks. Matt and Solly each carried a sten gun and four spare magazines in their rucksacks. After about five minutes Matt hand-signaled his party to halt. Close by was a shape that had to be the fuel tanks. Listening carefully, they could hear voices coming from somewhere beyond their target. Trench and the Shona soldiers moved forward purposely, while Matt and Solly kept an eye open for any movement to the south.

Ten minutes and Trench had placed all fifty pounds of explosives in and around the incomplete fuel tanks. They were all wired to a single trigger mechanism. At a signal from Matt, Trench bent over to push down the handle of the detonator when all hell was let loose. Firing was coming from a group of figures barely visible, shouting in German. Trench was hit and fell. Matt saw what had happened and rushed over to the detonator and pushed the plunger down. The subsequent explosion was massive. The Germans stopped firing.

Solly and one of the Shona rushed to Trench who had been shot in the leg and helped him to his feet. With one on each side they half carried and half dragged him along the beach towards where they had left the dinghy The others formed a rear guard. Once on the dinghy Solly proved to be a capable medic as he put a tight bandage from the first aid box round Trench's leg. The dinghy headed north and then after ten minutes west as it cleared the island. The return trip to Vilanculos was uneventful and took six hours against an outgoing tide.

Solly gave his first injection of his life in the back of the truck. He gave Trench a shot of morphine and changed his bandage before they set off on the long journey back to Salisbury. When they reached Salisbury, Trench was sent straight to hospital to have a bullet removed from his leg. The rest of the group were given a good meal and a night off to sleep at the RAR barracks. De-briefing took place the following day. The nameless man, Smith and Sommerville listened to Matt's report and announced that the mission was a complete success as judged by new aerial photographs. Sommerville thanked all the seven men for what they had done. He said that he expected some 'gongs' would be handed out. He addressed Matt saying," You will probably get a bar to your DSO. He then turned to Solly and said," and you Solly, I am afraid will get nothing."

Solly smiled and said," Not a problem. You can't bank a medal."

Solly was glad to be back home with Jennifer and Marcus. He wished he could tell her where he had been and what he had been doing.

She did mention that when she went to wash his clothes there seemed to be sand in the turnups of his shorts, Solly just smiled.

Johan was sitting in the office he shared with two other junior officers when a corporal approached him and gave him a message that he was to go and see the Colonel. The colonel was very affable and told Johan that his talents were being wasted in the job he was doing. He had therefore decided that he would be an ideal person to run a new government explosives factory that was due to be commissioned. The factory was going to be vital to the war effort in providing the high explosive munitions. He went on to explain that Johan would continue to serve in the army and would receive army pay but would receive a travelling allowance to cover the cost of commuting to the factory site. The new factory had been placed in the grounds of an existing fertilizer factory outside Somerset West about thirty miles south of Cape Town.

Johan left the colonels off ice with a smile on his face. His current job was boring and the new one would enable him to use the knowledge he had gained at university. He couldn't' wait to tell Molly. The afternoon dragged as he barely wrote a dozen words on a manual. When he got back to La Mercy he told Molly all about the job. She was pleased as she had never felt that Johan was an 'army' man. He would not have to wear army uniform while he was at the explosives factory. The time he could devote to helping Molly with the school would be marginally less due to a slightly longer commuting journey The following Monday an army car picked him up at La Mercy. The colonel had said he would be taken to work the first day to show him the way and so the driver could give him his pass into the fertilizer factory. It was pleasant drive from Newlands down onto the Cape Flats and then along a fairly quiet road towards the Helderberg Mountains. A few miles short of Somerset West, the car turned off the main road and then travelled through an unusual closely planted gum plantation in the middle of which was a large fertilizer factory, to one end of which was aa new extension, the explosives factory.

To enter the new building Johan showed the card the army driver had given him. He was met by a middle-aged man with thinning hair and steel framed spectacles. He introduced himself as Major Disaster, as that was what the men around him called him. Johan liked the man and subsequently liked the other staff he was introduced to, all seemingly more scientists than soldiers. He was given an office twice the size of the office he had just left and his duties were explained to him. It was over lunch that Johan learnt the rather ominous reason for the closely planted gum trees. They were there to help dissipate the blast in the case of an explosion at the site in order to protect the people who lived near the factory. His lunch companion laughed at Johan's reaction to the explanation of the gum tree barrier and comforted him with the observation that the gum trees were still there so nothing bad had happened yet.

Johan did not tell Molly about the gum trees, but described his new position with an enthusiasm which had been absent all the time he had worked at the castle. He ended the description of the new job and his new workplace with the comment," and the free food at the cafeteria is good and I don't have to wear a bloody scratchy bum freezer jacket to work!".

Ian had settled into a quite pleasant steady routine at Llewelyn Barracks. They were rarely serious medical or surgical cases as the small medical wing was too far from any battlefield. There were occasional accident cases, mostly motor accidents involving men returning to camp at night, highly intoxicated. Ian treated these men as best he could. He was nonjudgmental on their drunkenness as he wondered how he would behave knowing that in the near future he might be involved in the frontline of the war against Hitler. It therefore came as a shock when he was called to see the CO to be told he was being seconded to No.1 Army Hospital in Alexandria in Egypt. The CO told him that he had been selected for the transfer as he had acquired considerable skill in surgery during his time at Llewellyn.

Ian could have done with a poorer assessment of his surgical skills and a continued stay in Bulawayo. He dreaded telling his mother of his transfer. She was visibly upset but restrained her tears at least on front of him. She did cry when she said goodbye at Bulawayo Airport, as an overloaded Airforce DC3 lumbered into the air carrying Ian almost the length of Africa to his new place of work. The seats in the aircraft were nothing more than pieces of canvas strung on aluminium frames that, as he sat, dug into the undersides of his calves. The plane stopped to refuel at Nairobi and then again at Khartoum. Ian was aware that at each stop the weather was getting warmer and warmer. By the time the plane reached Alexandria and the door opened, walking down the steps into an Egyptian summer was to Ian like walking into an oven.

The airport was not large but very busy. Ian and four other doctors who had been with him on the plane were collected by a military policeman and taken in 4x2 Ford truck and dropped at the hospital which was a large two-story building of no great architectural merit and seemingly in need of a coat of paint. The five Rhodesian doctors were met by an obviously very harassed senior doctor who told them where the doctors' home was and told them to report ready for duty in twenty minutes. Ian's room could only be described as a utilitarian Buddhist monk's cell. There was a narrow iron framed bed, a thin coir mattress and one pillow whose kapok stuffing had settled in a serious of golf ball sized hard lumps. There was a simple stand with a chipped enamel basin and equally chipped water jug.

Ian surveyed the room in some despair little knowing that in the days to come his awareness of his surroundings would take second place to the need for sleep. He placed his tog bag on the bed and put on a clean sweat free uniform and reported for duty. At the reception area the place was a scene of chaos. Trucks and ambulances were stopping outside the entrance and the bodies of wounded men were being transported into the reception area as fast as the gurneys could be rotated. A doctor assessed each patient quickly and then directed them to various parts of the hospital. There was blood everywhere, on the floor and on the wall and the air was full of the sounds of the agony of the injured soldiers.

Ian was obviously expected and was ushered into an operation theatre ante-room where a nurse merely said "hello" and quickly fitted him with a gown and told him to sterilize his hands. His hands were then sprinkled with talcum and gloves pulled on. In the operating theatre there was a sheet covered body already in the process of being operating on. A masked figure told Ian to step forward. "Your file says you are a good surgeon, Negrini. Prove it. Take over suturing this poor fellow's femoral artery before he bleeds to death and then close up." said the oldest looking of the masked figures. Ian did what he was asked to do as quickly and carefully as possible under the eye of the doctor in charge, He found that once he got a surgical tool in his hand any nervousness disappeared. When he had finished, the senior doctor turned to the anesthetist and said," We got a good fast one this time, George. We might still get a game of golf in." To Ian he said," Good job, Negtini."

Ian remained in the operating room for another six hours leaving only twice to snatch a drink and relieve himself. He saw more blood and suffering in that one shift than he had seen in all the time he had been at Llewelyn. When eventually he was told to finish for the night, Ian was too tired to go to the hospital cafeterias to get a meal, He ate four of the homemade oatmeal biscuits his mother had made for him and fell asleep in his uniform.

The next morning an orderly woke him at six o'clock and told him that he was to be ready at the reception area by seven o'clock. Ian found himself in the same operating theatre with the same surgeon who greeted him quite affably," more casualties from Mersa Matruh. The Iti's are still trying to get through, the bastards. Mind you they won't as they are better lovers than fighters. Sorry, you're not Italian are you, Negrini? Your name sounds Italian."

Ian assured his new boss that he was a Rhodesian and not Italian. The day was much of a repeat of the previous day with operation after operation on soldier after soldier injured seriously in in one part of the body or another. He found it difficult to get used to the pronouncement, 'Just close him quickly. He's gone. Others are waiting.' Around midday he was told by Major Holloway, his doctor boss, to go and get a bite to eat. Sitting in the cafeteria eating a ham sandwich and drinking a cup of tea, he was aware that one of the two theatre nurses from Holloway's theatre had joined him. She was short and dark haired and without her surgical mask quite pretty.

"I'm Cora. I'm from Malta. You were sure dropped in at the deep end. It's not always quite so bad as the last couple of days. It's the fight for Mersa. The Iti's are desperately trying to get a foothold in Egypt." said the nurse.

"I'm Ian. I'm from Rhodesia. Nice to meet you. I guess I will get used to all the blood and gore."

The next three days were much like the previous two, though Ian did notice that Holloway was giving him more and more complicated surgical procedures to do. This pleased him and gave him confidence especially as he had yet to lose a patient except for the poor young body that had been pronounced dead before the anesthetic had taken effect. He was told by Holloway on the evening of the fifth day that he could have a day off. Apparently, there had been a lull in the battle at Mersa Matruh. He was eating a leisurely meal for the first time since he had arrived in Alex, when a voice next to him said "Can I join you." It was Cora. Ian half stood up and nodded to her.

The two young people talked, not of the war but home and their families. Ian found himself really liking this young woman and, when she suggested that they go to the beach the next day, he jumped at the idea, The next day Cora picked Ian up in an old Austin 7 that had an unusual ownership. It belonged to whoever were the current staff of the operating theatres as long as they put money in a jar for licence and repairs. The journey to a quiet beach did not take long. To start with the two lay on towels on the sand and enjoyed the sun. Then they both got up and ran down the beach and into the clear cool emerald sea.

They splashed each other and found themselves playfully wrestling each in the shallow water. Ian could not help himself from tilting Cora's head back as he held her and he kissed her. Cora responded and the two made their slow way back to their towels on the hot sand. They made love on the deserted beach and then lay sweating, lying next to each other. Ian said," I'm sorry. I took advantage of you."

Cora laughed and said, "Let's settle for taking advantage of each other."

The relationship between Cora and Ian was good for them both. Though they kept their affair a secret from their colleagues at the hospital. They found that involving themselves in each other's lives was a distraction from the ongoing pain and carnage that they witnessed day after day in the operating theatre. They went back to the beach often and when they had the beach to themselves enjoyed being intimate. They also ventured further afield when they got a shot at the Austin 7 and went to Cairo, which they thought was dirty, noisy and the fly capital of the world. They did enjoy going to see the pyramids at Giza in spite of the unwanted attention of a myriad of Arab boys trying to sell them everything from hashish to their sisters. Ian wrote to his mother every week with a severely censored version of his life in Egypt.

Chapter 25

Emily put her paints away and her visits to her tamarind tree were now few and far between. The war being fought so far away had made life difficult for the people of Leopard Ridge and Mary's Nest. Emily, Mariette, Abe and Rebecca had had to involve themselves more and more in the running the farms and the family businesses. They were ably supported by Aaron, Thomas and their wives but the absence of Matt working in Salisbury and only returning to the farm had increased the workload on the others. Giles was away most of the week and even on weekends if there was an emergency cabinet meeting he had to attend. The mines, ably managed by Hennie van Rooyen, continued to produce a steady flow of the precious metal even though the reefs were become deeper underground but still viable with the use of two crawler tractors.

Solly's businesses still provided his family with a good income under the stewardship of Jennifer, who had learnt how to balance the needs of the businesses and a rapidly growing son. Solly was able to help her less and less as he was asked to do more undercover work in Mozambique. He was also appointed as an adviser to the Prime Minister where, after some meetings, he was often able to exchange family news with Giles. He never gave the matter of medals another thought, but was secretly rather proud of himself when he eventually got a hand signed letter from Winston Churchill thanking him for his assistance in the wat effort. Since it did not mention any details of his assistance, he was able to show it with some pride to Jennifer.

Sommerville called Matt to his office on a hot summer's day. "I guess that life is getting a bit boring again with no excursions to Mozambique on the horizon. How would you like to take a detachment of the RAR to Kenya to deal with the remnants of the Italian forces who have joined up with Somali guerrillas and are tying down a lot our forces. We are worried that there might be another attempt to invade Northern Kenya."

"Would love to. Had an interesting time when I was last there." replied Matt.

Somerville went to outline what had happened in the immediate past in the NFD {Northern Frontier District} in northern Kenya. In 1940 after the Italians had captured Abyssinia and Somaliland, they had turned their attention to Kenya and had bombed the British detachment at Wajir in the north. This had brought about an immediate response from the British who had relatively easily defeated the Italians in Abyssinia and Somaliland in what was in effect the first Allies victory of the war. However, Sommerville went on to explain, that groups of Italian soldiers remained in the area and had in many cases joined up with groups of Somali bandits called the Shifta. These guerrilla groups were using hit and run tactics on isolated army and police posts in the far north of Kenya.

Matt was promoted to Lt. Colonel before his company of recently trained black soldiers were deployed to Kenya in February of 1941. Mariette was not happy at him going to serve his country again but, again, obtained some solace at his remaining on African soil as though this might protect him from serious harm. Matt and his troops travelled by train to Beira and then by ship to Mombasa. Matt never knew the identity of the ship as all identification had been removed, but it seemed familiar.

From Mombasa Matt's detachment was trucked all the way to a place called Marsabit far north in the NFD. Marsabit was nothing more than a couple of 'dukas', small general stores in the middle of a semi-desert whose only vegetation was a scattering of thorn trees and seemingly dead grass. The place was hot and unpleasant and Matt wondered if it had been the imagined setting for Dante's Inferno. Tents were ready for his men and not much else. Matt surveyed his new kingdom. His subjects were a hundred and twenty recently trained Shona recruits, four experienced black sergeants and two young untested white second lieutenants. His company was equipped with six Chevrolet 4x2's.

The brief given to Matt at EAF headquarters in Nairobi was to patrol the northern Kenya border from Moyale about a hundred and fifty miles north of Marsabit to Mandera about two hundred odd miles to the east. The patrols were to find and engage any small groups of Italians and Shifta, but back away from any large forces and inform HQ. Once his troops were settled in to the camp Matt addressed his troops in Shona and explained their mission. His troops who were strangers to him were surprised that he spoke good Shona. Matt had previously briefed the two white officers in English.

The day after their arrival at Marsabit, the first border patrol set off for Moyale commanded by Matt who sat in the front of one of the Chev trucks with a lieutenant and a sergeant. The lieutenant drove. Behind them were two other trucks. The total force was about sixty men. The black privates were each armed with Lee Enfield .303's and the lieutenants each had a sten gun. Matt had a holstered Webley Scott 45 at his waist. Matt had briefed the other lieutenant, the hopefully brighter of the two, to leave the camp as soon as he had gone with the other three trucks and the rest of the men less six to guard the camp under a sergeant. They were to take a slightly more easterly track and head for Mandera.

Matts convoy travelled slowly along a track deep in sand that was ill defined in places. The track occasionally crossed what might have been a dry river bed in a different age. They saw a few people herding emaciated goats. They were mostly Turkana, but a few appeared to be Somalis. Communication with the locals was difficult until Matt came across a man who spoke good English. Matt immediately engaged him as an interpreter even though he accepted that he would have to pay the man out of his own pocket. This man was to prove to be a useful addition to Matt's cohort.

They reached a track running at right angles to the one they were on just before nightfall. From the poor set of maps he had, Matt assumed that this was the northern border of Kenya. They set up camp and Matt set guards round the camp during the night hours. The next day the three trucks drove eastwards. The heat was draining and they went through a swarm of locusts so thick that they put on the windscreen wipers, a move they soon regretted as they had to stop and waste valuable water cleaning crushed locust innards off the windscreen. On the border track they passed not a single person all day. Matt stopped the convoy periodically and let one of his Shona soldiers, a skilled tracker, examine the sand on the track. The tracker announced each time that there had been no traffic along the track for weeks.

Matt was looking for a few larger thorn trees on the side of the road to give some shade to a potential camping site when the other three trucks came into sight. The lieutenant reported that they had reached Mandera and then headed west. They had seen only a few goatherders on the way to where they were now. The two groups of men camped for the night. Matt shared a tent with the two lieutenants. The two young men told Matt of their homes and families in Salisbury. The two young men soon discovered that Matt had more to relate than they had and he regaled them with stories of his family going back to Giles and the Pioneer column. The nights at Marsabit were hot but the skies were the clearest Matt had ever seen.

*****

With the defeat of the Italians in Libya there was a sudden decrease in the number of casualties arriving at the hospital in Alex. Many of the new patients had come from theatres of war further afield who had had initial treatment but needed restorative surgery. Ian, with Cora next to him in the operating room, found that he was actually enjoying repairing the bodies of patients hastily patched up near the battlefield. He liked to see the appreciation of some young soldiers when they looked in a mirror, weeks after Ian had operated on them, and saw how his grafts returned their faces to some semblance of their past looks.

Ian and Cora continued to spend their working hours together in the operating theatre but also continued to share their leisure time. They returned to the beach as often as they could as it was one of the few places that offered an opportunity to be alone. They never discussed the future. It was as if their relationship was a happy arrangement to help each other face the horror of war. Ian had a love of a kind for Cora but knew that, deep down in his heart, she was not the one and only life partner for him. It was then that, when Ian received orders in September 1941 to report to Alex airport for onward transport to Singapore, he was not left broken hearted. Cora and Ian said their goodbyes at the hospital. They both promised to write to each other, both knowing that it was not going to happen.

The first stage of his journey took Ian as far as Bombay where he had to spend three days waiting for an ongoing aircraft. These three days were to be the happiest days of the war for him. He was billeted near to a resort on the beach near Bombay called Breach Candy. There was a club there that was open to the forces and Ian spent hours there either on the beach or in the sea or at the bar sipping cold beers under a giant fan.

The onward journey was uneventful and Ian found himself being carried from the airport to Queen Alexandra hospital, also known as Singapore Army Hospital, in a rickshaw, his duffel bag on the seat next

211

to him. The hospital seemed to be in the same a state of chaos as had been the Alex hospital. He was soon to learn that the war in Malaya against the Japanese was not going well and the British and Indian ground forces were being slowly, but inexorably, driven down the peninsular towards a dead-end Singapore.

Ian was given an hour to settle into his room at the doctors' quarters and then ordered into one of the several operating theatres. He was told by a senior surgeon, an older man, that he would be senior surgeon and in charge of one of the operating theatres. He was hastily introduced to the theatre staff and told to gown up to operate on the man already lying under anesthetic on the operating theatre. He could not really distinguish the faces around him, but instruments rapidly appeared in his hand when asked for. His patient had a massive wound in his side that required intense work not only on severed muscle but also on a damaged liver. His surgeon assistant told him that it was probably damage from a Japanese sword or bayonet.

The rest of the day passed with only brief breaks between patients, in a whirl of blood and torn bodies. Ian wished that he had Cora by his side, if only to cast a spell of sense of normality on his current situation. He had a meal in the hospital rectory and went to bed. That night he dreamed of thousands of white chickens and in the middle of them was his mother. The next day was the same as the previous day. Patient after patient was wheeled into the theatre at a rate that barely gave him a chance to talk to his colleagues. Over a period of days, he learnt that the broken bodies being brought to the Alexandra, were the casualties of battles raging in that area of Malaya to the north of Singapore. The Japanese were winning the battles and slowly marching on Singapore. The Japanese were well armed and were using bicycles for rapid troop transport, an ideal method along the narrow paths in the jungle.

In Alex there had always been an atmosphere of optimism as the Allies crushed the Italians to the west, but here, there was a sense of depression and apparent acceptance of the inevitability of the over running of Singapore by the Japanese. Day passed into day and the only one of his theatre staff that Ian got to know at all was one of the theatre nurses called Noor. She was in her early twenties and a war widow with no children. She spoke good English and in odd moments of respite in the operating theatre told Ian about Malaya and its people. Ian told Noor about his homeland and its people.

1942 came and the flow of injured bodies passing through the doors into the Alexandra Hospital reached a level like Ian had never seen before. Working up to sixteen hours a day trying to repair injured bodies and staring at faces of men who knew they had no hope, drove Ian to retreat into himself. Apart from responding to conversation related to his work, he talked to nobody except Noor. He felt for her when he heard how she had watched her husband shot and then bayonetted by a Japanese soldier. She believed that she only survived because she had fainted and had been left presumed dead.

It was in the second week of February that Noor took Ian aside and told him that she was making a plan to escape from Singapore when the Japanese arrived. She had a cousin who had a prau, a fishing boat, that was moored off the seafront not far from the hospital. She would not leave the hospital until she knew the Japanese were coming, but would then go with her cousin and his family and sail north along the Malayan Peninsular as far as a place in Burma not occupied by the Japanese. From there she was determined to walk to the nearest point in India where she could seek sanctuary. She invited Ian to join her when the time came. Ian accepted her offer.

As the days passed the sounds of warfare became louder and louder. Water at the hospital became desperately short after the British blew up the land bridge between Singapore Island and the mainland in order to slow the progress of the oncoming Japanese. As suggested by Noor, Ian had packed a small duffel bag with a few clothes, some basic medicines, some biscuits and chocolate, a water bottle, matches and a spare set of shoes, his tennis shoes. From then on, he kept the bag with him at all time, even in the operating theatre. When he had the chance, he drew as much money as he could from his account in Singapore.

They were in the middle of an operation when they heard the sound of gunfire close to the hospital. Noor whispered to Ian that they must go. Ian insisted on closing the operation site. By this time bullets were flying around and over the hospital. Noor grabbed Ian's hand and ran with him out of the hospital across the garden and into the street. The two of them continued to run, bags in hand, towards the sea. The sound of gunfire had lessened slightly. At the seafront Noor looked quickly for her cousin's prau and, having seen it, guided Ian to the roughly twenty-foot boat already loaded with about fifteen people.

The boat had a small outboard motor which was used to get the boat away from the shore as quickly as possible. Once about a mile from the shore, the lateen sail was raised and the boat headed north keeping parallel to the mainland. Ian surveyed his fellow passengers. They were people of all ages who had one thing in common, a look of relief which Ian shared with them. He sat on the gunwale of the boat next to Noor for hour after hour. She introduced him to her family. She pointed out to him that they were sailing up the, Malacca Straits along the coast of Malaya and hoped to get reach the Thailand coast in about four days.

For days the sea was calm and days of sun were interrupted by occasional heavy downpours of truly tropical rain. Periodically the boat put into shore in less populated areas where water and food was purchased. Ian provided most of the money for the supplies. When Noor's cousin reckoned that the boat had reached Thai waters, he put in to land and here all the passengers went ashore to find a safe place to mingle with the locals. Ian produced a big wad of money which eventually persuaded the cousin take him and Noor as far as Burma.

For the best part of two weeks the prau sailed slowly north. They twice saw what they assumed were Japanese warships, but these sailed past them. Noor's cousin seemed to know the waters all around Malaya, Thailand and Burma which Noor explained was because he had been a successful smuggler before the war. It was with relief that the boat eventually was landed on a quiet beach apparently about twenty miles west of Rangoon. Ian paid off Noor's cousin and he joined her on the beach. The cousin turned his boat around and disappeared in the direction in which he had come. Even though the beach was deserted Noor hurried Ian off into the vegetation along the shore.

From where Ian and Noor stood, their destination, the nearest part of India was about six hundred miles. They both felt the enormity of the task ahead, bit realized it offered a chance to keep from being captured by the Japanese and ending up with a bayonet in the stomach. They started walking slowly northwards, sometimes on the beach and sometimes in the coconut plantations that fringed much of the beach. They were well aware of a Japanese presence along the coast, but also knew that most of the Burmese were against their invaders and would most likely help them. When they met locals, Ian left Noor to do the talking. He did not think he looked like a European any more. He was tanned, a quite dark brown, by the sun.

The two travelers only saw Japanese soldiers on two occasions in the first two weeks. On the one occasion local fishermen had called them over to their boat and quickly covered them with a net just before two soldiers walked past down the beach. Water was not a problem as there were lots of streams and sometimes substantial rivers that flowed out of the jungle into the sea. Food however was a problem. Most of the locals had little food themselves. What they had; the Japanese took from them. Noor had a knowledge of local plants and occasionally they found fruit which were edible. Mostly they lived on coconut milk that they got from trees bent near enough to the ground for Noor to reach the coconuts helped by Ian. The coconuts were cut open with a machete like knife that Ian had liberated from its absent owner near the beginning of their journey. Ian and Noor got thinner and thinner as their journey progressed.

Day after day Noor and Ian walked often through streams and sometimes in the sea round rocky outcrops. Their feet never seemed to be dry. By the end of the second week their shoes were rotting as were their feet. Ian tried to deal with the fungus diseases with his modest medicine kit but failed. They both threw away their shoes and put on their tennis shoes. Ian estimated that they were only covering less than twenty miles a day and would take much longer than he had estimated. One day in the third week they passed through a deserted village. Ian looked in the small empty school and saw a map of Burma on the wall which he removed, folded and put it in his pocket. Up to this point in the journey, he and Noor had only had an approximate idea of where they were. Having a map was a vast improvement.

Chapter 26

Matt and his men settled into a tedious routine of travelling north and then east to west two times a week. In between the motor patrols his men either lay and smoked in their tents or played endless games of soccer on a sandy pitch with thin crooked tree trunks tied together to make the goals. Matt and the two lieutenants took the opportunity to get tracking lessons from their experienced tracker. Weeks passed and Matt and his men saw nothing more exciting than a few Turkana tribesmen, a scattering of sullen Somalis with either cattle or camels and a single, aged prospector who had apparently lost his way somewhere south of Marsabit. An instruction came to Matt to send half his men back to Nairobi with three of the trucks for re-deployment.

It was the following day that Matts convoy of the three remaining trucks was travelling eastwards about ten miles from Moyale when they stopped to examine the track, and it was Matt with his new found tracking skills, that pointed out to his lieutenant and tracker, what appeared to him, were fresh tracks yet to have the crisp outlines of tyres smoothed by the wind. The tracker agreed with Matt and went further to suggest from a broken twig of a thornbush on the road verge that the truck that had made the tracks was moving away from them. Not only that, he offered the opinion that whoever it was, was very near as he could smell petrol. Since there was no sound of a engine but very faint sounds of faraway voices, it was possible that their target had stopped for some reason. Matt discussed the situation with his men and then acted by sending his lieutenant with twenty men to the east but in a wide arc south of the road to set up a road block a couple of miles to the east.

Matt's men debussed and then took to the bush in silence and moved under cover to the east. As they went, they could definitely hear voices. Matt and the tracker moved slowly and silently towards the road. There was an Italian truck stopped just off the track. Near the truck was an Italian officer of sorts sitting next to a camp table, drinking tea from a china tea service. Not far from him were his men drinking tea from tin mugs. Matt was amazed to see that the entire contingent of about twenty men had leant their rifles against the truck some yards from where they sat drinking tea. Matt reversed back to his men and gave them instructions the whole group crept quietly to the road and on a signal

216

burst onto the road with rifles pointed at the tea drinking Italians. Matt didn't know what to shout at the enemy. He couldn't say, 'put your arms down,' as they already were.

The Italians solved the problem by putting their arms in the air. The Italian officer walked over to Matt and handed him his Beretta side arm and said in almost perfect English, "Mario Cassini, I surrender, thank God. Had enough of running around forced to help the German Barbarians. I am happy to be your prisoner until the end of the war as long as you treat me well." The prisoners were distributed amongst the four trucks under guard. Major Cassini sat in the front of one truck with Matt and the two of them had an enjoyable conversation all the long way back to Nairobi where Matt handed over the prisoners.

It turned out that Mario Cassini had been a well-known artist before the war into which he had been forced. There were a couple of surprises for Matt in Nairobi. Firstly, the NFD border patrols were suspended. Secondly, he was being sent back to Salisbury as Brigadier Sommerville's Aide de Camp. Before he left Kenya, he was pleased to hear that Cassini had given up all information he could on the Italians forces and was happy at being sent to the Rift Valley to work on murals in the little Catholic church that prisoners of war were building for themselves half way down the Rift Valley.

*****

Three months of walking on fast failing feet and Ian estimated that he and Noor were somewhere on the coast of Chin State. They were both looked like skeletons but drove each other on. They had both had several bouts of malaria. Ian's supply of quinine had long run out. Noor took a chance and went into a nearby village to try and establish how far they had to go to the India border. An old man seemed happy to tell her that the village was within two miles of the border. He showed her a path that lead down into a heavily wooded valley with a stream that was the border. Noor returned to Ian and the two set off on the path to the valley pointed out by the old man. Their progress was slow as the soles of their tennis shoes had worn through. Ian had tried to make repairs with a rubber inner tube found on the beach but without much success.

It was raining as the two figures trod their way carefully down the muddy forest path leading to the river in the bottom of the valley. It was as Ian slipped and fell, that the shots rang out. Noor screamed. As he fell, Ian glanced back and saw Noor fall and then, as if he was watching something in slow motion, he saw a khaki figure stand over Noor and stick a bayonet into her stomach. Noor didn't cry. She was already dead. Ian turned and started forwards and down again. He was oblivious of the bullets flying over his head. He reached the stream and crossed it and went as fast as he could into the thick bush on the Indian side of the valley.

The doctor looked down at Ian as he lay in a military hospital outside the Indian town of Cox's Bazaar. "He was bloody lucky one of our border patrols found him. From his dog tags, he appears to have been a doctor in Singapore when the Japs overran it. God knows how he did it, but he must have walked here," said the medic to his colleague. Ian hadn't said a word from the day he had been admitted to the hospital. He was painfully thin and was periodically racked with malarial fever. He was treated at Cox's Bazaar for a month before being sent to England to a convalescent home. After two months he had responded to treatment for the malaria but still hadn't spoken a word. He sat all day. He responded to orders but seemed to have totally withdrawn.

The doctors decided that he might respond to being sent back to his home, Rhodesia. As it happened this decision coincided with the opening of the dam rondavels which were to be used as a place of peace and tranquility for Rhodesians suffering from shellshock. Ian was one of the first servicemen to be sent to stay at Leopard Ridge. MJ was down by the dam when Ian arrived. She had just finished school and didn't know what she wanted to do, so, at Mariette's suggestion, she agreed to help the new residents of the rondavels. She saw a man who was quite young but had an old and worn body. She looked in his eyes and saw nothing, as if he had put up an invisible wall against the world. M J had to go down to the water's edge away from Ian in order to restore her composure. She wondered what this man had seen or done to cut him off completely from reality.

Gladys Negrini was informed of Ian's current whereabouts and she phoned Leopard Ridge. She spoke to Mariette who was honest with her and described how Ian was healing physically, but was still in a state of mental isolation. Gladys decided to postpone any visit to see Ian and asked Mariette to let her know if and when Ian was communicating normally again. She thanked Mariette and the family at Leopard Ridge for caring for her son. Mariette went down to the dam and told Ian that she had spoken to his mother but got no response from him

MJ found herself drawn to the sad young man in rondavel 4. The work she taken on as she didn't know what she wanted to do after school, found her catering to the needs of six men both young and old, but she found herself gravitating towards Ian to a greater extent than any of the others. She would take him a cup of tea midmorning with a couple of biscuits and she would talk to him while he sipped the tea and chewed the biscuits. She didn't try and ask him any questions as she didn't want to be disappointed when he didn't answer. She held long one-sided conversations about the farms and the mines and the people who lived in this corner of Mazowe. She wanted to believe that now and again she could see a glimmer of light in his eyes. She talked to the army doctor who came once a month to check on the convalescents. She asked him how long it might be before Ian came to terms with reality. He said he didn't know, but that it could be at any time if something was said or Ian saw something that could act as a trigger to switch his mind into the present.

Matt was back living at Leopards Ridge and commuted every day to Salisbury. As Sommerville's assistant he had an interesting but relatively easy job. He related well to his senior officer who never ceased to take the opportunity to joke about Matt's famous battle against the Italians. This was usually when they were sitting next to the huge granite boulder in the bar garden of the Forces Club. Matt admitted to Mariette that he felt slightly guilty that he had now got a cushy job under Sommerville. Mariette had to remind him of the DSO in the safe at Leopard Ridge.

Solly was in Salisbury when the news came to him from Mary's Nest that Abe had passed away in his sleep. He was devastated as were all the Gold and Elliott-Smith families. Giles took the news worse than anybody. He could not accept that his friend and partner of close to sixty years, with whom he had shared a corner of Africa and whose families were intertwined forever, could possibly die both before him and without him. Rebecca took her loss more acceptingly and calmly than everybody. She just thanked the Lord that he had given her a life partner who had always accepted her imperfections. She had no objection to

Abe being buried next to Mary. Solly took charge of the funeral. A service was held at the Anglican Cathedral and a long snake of cars made their way to Mazowe to lay Abe's body to rest on his beloved farm.

*****

It was during the summer holidays of 1944 that a dreadful event occurred at La Mercy. The school was closed for the holidays. Molly was in Stellenbosch with Abigail attending a small exhibition of her paintings that she had accumulated over some five years. On a hot but windy day La Mercy went up in flames. It was nearly a hundred and fifty years old and had lot of wood in its construction. Many of its rooms had wooden paneling. It was later surmised that the fire had been started by an electric fault in the distribution box in the kitchen. The fire took hold quickly fanned by the south easter and the grand old house was almost totally destroyed before three fire engines arrived on the spot. Nobody was hurt. Only two gardeners had been on the property at the time of the fire.

Johan, Molly and Abigail were upset at the loss of all their possessions, but relieved that there had been no loss of life. The property was insured and Johan and Molly were paid fair compensation for what they had put into the school, enough to buy a modest property in Somerset West close to where Johan worked. Abigail soon settled at a local school. Not long after the fire, the manager of the fertilizer company retired and Johan was appointed in his place to run both the fertilizer and explosives companies. Molly had had such a success at the exhibition in Stellenbosch that she was able to paint full time in a little studio that Johan built in the garden where she could see the Helderberg Mountains not far away.

*****

Not really knowing why, MJ persisted in her efforts to help Ian. She continued to talk to him on a daily basis to the extent that Mariette had to remind her that there were other recovering soldiers in the rondavels at the dam. One day without permission, MJ took one of the family cars and drove down to Ian's rondavel where she told him to get in. He got in without expressing much interest in what was going on. In the back

220

she had put one of her Uncle Solly's tractor tubes, a rug and a blanket. She had only just got her driving licence but managed to safely navigate the way to Mermaids Pool. Being a week day, the place was deserted. MJ placed the tube at the top of the waterfall and got on, her foot stopping the tube from going down the waterfall. She told Ian to get on. He shook his head and started shaking. MJ could not help herself and got off the tube and going up to Ian put her arms round him. Slowly Ian stopped shaking. After a few minutes MJ realized that Ian was talking. She heard him say," I am sorry, Noor, I should have stopped to help you.". He kept repeating this and MJ just held him harder.

They lay on the rug in the sun and MJ saw that his eyes were now seeing her. Ian started to talk as if a verbal torrent that had built up inside him had burst out into the present. MJ just let him talk. He recalled the last day in the valley on the Indian border. He recalled in detail the sarong that Noor was wearing that day. He started shaking again when he told MJ of the red blood rosette that had appeared on her forehead and then the khaki clothed devil who had plunged a bayonet into her belly. It took time before Ian stopped shaking again and he carried on talking. He said that he had no memory of what he had been told had happened from the minute Noor died until a few hours ago.

MJ felt joy in her heart. She hoped, no she believed, that Ian was on his way to full recovery. Ian was not a happy soul but at least a talking soul. They drove home in silence as if by silent consent they agreed that enough had been said for one day. MJ was in trouble when she got back at Leopard Ridge but she didn't care.

MJ spent more time than she was expected to do with the convalescents, but especially with Ian. She sensed that Ian actually looked forward to her arriving at the dam. She raided the larder at the farmhouse for treats for Ian and brought him books to read. He taught her how to play chess. Gladys came to stay a week with Ian. MJ liked her from the start. Solly came to see Ian often and met up with Gladys who embarrassed him by kissing him over and over again.

It was not a sudden passionate moment but rather the sure and steady growth of a small emotional seed that saw MJ fall in love with Ian and he with her. The family watched and approved. Ian became a partner in the Mazowe doctor's practice and six months later as the war clouds over Europe were starting to disperse slowly, MJ and Ian were married in the little church in Mazowe. All the Elliott-Smith and Gold families were present. Eighteen-year-old Giles junior was proud to be best man at his sister's wedding. Matt was happy to escort his daughter down the aisle. The reception could not be held at any venue other than under the tamarind tree. There was to be no honeymoon. MJ and Ian were too thankful to need one. They just wanted to be with each other.

Chapter 27

On May the eighth 1945 the war ended and church bells rang out across the world. A week later a memorial parade was held at the Drill Hall in Salisbury. Emily sat on the VIP stand next to Giles, resplendent in his Colonels uniform. He had wanted to march with his old regiment, but realized that even on his very recent new prosthesis, he was not up to marching and standing in the hot sun. Emily looked at another Colonel, this one leading his regiment. It was Matt who smiled up at his mother and his wife standing next his father. Emily felt so proud of the two colonels and two DSO's on show amid two good displays of other medals. She also felt also thankful that the two families had survived the war in one piece.

The Governor General of Southern Rhodesia took the parade salute and then awarded medals to some members of the parade. That afternoon the prime minister held a garden party at his official residence. The Police Band played on a raised platform and politicians, soldiers and the key members of the mining and farming community mingled and celebrated peace in their country. Rebecca stayed close to Giles and Emily as she didn't know many of those present. The PM came over to them and thanked Giles and his family for what they had done during the war. He surprised Rebecca by thanking her as well and expressed his gratitude to her son, Solly, for what he had done for his country behind the scenes.

War had been a time of hardship, but peacetime also brought with it problems of a different kind economically and politically. Many black soldiers, those that survived the battlefields, returning to Southern Rhodesia, had tasted a political freedom that did not exist in their country. This started the first rumblings of political discontent. Their white counterparts, more especially the soldiers from working class Britain had traveled to various war theatres and had sampled life in countries where there was wide open spaces and sunny skies so often absent in their country. This nurtured the beginning of mass migration from Britain to the dominions and the colonies of which Southern Rhodesia was to have more than its fair share.

Solly, ever on the lookout for business opportunities called the senior members of the two families to a meeting at the Salisbury Club. He explained to them that, in his opinion, there was going to be a lot of immigration to Southern Rhodesia in the coming years and that would create a need for housing which in turn meant a need for more residential land to build on. He told them that he had sold his remaining land at the Victoria Falls for a very healthy amount and was going to invest in residential land round Salisbury. He was going to hedge his bets by buying land south of the railway line for development of a working-class suburb and he was going to look for vacant land north of Salisbury on which to develop a middle to upper class suburb. Rebecca, Giles and Mariette agreed with Solly's thinking.

The four of them sat for over two hours in the club planning and horse trading until a decision was reached. A new property development was to be set up with Solly and Jennifer as fifty percent shareholders with twenty five percent of the shares to be held by Matt and Mariette and the same by Rebecca. After much discussion it was decided to call the company, Goldsmith Property Development incorporating 'Gold' and 'Smith' from Elliott-Smith. Emily suggested that Gladys be also considered to be a partner in the business. She had, the previous month, sold the chicken farm at Essexvale as she was very tired of eggs and gizzards and chicken livers and she had been invited to go and live with MJ and Ian in Mazowe. Furthermore, she was offered a job as a part time receptionist at Ian's surgery. Gladys moved gladly to Mazowe. When offered the chance to be a shareholder in the new company she jumped at the chance and sank the entire proceeds of the chicken farm sale into Goldsmith.

Raising money for the new venture by Rebecca, Emily and Matt was to prove easier than expected, when a large multinational food company made a very acceptable offer to buy out both the food companies in Mazowe. A condition of the sale was that Leopard Ridge and Mary's Nest farms both continue to sell their oranges to the new owner. Chief Madire was very happy to take a cash payment for his small share in the food companies as it would supply him with millet beer for years to come and even stretch as far as a new young wife.

Solly left the club in an exhilarated mood and went home where he persuaded Jennifer to go with him into Salisbury where he drove directly to Sagetts the new car dealer, In the showroom he stopped Jennifer in front of a sleek white sports car, a Jaguar XK120. " Just look at that and imagine us flying down the Enterprise Road to Mermaids Pool. The 120 in the name means that it can do a hundred and twenty miles an hour."

Jennifer looked at Solly and asked," you're serious aren't you. Where do we put our son and the police are up to your speeding on Enterprise Road.?"

"Oh, come on Jen, we aren't that old yet. Marcus can take turns with you and when he's got a licence, he can have the Stutz".

Elias Sagett the car dealer introduced himself and said," Mr. Gold, this is the first XK120 in the country. It's a real eye turner. As I know you will advertise the car all over Salisbury and I have another five arriving from Beira, I'll give you a five percent discount,"

Solly replied," make it seven and half and I'll take it off you and show it all round the city."

"Done." said Sagett.

Jennifer just shook her head but didn't look too upset at the thought of driving along Jameson Avenue in the sleek white Jag.

For two weeks Solly drove the roads and side roads of Salisbury both to the north and to the south. He found an undeveloped tract of land next to the area called Hatfield after Lord Salisbury's ancestral home, Hatfield House. The piece of land was about four hundred acres in extent and would, when allowance was made for roads and a school, give about five hundred saleable half acre plots. The land was in a deceased estate and due to go on auction the following week. After getting the approval of his business partners, Solly attended the auction and bid fiercely for the land. He opened the bidding and bid relentlessly until the last opposition bidder dropped out at a hundred thousand pounds. Raising the bid another ten thousand and Goldsmith had their first suburb to be. The next day he had engaged a surveyor and a town planner. The shareholders of Goldsmith agreed to call the township Southside.

Solly now moved his efforts to the north to a place called Borrowdale after a pioneer, Henry Borrow. It had once been a huge farm that at one stage had been owned by United Goldfields Company, but was currently part developed into several suburbs. Solly found a subdivision of one thousand two hundred and sixty undeveloped acres in the north west part of Borrowdale. He found the owners and offered them three hundred thousand pounds cash. They hesitated and refused.

Solly rather liked the old couple, the Martins, who owned the land, so he raised his offer to three hundred and twenty thousand pounds and a five percent stake in Goldsmith and a seat on the board. He would sell them one tenth of his shares. The Martins son, Martin, advised them to sell and they did.

Goldsmith was off the ground and the same surveyor and the same town planner who were working on Southside had another job to do. The new suburb was to be called Northwold. Solly arranged a party at his house in Second Street Extension to celebrate the launch of Goldsmith. All the shareholders were there including the Martins and also family from Mazowe. Jennifer arranged the catering for the party and Solly arranged the drinks. The Martins seemed lost amongst a group of people who all knew each other and so MJ took them under her wing. One star of the party was undoubtedly the XK 120 that stood in the drive, Jennifer felt almost sorry for the Stutz Bearcat languishing in the garage. Solly took centre stage just after ten o'clock and called for a toast first to a new wave of prosperity in Rhodesia and secondly to continued good fortune for the Golds and Elliott-Smiths and the Martins of course.

Emily had always longed to be able to spend more time with Molly. She was very close to MJ but as she got older felt the need to be close to her daughter. Her wish was to be granted when, in early 1947, the fertilizer company that Johan worked for decided to open a fertilizer factory in Salisbury to cope with the increasing demands of the local farming community. The site selected for the new factory was on the eastern outskirt of the city on the road to Umtali. Johan was asked to be the managing director of the new Rhodesia Fertilizer Company and he happily accepted. Within three months of receiving the offer, Johan and Molly were in Salisbury. Abigail stayed in Cape Town to finish her education. The family gave them a plot at Northwold and they had a house built designed and built to their specification. Molly and Emily, both established artists, were able to get together to share their enthusiasm for the Rhodesian countryside and were to get together on several occasions to hold joint art exhibitions.

Emily's happiness was to be cruelly interrupted when on the ninth of January 1948 Giles passed away. On a hot summer night Giles had retired to bed and Emily was putting the finishing touches to a portrait of him, the first portrait she had ever done. Giles called Emily and asked her to call Ian as he didn't feel very good and had a bit of pain in his chest. Ian arrived and after examining him gave him a nitroglycerine tablet. The heart pain went quickly away. Ian left promising to call in the morning. Emily joined Giles in bed. Giles turned to Emily and said," I always decided that when the time came I would be brave. I think the time has come and I am trying hard to be brave. I don't want to leave you Emily. I don't want us to be separate. We have been so close together for sixty years."

Giles closed his eyes and lay still. Emily leaned over him, stroked his head and then his cheek. She kissed him gently on the cheek and at that moment somehow knew that he had left her, at least in a physical sense. Emily stayed where she was next to Giles until the next morning. She cried silently for a long time and then lay there remembering the events of all the years that she and Giles had been together. In the morning, she called all the family.

Emily insisted that Giles had made it known to her that he did not want a large fancy funeral and wanted to be buried on the kopje beyond the tamarind tree. On the day, only family were invited to the funeral. Giles's coffin was carried by Matt, Solly, Giles junior, Ian and Chief Madire and his oldest son. As the pall bearers carried the coffin across a large slab of rock to its final resting place, Emily remembered another time and another funeral among granite rocks, that of Giles's hero, Cecil Rhodes.

The public may have been excluded from the funeral but that did not stop Giles being given recognition by the people of Salisbury. The Herald devoted a full front page to his death, outlining the colourful and productive life he had had. The mayor of Salisbury announced that a hereto unnamed street just north of the avenues would be named Elliott-Smith Street. Emily smiled when this information was relayed to her. She thought that it was ironic that a two-shilling name was now on a street sign in the capital. Emily finished her portrait of Giles and gave it to the Forces Club where it was to hang for many years. She carried on painting. She liked to do it but only sitting under the tamarind tree. She explained to MJ that she felt that there she was within thinking distance of Giles.

Solly's prediction about immigration proved to be right and within a few years after the end of the war people were pouring in from not only Britain but also other parts of Europe. Goldsmith's plots in

Northwold and in Southside sold fast. The sales were all handled by Caldicott and Gold, the dormant company having been revived.

Solly foresaw that Salisbury would become an important centre for the sale and processing of the tobacco which was being grown in bigger and bigger quantities in Southern Rhodesia, so he bought land in the Lytton industrial area of Salisbury and bought a half share in an up-and-coming tobacco auction company. Solly became a relatively wealthy man, but never forgot his family's humble beginnings in a poor street in Cape Town and funded a home there for orphans. In 1949 he was elected Mayor of Salisbury. A very proud Rebecca and all the Mazowe crowd attended his inauguration.

It was Emily's idea to hold the family get together to celebrate the sixtieth anniversary of the arrival the Pioneer column in Salisbury but, more important to her, the arrival of Giles and Abe at Mazowe where the seeds of the family had been sown. Giles and Abe no longer wandered the grassy plains and rocky ridges of Leopard Ridge and Mary's Nest but their spirits surely did. The whole of the Golds and Elliott-Smith families descended on Mazowe that weekend. Molly and John arrived from Northwold. Solly, Jennifer and Marcus arrived from Salisbury and came for the weekend. Giles junior was home from Natal University on holiday. The family occupied several of the rondavels at the dam.

On the Saturday afternoon a braai was held under the tamarind tree. Emily had organized it from the wheel chair that she had been forced to use as her body fought the ravages of old age. Food and drink flowed as music from records played. Marcus chose the records that were played. Chief Madire was there with his new wife, eating lots of meat and getting quietly tipsy. Emily and Rebecca sat together and relived their experiences as they watched their extended family circulate. They shared a sense of success as they saw three generations, if they counted themselves, mixing happily. It was almost four generations if one counted the unborn baby being carried by MJ who waddled around carefully shepherded by Ian.

As the sun sank towards the ridge, the party dispersed knowing that the next day they would meet again for a roast lunch. Rebecca was the last to go leaving Emily alone in her wheelchair next to her tree. As the sun went down MJ went to her grandmother to try and get her to agree to return to the house. Emily insisted on a few more minutes. MJ went back walking slowly to get Emily a shawl to keep out the chill wind that had started to blow. She turned and noted the figure of her grandmother sitting close to the tamarind tree. She felt such love for her favourite person in the whole world.

Torch in one hand and shawl in the other MJ made her way back to her grandmother. She felt a pain in her stomach but ignored it. As she got near to Emily, she shone the torch on her and firstly saw that she was clutching something in her one hand. She then saw that Emily had partially slumped against the tamarind tree. Her eyes were closed and she was not moving. At that moment a terrible pain took hold of her belly and she doubled over screaming for Ian.

Epilogue

I didn't remember much of the next twenty hours. I was in agony lying on my grandmother's bed. I was concerned for the safe arrival of our first child, but somehow in the background was another concern, that for my grandmother, who I had left uncared for next to her tree. At the time I didn't know that my Mom and Dad had taken care of their beloved mother. Our baby, a beautiful little boy, eventually arrived thanks to my caring husband, the doctor. As I lay with my son suckling on me, I looked at him and wandered if he was the incarnation of my grandmother arriving when he did. I then decided that that could not be, as there could never be a copy of my grandmother, she was unique.

Mom handed me a little wooden box and said ," this is for you, MJ. Your grandmother must have been holding it when she died and we opened it and inside was a short note that just said that it was for you, Emily Jane."

I took the lovely little wooden box and opened it. Inside was a shriveled mealie pip and a small gold ingot. I didn't understand, but somehow, I actually did.

I often walk the veld holding hands with my husband and my young son. I do it often to remind me and them of the privilege we enjoy to be able to walk free across this corner of Africa. We walk carefully to avoid the puffadder, we listen to the strident call of the grey go-away bird and, if it has just rained, we inhale the distinctive heady smell of rain on arid red earth. I and mine are blessed.

About the Author

Mike Paterson-Jones was born in the UK but went to Kenya as a baby. He was raised there and in Rhodesia. After attending university in South Africa. he worked in Rhodesia as an agronomist, industrial chemist and teacher before buying, with his new wife, Thora, a coffee farm on the Mozambique border. For seven interesting years Mike and Thora raised five children, grew coffee, got bitten by a mamba and dodged bullets and mortars and rockets. The couple then moved to South Africa where Mike worked as a teacher, lecturer and eventually chemistry professor. Because of the increasing violence in post-apartheid South Africa, they moved to Upstate New York for seven years before retiring to the UK.

Mike has had three novels published, many short stories and even a few poems.

About the Publisher

Creative Texts is a boutique independent publishing house devoted to high quality content that readers enjoy. We publish best-selling authors such as Jerry D. Young, N.C. Reed, Sean Liscom, Jared McVay, Laurence Dahners, and many more. Our audiobook performers are among the best in the business including Hollywood legends like Barry Corbin and top talent like Christopher Lane, Alyssa Bresnaham, Erin Moon and Graham Hallstead.

Whether its post-apocalyptic or dystopian fiction, biography, history, true crime, science fiction, thrillers, or even classic westerns, our goal is to produce highly-rated customer preferred content. If there is anything we can do to enhance your reader experience, please contact us directly at info@creativetexts.com. As always, we do appreciate your reviews on your book seller's website as well.

Finally, if you would like to find more great books like this one, please search for us by name in your favorite search engine or on your bookseller's website to see books by all Creative Texts authors. Thank you for reading!

Find us on Social Media

@CreativeTxtsPub

/CreativeTextsPublishers

Printed in Great Britain
by Amazon

38238691R00136